ESCAPE FROM

DEATH ROW

Also by Stanley Salmons

ESCAPE FROM DEATH ROW

Stanley Salmons

Stanley Salmons was born in London. He is internationally known for his work in the fields of biomedical engineering and muscle physiology, published in over two hundred scientific articles and twelve scientific books. In his parallel existence as a fiction writer he has published over forty short stories in various magazines and anthologies and two children's books. This is his seventeenth novel.

ACKNOWLEDGEMENTS

I'm grateful to my wife Paula, and members of the Chester Fiction writer's group, Russ, Fiona, Kath, and Sue, for providing invaluable critical comments on the draft manuscript.

GLOSSARY

ADC	Aide-de-camp
Black ops	Covert, deniable operations
claymore	An antipersonnel mine
good-nite	A (fictional) grenade that disperses a short-acting anaesthetic gas
ICBM	Intercontinental Ballistic Missile
Infil/exfil	Infiltration/exfiltration
LZ	Landing zone
RPG	Rocket-propelled grenade
tab	March or jog with heavy equipment over difficult terrain
USACID	US Army Criminal Investigation Division
USCYBERCOM	US cyberspace intelligence and operational command
WARCOM	US Naval Special Warfare Command

WASHINGTON

President Harriet Nagel

Admiral Mike Randall, Director of the National Security Agency

Joe Templeton, Director of the CIA

Hunter Freeman, Director of National Intelligence

Bob Cressington, Secretary of State for Defense

General George Wagner, Chief of Staff of the Army

AUTHOR'S NOTE

This novel is set four decades in the future at the time of writing. It is not, therefore, a commentary on existing regimes. Nonetheless readers will be aware that there are, even now, countries where human rights are routinely violated, and where political opponents and dissidents of any kind may be brutally attacked, illegally detained, tortured, or killed. This is a work of fiction, but it is by no means a work of fantasy.

1

20th April 2062

They all heard it – footsteps approaching along the corridor. Heavy boots. Guards' boots. Two prison guards, walking in step. Why? Not a mealtime, it wasn't that long since the trays and the paper cups of coffee were taken back through the slots, the trap doors banged shut and padlocked. Not someone going for the long walk, either; that always happened in the small hours. Anyway the prison governor always came beforehand and he hadn't been down. A visitor? You never got visitors on Death Row. Did you?

*

The small cell echoed to the sound of multiple latches slamming back and the door opened.

'Dexter? Visitor for you.'

Maynard Dexter rose slowly to his feet. 'A visitor? Who?'

'You'll find out soon enough. We'll leave the shackles off but you need to have the cuffs.'

Dexter held out his hands and one of the guards clipped his wrists with the handcuffs. Then, without a word, the three emerged into the corridor and began to walk. Behind small

1

armoured glass windows in the walls high-resolution video cameras swivelled to follow them. The moving images were transmitted to a screen in the Central Security Office, labelled by facial recognition software with the names of the two officers and the prisoner.

They stopped at the massive barred gate at the end of the corridor. The guard on Dexter's left placed his hand on a reader and spoke into the box. 'Jason here. Open door East-13.'

There was a short pause while the software added his voice and the handprint to the facial recognition data, then the barred gate disengaged and slid back. They went through and Dexter heard the gate slide back and lock behind him. They passed through two more gates in the same way and finally reached the visitors' room. It wasn't large. Most of it was taken up with the table and two chairs, a single assembly bolted to the floor. The chairs faced each other with a glass partition between the two sides. Contact was strictly forbidden. Dexter wasn't regarded as violent but they padlocked the chain between the handcuffs to a hasp on the table just the same. Normal procedure. He sat down.

The man sitting on the other side of the table hadn't moved. He wore a navy suit, shirt and tie. His hair was smooth and dark, the face clean-shaven. About forty, Dexter thought, and almost certainly an attorney. By this time he'd seen enough of them to know.

Jason said, 'I'll be right outside.' He left the room and the door closed with a dull thud.

The man clasped his hands and placed them on the table. 'Mr Dexter, I'm from the US Department of Justice.'

An attorney. He'd guessed right.

'In two weeks' time you will be taken from your cell and led to a room where you will be placed on a gurney, sedated and anaesthetized. You will then be wheeled into an operating theatre where surgeons will remove your corneas, kidneys, heart and lungs, for use in organ banks. At the end of this time you will, of course, be dead—'

Dexter glared at him. He half-rose but the handcuff chain rattled taut. 'You came all the way here to gloat?'

'On the contrary, I'm here to tell you that there is a way of avoiding all that. Please sit down, Mr Dexter.'

Dexter took his seat again warily. 'Who the hell are you?'

'You don't need to know that. In fact this conversation is not taking place. Do you understand?'

Dexter shrugged.

The man went on, 'You're intelligent enough to know the sort of people you have for company in this Special Confinement Unit. Serial murderers, rapists, cop-killers. The only way any of them will be leaving here is by the route I've already mentioned. You, on the other hand, could be an exception. You're a well-educated individual from a good background, you've had a successful business career and a government appointment.'

'We've been through all this before during the appeals – and a fat lot of good it did me.'

'Please hear me out, Mr Dexter. The fact remains that you have taken the life of a man. It appears to have been premeditated and there's no question of your guilt, which is why you find yourself in here. There's very little latitude in such matters these days, and that's a pity because,' he leaned forward and tapped the table with a finger, 'because you are in a position to render a service for your country.'

'A service for my country? The country that's been so good to me?' Dexter sighed. 'Get to the point, will you?'

The man nodded. 'Very well. You lived in Venezuela for many years. You conducted business there. You know the country and its politics extremely well, and you are fluent in Spanish. For that reason you were appointed as an attaché when a US Embassy was briefly reinstated and you served – with some distinction, I may say – until they had another change of President. Correct?'

'You know it is. In 2050 they ordered the withdrawal of all staff. That was more than ten years ago and the Embassy's been closed ever since.'

'Just so. You'll be aware that during that time we have not been on good terms with Venezuela.'

Dexter huffed derisively. 'That's one way of putting it.'

'Mr Dexter, for various reasons the US would like to normalize relations with Venezuela. There are things we want from them, and we have a substantial package that we can provide in return. But without a diplomatic presence we do not have a representative in that country. We would like you to act as a Special Envoy to present the deal to whoever President Aguilar appoints as his negotiators.'

Dexter's eyes widened. Then he laughed, a short bitter laugh. 'Are you nuts? Those guys are rabidly anti-American. I wouldn't last five minutes!'

'We'd prepare the way for you, of course, and you'd be presenting them with an attractive offer. Look, clearly you need an incentive to act for us in this way. I'm in a position to tell you that if you succeed you will receive a Presidential pardon.'

Dexter blinked. 'And if I fail?'

'If you fail your sentence will be commuted to eighteen months. As you've already served nearly two years you will be released. Either way you'll be a free man.'

'And if President Aguilar sends me to jail? This place is no holiday camp but Venezuela's prisons are the worst in the world.'

'We would, of course, make strenuous diplomatic efforts to get you released. The US does not take acts as hostile as that lightly.'

Dexter shook his head. 'This is crazy.'

'Not so crazy, Mr Dexter. Look, I won't minimize the risks. In the very worst case you may end up dead. On the other hand if you turn down the offer you will most certainly end up dead, right here in two weeks' time. Please think it over. I'll come back in three days to get your answer. If you say yes, you'll be released under supervision, given a full briefing, and prepared for the mission.'

He rose, went to the door and banged on it. The door opened and when Dexter looked up again the man had gone.

2

There was a grunt and the man fell heavily. Jim Slater helped him up.

'Get the idea, Mason?'

'I think so, sir.'

'Good. Remember, you have to move that foot fast. Now you try it with one of the others.'

Jim left the mat and joined the other instructor, Ned Howells. No one would expect a Colonel to share instruction duties in unarmed combat, but it was something he liked to do. He'd learned his skills first in the British Army, then the 22 SAS, then the US Special Assignment Force when he was first inducted as a Captain, and later, during his rehab. He'd had the benefit of different instructors every time, each with their own tricks and specialities, and he'd be hard put to count how many times his survival had depended on it. Now he was CO of the SAF and he was keen to bring his men up to a similar level of proficiency. He was well qualified to do that. Even Ned couldn't rival him on the mat.

His stints down here in Fort Piper's well-equipped gym kept those skills fresh, and on other days the morning run with the men, fully loaded, which he still referred to as a tab, helped to maintain fitness and cleared his mind.

At the end of the session Jim showered, dressed in his combat fatigues, and walked back to his office, enjoying the warmth of the sun. Soon enough the stifling humidity of summer would descend on North Carolina, so it was worth savouring these fresh Spring days while they lasted. Bagley, his aide-de-camp, looked up as he came in.

'General Harken phoned, sir. He wants you in Washington.'

'When?'

'As soon as possible. I took the liberty of booking the nine-fifty flight. A pool car is standing by for you.'

'Did he say how long I'll be there?'

'I asked him if you should pack an overnight bag and he said there was no need.'

Jim glanced at his watch. 'If I'm quick I should be able to make that flight. Well done, Bagley.' He knew very well that the accolade would fail to shift the long-suffering, put-upon expression that was a permanent feature of Bagley's face. It no longer bothered Jim. For all his gloomy disposition Bagley was a good ADC.

He collected some paperwork from his office and stuffed it into a slim document case. Then, after casting a quick look around the room, he headed straight to his quarters to change into a more formal uniform.

*

The flight landed at Washington's Dulles international airport and he took an autocab to the Pentagon. They were passing through Ashton Heights when a female voice announced, 'There is a collision on my normal route. To avoid delay I will make a diversion around Arlington Cemetery.' He smiled. The voices the robots used these days were so seductive you found yourself simply dying to meet their owners.

When it – or was it she? – pulled up near the Metro station he showed his credit token to the reader, the doors unlocked, and he got out.

The road and sidewalks were still shining from a recent downpour, but this hadn't lowered the temperature, merely served to raise the humidity. It wasn't the first time he'd left better conditions behind in North Carolina.

He went in at the Concourse entrance and crossed the foyer to reception. It seemed to him they had an endless supply of young men and women to staff the desk; he'd certainly never seen the same one twice. Their response to him, on the other hand, was always the same. They'd take in the rank insignia and medal ribbons and greet him with a polite:

'Good morning, Colonel. May I help you?'

And he'd answer:

'I'm here to see General Wendell Harken.'

And they'd say:

'May I see your I.D., sir?'

And then they'd spot the SAF flash on the shoulder of his tunic and there'd be a subtle change. For anyone within the armed services that flash meant two things: elite force and black ops. They would stand taller and straighter and there'd be a look of appraisal in their eyes. The response wasn't important to him personally, but as the CO of the Force he was glad that his outfit had the reputation to prompt it.

It was no different today. The young soldier handed back Jim's I.D. with a new deference and said:

'Do you know your way, Colonel?'

'Yup, I know my way.'

'You have a nice day, sir.'

'Thanks, you too.'

He took the lift to the third floor and went through a further layer of security at D-ring. Then he walked the long corridor to Wendell's office. Outside the office he glanced at his watch, brushed his tunic straight, and checked his tie, then knocked on the door.

'Come.'

He went in and Wendell waved a hand to a chair and finished going through a document, the familiar red fibrepoint poised. Legal and high security documents were always delivered as hard copy.

Wendell looked older. His buzzcut was greying at the temples and there were creases around the eyes and on either side of his mouth. When Jim thought about it he realized that he still had a mental image of Wendell as he was more than ten years ago, when he was CO of the SAF and Jim had just transferred to them from the 22 SAS. Despite these signs of the administrative burdens of his current post, Wendell looked as physically fit as ever. Jim guessed he was still making time to go for a run each lunchtime with Bob Cressington, Secretary of State for Defense.

Wendell closed the pen and pushed the document to one side. Then he placed his hands on the desk and looked up. 'Sorry to drag you up to Washington, Jim. We've been asked to undertake a covert mission and I didn't want to do this by holoconference.'

Jim waited. Holoconferencing was the most secure communication system ever devised so there had to be a damned good reason for a face-to-face.

'The government is keen to regularize its dealings with Venezuela.'

'Venezuela? Good God, why on earth would anyone want to do that?'

'That part hasn't been shared with me, but I'm told it's not relevant to the mission.'

Jim's eyes narrowed. Wendell had a very high security classification. If they weren't giving even him the full picture it must be an extremely sensitive issue, one that wouldn't have gone far outside the White House.

Wendell continued, 'We may assume that the US wants something from Venezuela, and is prepared to offer them something in return. They're sending a Special Envoy to put the deal to them.'

Jim whistled softly. 'They found someone who'd actually go there?'

'So it seems.'

'Do we have a name?'

Wendell shook his head. 'His name is on a need-to-know basis, and apparently we don't need to know. Let's call him Mr X.'

Jim was still waiting to find out how the SAF might be involved. 'I take it this guy will have a US military escort.'

'No, there'll be no US escort but he'll be flown in a military aircraft to Aeropuerto Internacional de La Chinita.'

The name rolled easily off Wendell's tongue. Evidently he hadn't lost his facility with Spanish. When he'd been CO, fluency in at least one foreign language was something he'd demanded of any soldier who applied to join the SAF. He'd made that a requirement because the Force never knew where they could be expected to operate. Jim had continued the practice.

'That's not Caracas,' Jim said, frowning,

'No, that airport serves Maracaibo. He'll be met by a contingent of the Venezuelan army and they'll escort him to the Mayor's Residence. The envoy will meet there with the negotiators. As I understand it, they'll include the equivalents of our Secretary of Commerce and Secretary of State.'

'Not the President?'

'No. President Aguilar wouldn't want to be seen anywhere near an American. He wouldn't even allow the conference to take place in Caracas.'

'So how does this Mr X get back – that's if they fail to kill him?'

Wendell gave him a one-sided smile. 'He has a reserved number to phone. The military aircraft will return to pick him up.'

'Right…' Jim said.

'The US government needs to be completely up-to-the-minute on what's happening from the moment the envoy lands, but it could jeopardize the whole operation if we are spotted on the ground. USCYBERCOM have a unit out there with a small base in a house in Maracaibo. They've been briefed but they need some trained observers on the ground. It's been suggested that this is something the SAF should handle.'

'Why us? I would have thought Special Forces Reconnaissance Detachment Alpha could manage something like that.'

'Yes, but on the other hand I'm gratified that someone's noticed that we're more experienced in covert operations. And we do have a number of fluent Spanish speakers in the Force.'

'True.'

'Jim, my understanding is authorization for this mission comes from a high level. If it's that important we can't afford to slip up, so I'd like you to take charge.'

Jim raised his eyebrows, then shrugged. 'Okay, I can do that.'

'When you get to Maracaibo, go to that cyber base. They'll give you all the details. The address is on here,' he opened a desk drawer, withdrew two sheets of paper and handed one over. 'Use that codeword and cryptic exchange or they won't let you in.'

Jim picked up the sheet. It was headed in bold red capitals: READ, MEMORIZE, BURN. Below that was the address, the codeword and the exchange.

Wendell continued, 'The crucial moment is when the envoy leaves the Mayor's Residence. We have to know if they'll be taking him to the airport or to jail.'

'Jail? What about diplomatic immunity?'

'May mean something, may mean nothing – that's what you're there to find out. The cyber unit can't observe the whole route. That's where you come in.'

Jim raised his eyebrows. 'We're supposed to be invisible. How many people is this going to take?'

'Four should be enough.'

'Four?'

'Yes, the cyber unit will brief you on it. Choose three fluent Spanish speakers, preferably ones familiar with the local accent. You speak pretty good Spanish yourself, don't you?'

'I can get by.'

'Good. I've arranged for you to have full access to a section in Virginia that can give you appropriate clothing, false identities, all that sort of thing. Their contact details are on this,' he tapped the second sheet of paper with the backs of his fingers, but continued to hold it. 'When you're in Maracaibo the cyber unit will provide you with communicators so you can stay in touch with the unit and with each other. They'll monitor the exchanges but they won't take any part; they'll just relay everything direct to Washington. That way we'll know where Mr X is being taken.'

'And if he's being taken to prison, probably in a convoy, just four of us are expected to extract him and head for the sunset?'

Wendell placed his forearms on the desk. 'Absolutely not, Jim. Quite apart from the risk to yourselves that would be seen as a show of bad faith.'

'What about the bad faith of people who imprison accredited emissaries?'

'That would have to be addressed through other channels.'

'Bit hard on Mr X.'

'Jim, I'm told it took a lot to get the Venezuelans to agree to this meeting at all. We can't do things that violate that agreement or give them an excuse to put us in the wrong light. Your brief is simply to report on what's happening, not to intervene.'

Jim shook his head. 'This is unbelievable. We can't carry weapons because we have to blend with the scenery, so it puts us in a major city of a hostile country, unarmed, for hours. All that just to tell someone over here what's happening. Why can't these cyber mavens use mini-drones?'

'You know why. Most military vehicles carry radar these days. Drones would be picked up instantly.'

Jim studied Wendell for a moment. He knew him well enough to recognize that pained expression, the face of a man who was trapped in the middle of something.

He said gently, 'Wendell, who dreamed up this whole caper?'

Wendell's mouth twitched but he said nothing.

Jim went on, 'It didn't come through Bob, did it? I'm guessing it came from SAD/SOG.'

Most of their missions came through the Secretary of State for Defense and Bob Cressington usually passed them to Wendell himself. But occasionally the SAF were called upon by the CIA's Special Activities Division, specifically their Special Operations Group, SAD/SOG.

Wendell took a deep breath. 'Yes, Jim, it did. Look, I don't know what's going on but there's not a lot I can do about it. Because of the diplomatic component it's obviously been cleared at the highest level but that's where it's stayed.'

Jim sighed. He was silent for a moment, then he said, 'What about infil? Do we parachute in or rope down?'

'No, the area around Maracaibo is intensively cultivated so there'd be too many eyes and ears. There's a suitable landing zone about thirty miles from the edge of the city. In the past there was some logging in that area but it's dormant now. I've written down the coordinates of the LZ here.' He pushed the second sheet of paper across the desk. 'You'll be flown from Raleigh-Durham to United States Air Force Base, West Texas, where you'll board a Rotofan. Give the pilots those coordinates – they won't know where they're going until that moment. Their instructions are to drop you at the LZ and wait there for your return.'

'And from there to Maracaibo?'

'You'll find that your Rotofan is in the military transport configuration – without markings, of course. An off-roader is being specially prepared at the section in Virginia I just mentioned. Don't worry, when they've finished it won't look any different to similar vehicles you'll see out there. It'll be on board that craft and you'll take it with you. Drive it on the old logging trail to get to the nearest road, which will lead you to Maracaibo.'

Jim took the sheet of paper from the desk and frowned at it. There was the usual line of sixteen digits with a dot after the first two digits in each group of eight and a dash in front of the second group. But below it there was another line of digits.

'What's the other grid reference, Wendell?'

'I insisted you had an alternative escape route in case things went pear-shaped. SAD/SOG obliged. There'll be a boat squad on a lonely stretch of the coast bordering the Gulf of Venezuela. It'll be manned by SEALs. That's the second grid reference.'

Jim said, 'Thanks, the way things are going we may need it. When's all this supposed to happen?'

'The Envoy will be flown out in a little over two weeks from now. I'll call to tell you when to leave. That way you can be in good time for his arrival.'

'And how are we supposed to watch him if we don't know who he is?'

'You'll be given a photo before your flight leaves for Texas.'

Jim was turning it over in his mind, but they seemed to have covered everything.

'Oh, just one more thing,' Wendell said. 'The whole operation has the codename Hallowe'en. It's spelt with an apostrophe – that's so if someone accidentally overhears it they still won't know about the apostrophe.' He opened his hands. 'And that's about it.'

They stood and shook hands.

'Good luck with this, Jim. And let me know if there's anything more you need.'

Jim nodded and left the office.

Bloody CIA. You just never knew where you were when they ordered something up.

3

Jim was still deep in thought about the mission as he descended to the ground floor of the Pentagon. In some ways the job resembled the initial surveillance they'd used any number of times during the preparation for a hostage extraction but there were two big differences: firstly, this operation was being conducted under cover in a hostile country, and secondly, there would be no hostage extraction at the end of it.

He hadn't operated in Venezuela before, although he was familiar with the problems and the dangers out there. He needed more background and Washington was the right place to get it. Perhaps Wendell had foreseen that and briefed Jim in the Capital for precisely that reason – Jim wouldn't have put it past him.

The Pentagon Press Office was a whole suite of rooms. The one the Reception desk directed him to was about five times as large as Wendell's office and full of people busy on phones or typing at computers. Perhaps it wasn't that usual to see a Full Colonel walk through the door because one of the press officers got up and came over to him. Her name tab read 'Kimberley'. She looked to be in her thirties.

'Can I help you, sir?'

'Yes, I'd like to know who your choice of reporter would be for a press item on Central or South America.'

She frowned. 'Do you have such an item for us to handle?'

'No, I'd just like to know who you'd send it to if I did.'

Her lips twisted. Then she said, 'One moment, please.'

He watched as she went to one officer, who waved her over to another. She came back.

'It would be best if you had a word with Max Burrows yourself.' She pointed to the person she'd just spoken to.

Jim went over. The young man looked harried and he spoke quickly. 'Whereabouts in South America, Colonel? Chile, Argentina, Brazil—?'

'No, the northern part, Colombia, Venezuela, maybe into Panama, Costa Rica.'

He thought for a moment. 'I don't know about Panama and Costa Rica. There's a real good man covers Venezuela, though – Aidan Somersby. He reports on that scene and I think he's done a little on Colombia, too. He'd be the guy I'd go to.'

'And where would I find Mr Somersby?'

'Well, if he isn't on location his desk is at the Washington Post.'

'Thanks.'

'No problem.'

*

A cab dropped Jim at 1, Franklin Square. He entered the Washington Post building and waited in the lobby for Aidan Somersby. It was after midday when he'd phoned The Post and asked to speak to the reporter, so he thought it was politic to offer him lunch in an establishment of his choice. That worked.

A man made his way across the lobby: medium height, clean-shaven, forty plus. He wore an open-necked shirt under a creased brown suit and his face was tanned and lined, probably from too much sun. He was very thick around the waist.

'Colonel Slater?' he said. 'Not hard to spot you. Aidan.'

Jim shook the hand offered to him. 'Jim,' he said, keeping things informal. 'Thanks for agreeing to meet up. Do we need a cab?'

'Nah, we can walk. My usual spot is a bar two blocks thataway,' he jabbed a thumb over his shoulder, 'but it'll be packed at this time of day. I'm guessing you'd like a little more privacy?'

'That would be good.'

'There's the St. Regis. Tables are well spaced and it's quiet. Costs more, though. Are we on Uncle Sam's dime?'

'Don't worry about it.' Actually Jim wouldn't feel justified in putting this on expenses.

'Okay. I booked a table there just in case. Hotel's on 16th and K, three blocks thataway.' He pointed.

'Fine. Let's go.'

The sidewalk was crowded so they didn't attempt to engage in conversation but walked briskly, often one behind the other, past Franklin Square, then McPherson Square, and arrived at the hotel at the next intersection. Aidan had evidently been here before because he led the way quickly through the cool, plush interior of the hotel straight to the Alhambra restaurant.

It wasn't busy and, as Aidan had said, the tables were well spaced. Jazz was playing softly in the background, but most of the normal sounds of conversation and cutlery on plates were absorbed by the high ceiling, heavy curtains, and soft carpet. The waiter checked the reservation and Aidan pointed to a table where they'd be away from other customers.

'Certainly, sir,' the waiter said. 'Please come with me.' He picked up a couple of menus and led them to the table, pulled chairs out for them and set the menus down. 'Something to drink, gentlemen?'

They both ordered beers, then opened the leather-covered menus and studied them in silence. There were a number of Mediterranean specialities, which suited Jim well. The waiter returned with two beers, already poured, the glasses sweating with condensation.

Aidan said, 'Ready to order, Jim?'

'Sure, you go ahead.'

Aidan had bypassed the specialities and ordered a steak medium-rare and fries. Jim ordered a brandade of cod and smoked trout, with a salad on the side.

The waiter repeated the orders and withdrew. Aidan took a pull at his beer, then set the glass down. 'So, Jim, what's on your mind?'

'Did you gather that I'm with the SAF?'

'Yup, and I looked you up. You're the CO.'

'That's right. Let me say something right here, right now. We keep a tight lid on our operations, Aidan. That's not for fun, it's to protect men and women who could be putting their lives at risk on every single mission. So what you and I discuss here has to be in the strictest confidence. You're not at liberty to report or hint at any part of this conversation, much less quote me as a source.'

'Okay, I expected that. It won't go any further.'

'Good. And that includes the in-ear devices you're wearing, which probably transmit to a recorder in your pocket.'

Aidan exploded in laughter and slapped the table. Two businessmen sitting a few tables away looked up.

'How in hell's name did you know that?'

Jim said quietly, 'I've been trained in counter-surveillance, Aidan.'

'Well you needn't worry, they're switched off. I'm only wearing them out of sheer habit, but if it makes you feel any easier…' He removed the earpieces, brought out the recorder and showed Jim that it was indeed switched off, then pocketed all three. 'Okay?'

'Okay, let's talk.'

4

Jim initiated the conversation. 'The SAF operates all over the world: the Middle East, Africa, Central and South America, and so on. That means I have to be on top of any situations we're likely to encounter if we go in. I have some holes in my knowledge of South American countries and I was hoping you could help me fill them in.'

Aidan studied him carefully. 'But you've come to me, so I assume you're undertaking a mission in Venezuela and you want the latest on what's going on there.'

Jim side-stepped the implied question. 'In some circles you're known for your inside knowledge of that country.'

'Not too many, I hope. I need to protect my identity. I even report without a byline.'

'Go on.'

He shrugged. 'I guess you know some of it, but these days Venezuela is a kind of black hole when it comes to news. I expect the US has spooks operating out there but whatever they find never makes it to the media. And it's dangerous, so it doesn't appeal to most correspondents. Gives me something of a niche.'

'You're fluent in Spanish, obviously.'

'Oh yeah, and I have a knack with local accents. When I'm out on location I dress like a local. Trouble is, I don't exactly look like one – too many skinny people around. I should try to lose this.' He slapped his stomach. 'It's a problem. I lose weight when I'm there – I do a lot of walking. Then I come back to Washington and put it all back on again.' He gestured at his beer glass, which was already half empty.

'So how do you gather information?'

'Not by going around talking to people – that would attract too much attention. And with this gut someone could take me for a member of a cartel, which could be one helluva problem. No, I use my eyes and my ears.' He smiled. 'Every day I go out and buy a local newspaper. They're government-controlled, of course, full of crap about the wonderful things the President is doing for them. But that also means they report on major infrastructure projects. If it's a hospital or a school or something like that they're thrilled to bits to let people know. But it doesn't really matter what the hell it is, so long as it'll sound good to the reader and looks like it may create jobs. I go to the vicinity of those projects and find myself a coffee bar. Sit there reading the paper and using these.' He dipped into his pocket, and brought out the in-ear devices again. 'Let me show you how it works.' He plugged them into his ears, turned on the recorder and passed his thumb over a knurled wheel, presumably to adjust the volume. He listened for a few moments, then said, 'The two businessmen on that table over there? They're discussing a hostile bid for a rival company. And I hear footsteps. The waiter's coming this way.'

Jim looked up. The waiter approached the table with their two meals. Jim pointed to Aidan's almost empty glass. 'You want another of those?'

Aidan winced. 'Shouldn't really, but yeah, okay.'

The waiter gave Jim an enquiring look but he said, 'No, I'm good, thanks.'

The waiter left. Aidan said, 'See? Surprising what you can pick up just by hanging around.' He removed the earpieces, switched off the recorder and replaced them in his pocket. Then he set about cutting up his steak.

Jim knew that eavesdropping equipment like that was available in the services – Reconnaissance Detachment Alpha had them, for example. It seemed they were also available on the open market – if you knew who to talk to.

Aidan put down the knife, forked a piece of steak into his mouth, and continued to speak while chewing. 'If it's not productive I move to another bar.' He swallowed, then laughed. 'I drink a whole lot of coffee.' He forked another piece of steak.

Jim tried the brandade, which was very good, and for a while they ate in silence. Then Jim said, 'I know Venezuela's a basket case, financially speaking – has been for years.'

'Correct. Hyperinflation, repeated devaluations. People can scarcely afford to eat. The little that's available in the supermarkets is expensive. A bag of rice or sugar costs a week's wages. And that's in Caracas, where things are a bit better than elsewhere, because they like to show off to the occasional foreign visitors and correspondents. Outside the capital they're not even attempting to hide the problems and it's much worse. A lot of people emigrated to Colombia.

Some get by on farming. Others get involved in smuggling goods across the border. The rest stay put and go hungry.'

Jim shook his head. 'Why's the economy so bad? They have oil – don't they? – some say the largest reserves in the world.'

Aidan drank off the rest of the beer, put down the empty glass, and ran the back of his hand across his mouth. 'Yeah, oil would be a handy export if they had a market for it. A lot of countries are still operating sanctions thanks to the existing government. The US shut their doors to imports from Venezuela years ago. Any case we're a hydrogen economy. Oil's still a useful raw material for stuff like lubricants, paints, and petrochemicals but we can easily supply that market from our own reserves.' He forked up some fries, chewed for a bit, then said, 'Trouble is, in Venezuela the bulk of the industry's collapsed, and the equipment isn't being maintained. So even if there was an upturn they'd find it hard to respond now.'

'They must have other resources.'

'Oh they've got some other industry. Unfortunately a lot of that is destroying the country. They harvest timber and that means deforestation. They mine gold in the south and that pollutes the local water supply.' He tapped the tablecloth with one finger. 'The big problem, Jim, is the administration. It goes from extreme right-wing, corrupt, and hopelessly incompetent to extreme left-wing, corrupt, and hopelessly incompetent. Currently it's extreme left-wing, but so was Stalin. And, like Stalin, President Aguilar is the complete autocrat. He outlaws opposition parties and has political leaders arrested, imprisoned without trial, tortured, and killed. Civil protests are brutally put down by the army, and the leaders meet the same fate as the political opponents.' He picked up more fries.

The waiter came with another beer and removed the empty glass. Aidan nodded to him, then waited until he was out of earshot. He lowered his voice, 'Aguilar denies responsibility for the economy, of course. Like some of his predecessors he blames the whole mess on the US, rails about it for hours in his public speeches. Meanwhile he lives in his luxurious playpen and nothing changes.'

'So where's his money coming from?'

Aidan smiled, put down his fork, and tapped the table again. 'Look, if you want to understand Venezuela you got to reckon on the importance of the drug cartels. There used to be a whole bunch of them, like in Mexico. But there were mergers, so now it's just two main cartels and a few minor ones. The two main ones are Los Feroces and the Guárico Cartel. They're big, they're rich, and they influence everything that happens in that country. By the way, not many people use the name Guárico Cartel. Most of them call it *El Hombre Gordo*, The Fat Man. Heard of it?'

'Sure, I've heard of it.'

'Okay, Los Feroces supports President Aguilar and keeps him in pocket money. They're well-equipped and effectively they're an extension of the Venezuelan Army. The Fat Man cartel supports his rival, Delgado.'

'Why?'

'Think about it. Aguilar's in power, hand in glove with Los Feroces. If Delgado takes over, Los Feroces is out, and there's an opportunity for the Guárico organization to step in.'

Jim ate some more brandade, then sipped his beer. 'So Aguilar survives on drug money.'

'Partly. But there's another source: Russia. It suits Russia to have an influence in a country that's on North America's doorstep. Russia never signed up to sanctions. On the contrary, they still accept imports from Venezuela and support infrastructure projects. Of course some of that money goes to Aguilar and his cronies and some must go to Los Feroces as well, otherwise the projects would get held up by mysterious accidents.'

'This rival of his, Delgado...'

'Juan-Luis Delgado is recognized as the rightful President by more than fifty countries around the world, including the US. Everyone knows he would have won the last election if Aguilar hadn't rigged it, hence the sanctions. Aguilar's over seventy now, but he's not quitting.'

'From what you've told me I'd have thought Aguilar's people would have eliminated Delgado by now.'

'No, not even Aguilar's secret police could do that without it getting around. In any case they have another problem: he's alive all right, but no one knows where he is. Some say he's in hiding with the Guárico Cartel.' He shrugged. 'No one knows where they operate from either.'

Jim nodded. 'What about the Venezuelan army? Whose side are they on?'

'Officially they have to swear allegiance to the President.'

'And unofficially?'

'Unofficially? My guess is if Delgado came to power they'd follow him. It's human nature. The army is a good job and good jobs are scarce.' He put his fork down and took a long draught of beer. His plate was empty.

Jim sat back. He wasn't planning to finish the brandade or the salad. 'Coffee?'

'Sure.'

Aidan caught the waiter's eye and he came over to clear the dishes and took the order. While they were waiting for the coffee Jim said:

'I've heard Venezuela has the worst jails in the world. Is that reputation deserved?'

'Are they the worst? That I can't say. Are they bad? You bet. The Post did a piece on them a while back, and I helped on it. We couldn't get inside one but we managed to interview some of the people who came out. Even I was shocked: severe overcrowding, inadequate food, shortage of clean water, gangs in total control, drugs, weapons, violence – murders every day. The guards look the other way. So far as they're concerned an inmate gets killed, great, one less to look after.'

'My God, are they all like that?'

'Well, a while back they built a new one in Maracaibo: Buena Vista they called it. Government propaganda says it's a model prison and they send their political opponents to it. I contacted one ex-prisoner and it sounded like it wasn't a whole lot better than the one that was there before, worse maybe. He told me there was a special wing for systematically torturing prisoners to death. His cell was nowhere near that wing but even from that distance he could hear the screams.'

The waiter arrived with the coffees.

Jim had learned as much as he cared to.

*

During the flight back from Washington Jim had time to mull things over. He'd had personal dealings with President Nagel and he admired her quick grasp of issues and her ability to get things done. Even if it was the CIA who'd masterminded this scheme she would have had to give the go-ahead on this one. That could only mean there were issues of national importance involved. Wendell had been shut out of the loop; consequently Jim had no idea what those issues could be. But he'd been on missions ordered by the CIA before and he'd learnt not to take anything ordered up by them at face value. By the time the aircraft was on the final approach to Raleigh-Durham his thoughts had congealed into a kind of resolve.

What he'd decided was that he was not on any account prepared to stand by and let a US envoy be taken to a prison to be tortured to death.

5

Jim lost no time in selecting his squad. Sergeant Miguel Garzón had been with him on a mission in the Yemen. He was Mexican-born and ideal for this operation. Corporal Fernando Boudon was born in California but brought up by his Argentinian parents and they spoke both English and Spanish at home. He wasn't a great talker but if you wanted something done he was already doing it. Lieutenant Sally Kent still walked with a slight limp from the rounds that had shattered her femur in Northern Tanzania. She'd worked hard on her rehab, lost a lot of weight, and now she was even doing the ten-mile tab each morning, although without the full pack. Jim knew she was anxious to get involved in real action again. She was certainly fit enough for this assignment, and she was fluent in several languages. She was a fine officer, and he had a lot of admiration for her guts. It would be good to have her with them.

He gave them all a briefing on the nature of the mission. Then he told them to get some practice in right away by conversing with one another only in Spanish. Maybe Miguel could give them a steer on the local dialect, too. Jim said he'd join in himself whenever he could.

The more he contemplated the impending task the more uneasy he felt about it. They were dealing with a country that had a reputation for cheerfully imprisoning and torturing to death anyone who presented a challenge to the regime or wasn't sufficiently respectful of it: political opponents, protestors, journalists, writers, artists, and Americans – especially Americans. The entire exercise struck him as odd. Why was our government negotiating with this bunch of despots? What was it they had that our people wanted so badly? And what were we offering them in return? Over and above that, his squad would be going into this country's second largest city, four Americans walking the streets unarmed, and he was concerned for their safety. Above all he was troubled by the thought that something he may have overlooked, a detail here or a precaution there, could expose them to danger.

The only solution was to prepare even more thoroughly than usual. He learned something of Venezuela's history and geography. He spent a lot of time studying maps of Maracaibo, memorizing the major landmarks, and he encouraged the other members of the team to do the same. He planned carefully for every stage of the operation, with every alternative scenario he could think of, and he prepared to equip them accordingly. If something unexpected did happen, well, they'd have to deal with it on the spot.

After that he could only wait for the instruction to report to the people who were going to give them the right documents and clothes for the mission.

All I can say is, they'd better be good. Damned good.

*

The 'outfitting' section Wendell had contacted was located in McLean, in Fairfax County, Virginia, not far from the CIA's headquarters at Langley. No coincidence about that, Jim thought. The CIA's spooks probably kept them pretty busy.

Although the purpose of their visit was top secret this part of the assignment promised to be fairly routine. There was no need for military transport to Andrews Air Force Base. Instead they wore civilian clothes and took a scheduled flight from Raleigh-Durham to Washington Dulles, where they picked up a rental car. Miguel drove, taking the VA-267 toll route, and exiting onto North Madison Boulevard and Old Dominion Drive. The NavAid closed on the address they'd been given and signalled a left turn.

Miguel pointed. 'That can't be it. No sign. Just an alleyway.'

'Try going on a hundred yards.'

He did and the NavAid signalled a U-turn.

'Must have been it.' Miguel shrugged and made the turn.

The road was barely wide enough for two cars. After about a hundred yards it widened into a large turning circle, beyond which there was a pole barrier and a sentry post. The sentry came out. He was wearing Army Combat Uniform and the brassard on his left upper arm identified him as Military Police. He had one hand on the butt of his sidearm.

'This is a restricted area. You have an appointment?'

Jim said, 'Yes, orders of General Wendell Harken.'

The sentry extended a hand. 'I.D.s.'

They handed over their I.D.s and the man took all four and disappeared into the post for a while, no doubt to check the appointment on a monitor. Jim saw him lift a receiver.

He spoke for a while, then replaced the receiver and came out.

'Y'all stop at the first building on the right,' he said, handing back the I.D.s. He raised the barrier and they drove through.

'Security seems to be pretty low-key,' Miguel said.

After a further hundred yards the road ended at a twelve-foot-high chain-link fence topped with razor wire. Tall flood-lights were set along it at regular intervals. Full height electrically-operated gates were swinging slowly open for them.

'Not that low-key,' Sally commented.

Miguel parked the car at the first building, nothing imposing, just a long, low construction of magnoceramic blocks with a sloping felt roof. Beyond it was a line of similar buildings on the right of the access road, and several on the left, including a single long one which, Jim suspected, was a barracks. They went into the first building.

'Venezuela,' the portly ex-army man said by way of greeting.

'That's right,' Jim said.

'Yeah, that's what the General said. My name is Andy. We-all have what you need, and please believe me when I say I do know what you need. I served in surveillance.'

'Right,' Jim said, wishing he'd get on with it.

Andy took waist and inner leg measurements on the three men. He didn't bother with Sally, just looked her up and down, stated a dress size and Sally nodded.

They spent the next hour donning and doffing shirts and chino trousers while Sally tried on dresses. Finally Andy lined them up to check the chosen attire. The men were wearing thin open-neck shirts and chinos, each of different colour. As Andy said, 'You do *not* want to look like a goddamned football team.' Sally was wearing a long cotton dress patterned with flowers. She was tanned from the tabs and practice exercises in North Carolina, as indeed Jim was, so they wouldn't be too pale and conspicuous in a crowd. Fernando and Miguel had a natural Latin skin coloration.

Andy appraised the result. 'The clothes look good and they fit good,' he said. Then he pointed a finger first at Jim and then at Sally. 'You two. Blond hair.'

Sally's hair was still done up in the regulation bun. 'Do you want me to give mine a rinse?' she asked.

He grimaced. 'No, that'd be too obvious. Wear it in a ponytail, though.' He turned to Jim, whose hair was a straw blond. 'I guess you'll do,' he said. 'There'll be quite an assortment of folk out there. Just make sure you-all don't identify as Americans.'

'Yeah, we got that message,' Jim said.

'Good,' Andy said. 'Put on your own outfits now. You can take these and the changes of clothes.'

The next stop was the documents section, where they had their photographs taken and filled out some details. Half an hour later they were issued with fake passports, identity papers, and Venezuelan driving licences.

A man in a white coat emerged from a back room and gave each of them a cheap-looking watch. The watches were identical but the straps were of different styles.

'This here watch looks pretty ordinary, right?' he said. 'Don't let that fool you, it's real useful.' He then demonstrated its capabilities, which included a compass and geolocation functions. 'When you go in, dump those,' he pointed at their service watches, 'and use these.'

Each of them strapped the watches on their opposite wrist for the moment.

'Thanks,' Jim said. 'What's next?'

'I guess you'll be collecting some Venezuelan cash. The office is over there.'

The currency office was the next building on the same side of the access road. They were each issued with a large wad of bolivares, which they had to sign for.

Sally looked at the currency in consternation, then back up at the accountant. 'There are thousands here. Do we need this much?'

The accountant gave her a wan smile. 'Venezuelan currency is worth shit. And they have hyperinflation, hundreds of per cent, so this lot will buy you less at the end of your assignment that it did at the beginning.'

Sally turned to the others and shrugged.

Jim said, 'I'd like to have a word with the people who are preparing our vehicle.'

'Sure thing, that's across the road, further down. You'll see a lot of cars parked up there.'

'Thanks.'

They slung their backpacks with the clothes, identity papers, and currency over their shoulders and walked down to the vehicle centre. The man at the counter checked Jim's I.D., said, 'Venezuela, yeah,' and took them through to a large covered shed, something like an aircraft hangar, where mechanics were working on a range of different vehicles. There were smells of oil, ozone, and paint, and sounds of hammering. One corner lit up with a shower of sparks, outlining a heavily visored man with an arc welder. They stopped at an all-roader.

'This here's a six-year-old Toyota. You'll see plenty like this'n over there. Four seats, and a couple of extra seats in the back if you don't need the luggage space. Pretty standard. Main changes are under the loading bay.'

He took them round to the back, opened the rear door, then hinged up the floor of the loading bay.

'Normally you'd find a spare wheel in here. You won't need it; we fitted heavy-duty, run-flat tyres. We cleared out all the bracing, welded some reinforcement round the sides. Gives you a good space for whatever you'll be taking in the way of armaments.'

Jim nodded. 'Nice.'

'In the cubby: standard documents, couple of maps, manuals, maintenance records – not stamped, most of the folk there don't go in for regular maintenance or they do it themselves.'

'How about the numberplates?' Jim asked.

'Bona fide Venezuelan numberplates.'

'Where did they come from?'

'You don't need to know that.' The answer came without a smile.

'I say I do,' Jim said. 'If they've been stolen we could be in trouble.'

'That won't be a problem, they're not stolen. Let's just say we have a contact at a vehicle recycling centre.'

Jim nodded. 'Okay. Thanks, you've done a great job.'

'Just needs some finishing touches. We'll take some of the shine off the bodywork, put in a couple of dents, spray on a little dirt. And the sun gets hot out there, so the plastic under the windscreen gets bleached and cracked. We'll do something about that, too.'

'How will you get it to the Rotofan?'

'We look after all that. It'll be ready for you.'

Jim thanked him again and shook hands. Then he turned to the others 'I guess we're all through here.'

They drove back to the airport, checked their rented vehicle in and made their way to Departures.

'Good morning's work,' Jim said.

Sally said, 'Seems we're pretty well-equipped.'

Miguel said, 'When do we leave?'

'I don't know, I have to wait for the go-ahead. We don't want to be there too early or someone may notice us hanging around. Soon as I know I'll tell you. Between now and then I don't want any injuries or setbacks. You can do the morning tab but without the full pack. Some light gym work, no close combat training. Play with your new watches and talk to each other in Spanish. It shouldn't be long now.'

6

A week later Jim was in his office when a call came through on the secure line. It was Wendell Harken.

'You ready to go, Jim?'

Jim breathed out. 'Yes.'

'Good. There'll be a military transport waiting for you at Raleigh-Durham airport tomorrow morning, 0900 hours. The pilot will have a sealed envelope for you. Inside you'll find four copies of a photo of Mr X, one for each of you. Good luck.'

Jim sat back. The waiting for this one had been harder than usual, so it was a relief to be doing something at last. He looked at the wall clock. Seven pm. Wendell was evidently working late.

He went over to the mess, where the others were having dinner. They looked up expectantly.

'We're go for the mission,' he said quietly. 'Raleigh-Durham at 0900 hours. I'll order a people carrier from the pool.'

'Great,' Miguel said, and the others nodded.

'Do we wear civvies or combat uniform?' Sally asked.

'Best to wear combat uniforms on the way out, just in case that LZ isn't as deserted as they think it is. If all's clear we'll change into the civvies.'

*

They took off from Raleigh-Durham the following morning. Jim unsealed the envelope given to him by the pilot and handed three of the photos he found inside to his team. He examined the fourth carefully. It was not a distinctive face: hazel eyes, light brown hair, tinged with grey at the temples, skin creased a little around the eyes and lips, small nose, firm jaw. He returned the photos to the envelope and prepared for take-off.

Three hours later they landed at United States Air Force Base, West Texas. The engines wound down and there was a rattle in the cabin as they unfastened seat buckles. Fernando got to his feet.

Jim stood and held up a hand. 'Just stay put for the moment, guys. I have to check in with the base commander.' He took a carrier bag out of the overhead locker and went to the front.

The copilot came out of the cockpit, opened the door and lowered the stairs, and Jim emerged into the intense dry heat of a Texas day. There was, he saw, a single Rotofan parked not far away, rippling in the hot air coming off the apron. He crossed swiftly to the base commander's office and knocked on the door.

'Come.'

He opened the door and the commander drew his long legs off the desk and rose with a broad grin. Colonel 'Red' Nicholson was in his fifties but he still had the freckles and the brush of carrot-red hair that had earned him his nickname.

'Well if it ain't the Special Forces Colonel. How the hell are you, Jim?'

'I'm good, thanks, Red. You know, I haven't forgotten how you saved my ass when I was in a tight spot down there in Mexico. This is overdue but I hope you like it.'

Jim placed the carrier bag on his desk and Red drew out a bottle. 'Old Forester 1920 Prohibition Style – say this is seriously good stuff!'

'You earned it.'

'What say we give it a try?'

'Sorry, Red. Just passing through, but I wanted to drop in.'

'Oh sure, you'll be the party taking off in that Rotofan. They told me it would be special forces, didn't realize it would be you again.'

'That's right. I'll try not to get into trouble this time.'

'Shee-it, if getting you out of trouble gets me a bottle like this you can do it any ol' time you like!'

They shook hands.

'Red, I've got three guys back there in the transport. It's cooking outside. Anywhere cool I can put them while I sort out the route with the Rotofan pilots?'

'Oh sure, better'n that. Why don't they come to the mess and we'll fix them up with somethin' to eat.'

'Well I've never known them to pass up a meal.'

'Bring 'em over and I'll take y'all down there. And that'd be where the Rotofan guys are right now.'

'Great.'

Jim collected the others, introduced them, and Red led them to the mess. It was a large base and the mess hall was crowded at this time of day. The air was warm and heavy with the meaty smell of chilli con carne. There was a long line-up at the lunch counter but Red took them to the head of it, saying to the waiting personnel, 'These here guys are our guests.' Then he turned to Jim.

'The four over there are your Rotofan crew.' He pointed at a table quite close to the counter. 'I'll leave ya here, got stuff to do. Good to see ya, Jim!'

They shook hands again and he left.

When they'd loaded their trays Jim, who'd just picked up a couple of sandwiches and a Coke, said to Miguel, 'Can you take these and find a table? I'm going to talk to the Rotofan crew.'

He walked over to the table. He didn't know the two he could see. The other two had their backs to him, one of them a heavily built African American. They looked up as Jim reached them.

'Hayden! And Cliff!' he said.

'Jim, how're ya doing?' Hayden Robbins stood and extended a hand. The older of the two, he was almost as tall as Jim but broader all the way down. His colleague, Clifford King, was the polar opposite, a skinny, blond-haired twenty-something. They shook hands.

Jim said, 'I gather you're flying that Rotofan for us.'

'We sure are.' Hayden's voice was a rich bass. 'And this here's Kelly and Rafael. They'll be riding shotgun.'

Jim shook hands with Rafael. He had straight black hair, a dark complexion and a small flat nose suggestive of Native American ancestry. Then Jim leaned over to Kelly and she gave him a firm handshake. Her hair was chestnut brown, tied back in the regulation bun. To handle a fast-firing cannon you had to be strong. She looked like she was up to it.

Jim noticed that their plates were empty. They must have got here much earlier, which explained how they'd found a table so close to the counter.

'Are you based here now?' he said.

'Nah,' Hayden said. 'Flew in from Andrews. That's where your vehicle was loaded. They refuelled us here.'

'Right. But Rotofans? Last time we met you were flying Buzzards.'

'Yeah, well, Jim, they was short on Rotofan pilots so I thought, why not give it a whirl?'

'And?'

He screwed up his face, which accentuated the laugh lines around his eyes. 'Y'know I kinda miss the speed and that punch in the back when you flick in the ol' afterburners. But these babies are interesting too, 'specially hovering and landing. Give you plenty t'think about.'

Jim looked around him, then passed a piece of paper across the table. 'That's where we're going.'

Hayden glanced at the coordinates. Without moving his head he flicked up his big, bloodshot eyes. 'Which is where, exactly?'

'Venezuela,' Jim said softly.

'Jesus H. Christ,' Hayden said, equally softly. 'And the LZ?'

'About thirty miles outside Maracaibo. It's a clearing in the forest that someone's gone to the trouble of identifying for us.'

Hayden sighed. 'That'll be from an earth-observation satellite. They tell you shit about the terrain you're supposed to set down on. Those things can spot a centipede from 10,000 miles up, but can they say whether it's a clearing or just a bog? Can they hell!'

Jim shrugged. 'All I've been told is that the clearing was made by logging, which seems to have stopped.'

Clff said, 'We need to file a flight plan, Hayden. For Texas, at least.'

'Yeah,' Hayden said. 'But I'm not planning to cross half a dozen borders to get there. We'll leave the coast west of Houston, then head out across the Gulf. I don't want to fly over Colombia either if I can help it. I'll look out a better route, maybe come in from the sea.' He looked at Jim. 'There's an airport at Maracaibo, isn't there?'

'Yes.'

'Well, we'll come in to the north of that, too, so we don't get picked up by their radar.'

Cliff said, 'We expecting any opposition, Jim?'

'We don't know that. I shouldn't think they have ground-to-air but you never know. I think you should try to keep under the radar as long as you can.'

'Okay,' Hayden nodded slowly. 'Look, Jim, you have your lunch. I'll go over to the office, take a look at the latest digimaps and file the necessary.'

Jim said, 'Good idea. See you later.' He began to leave, hesitated, then turned back. 'Hayden, we need to keep a very tight lid on this. How much of the flight plan do you have to reveal?'

He smiled. 'Trust me.'

43

7

They came in over the Caribbean Sea, flying so low it seemed to Jim that they were almost touching the waves. At Hayden's invitation Jim had taken a jump seat so that he could be with them in the cockpit. He'd donned a headset, which snuffed out the distant double whine of the Rotofan's engines and enabled him to listen to their communications. Now he was looking through the big bubble of the cockpit, focusing on the forward view, where a line of green topped with clouds had materialized on the horizon.

Hayden said, 'Crossing the coast in a minute. Kelly, Rafael, stay sharp. I'm gonna gain some height to clear those cliffs.'

The gunners' voices came over the headset, 'Got that,' and 'I copy.'

Jim could visualize the two at the ports on either side of the forward fuselage, swivelling the cannon, scanning the terrain below.

They crossed a shoreline, the green water striped with a succession of rolling breakers, and almost immediately flew over cliffs. Below them now was a rugged landscape of alternating forest and bare ground. A coastal road passed underneath them and shortly after that a wide river. This gave way to a plain patterned with rectangles, clear evidence of cultivation. They left behind several smaller roads, then gained more height and Hayden skilfully banked the craft to fly along the tree-clad slopes of a mountain range. Finally he turned and began to descend. Jim's eyes were on the navigation panel now, watching their target, a small red circle within an upright cross, creeping in from the top of the screen.

Cliff said. 'I have a visual.'

Hayden's hands moved to a lever and Jim realized he was rotating the engine pods to a more vertical angle. They slowed and began a tight circuit around the landing zone, the trees below thrashing in the downdraught.

'Doesn't look like logging,' Cliff said. 'Usually those guys leave stumps and a lot of small branches behind. No vehicles that I can see. Looks okay to land, Hayden.'

'Yeah.'

Hayden reduced forward speed until they were hovering, then descended slowly. A cloud of dust and leaves rose all around them, obscuring the view, but Hayden continued the descent and they felt the contact as the Rotofan settled on the ground. With a swift movement of his big hand he swept the twin throttle levers fully back. The engines were barely turning over now and the dust began to settle.

'Nice touchdown,' Jim commented.

Hayden acknowledged this with a nod. He said, 'See anything move, Kelly?'

'Not so far.'

'Rafael?'

'Nothing.'

'Okay, I think we take a look.' Hayden switched off the engines.

'That's our job,' Jim said. He unbuckled his seat harness and went back into the main cabin. The others were already hauling down their packs from the overhead lockers and picking up their multirifles. It was a natural reaction to a landing in hostile territory. If someone's going to start tossing grenades you don't want to be caught inside a tin box.

Jim grabbed his multirifle and shouted, 'Miguel. With me.'

Miguel hurried forward grinning all over his moon face.

Kelly was still scanning the cannon back and forth. 'Cover us, Kelly,' he said.

'You bet.'

The loading door on that side unlatched with a metallic thud, presumably operated by Hayden or Cliff. A gust of hot, moist air met them as it opened, and a set of steps unfolded.

Jim clattered down them fast and threw himself to the ground.

Nothing.

Miguel did the same.

Still nothing.

Jim hand-signalled to take one way while he took the other. He crept low, treading stealthily, ears tuned to the slightest sound. The forest was dense and he saw nothing move. Minutes later he heard a soft crunch and swung the rifle round, but it was Miguel; they'd met half way. They continued past each other and back to the Rotofan.

'See anything, Miguel?'

'Not a thing.'

'Me neither. What about the logging trail?'

'What logging trail?'

'Damn,' Jim said. 'It's supposed to be here. May be overgrown. We'd better search properly.' He went up the steps again and took his pack from the locker 'Okay to disembark,' he said.

They assembled down below.

'Okay,' Jim said. 'First things first. Let's see if we can find this logging trail.' He checked the compass on the cheap-looking but deceptively capable wristwatch he'd been given at McLean. He pointed. 'It should be on that side.'

It was Fernando who spotted the path. Jim hurried over. Trees next to the cleared area had enjoyed more sunlight and their branches had grown vigorously and spread across the entrance. He ducked through. The rest of it looked passable, if a bit wet and muddy. He saw no fresh vehicle tracks.

'Okay,' Jim said. 'Let's get that Toyota down from the Rotofan. Sally, Fernando, stay clear. Miguel, you can come on board and do the driving.'

While Miguel climbed into the driver's seat of the all-roader Jim went forward to the cockpit. 'Can you lower the ramp now, guys?'

'Sure can,' Cliff said. 'Everyone standing clear out there?'

'Yes.'

'Okay.' He pressed a button. Electric motors whined and the loading doors of the Rotofan opened. The ramp slid out, then tipped down. The noise stopped. Miguel started the vehicle's engine. He had to back out, so Jim walked alongside, signalling him to come on. The ramp was steep but the all-roader was rock steady as it came down. The rear tyres met the ground, established a grip, and it moved back and off the ramp. Then Miguel manoeuvred to face the logging trail and switched off the engine.

They assembled again in the clearing. Jim said:

'Okay, we can change into the civvies now. We'll leave our uniforms in that compartment under the loading bay of the vehicle. The automatic rifles and other stuff will go in there, too. It's unlikely we'll be stopped on the way but in case we are, keep some small arms handy but out of sight. We'll stow those when we get to Maracaibo.'

Sally went back on board to change. The rest stripped down where they stood and changed into the local clothes they'd been assigned. Sally joined them and they laid their weapons in the space under the loading bay. Jim saw her putting in a walking stick.

His eyes widened. 'Do you need that?'

She held up the stick. 'This? No, I don't need it, but it's handy.' She pressed something on the handle and drew out a section about a foot long.

'What is it?'

'A taser. Bit of an advance on the old sword stick, isn't it?'

'Jesus, where did you get it?'

'I have a friend with connections.'

Jim shook his head and went back up the Rotofan's stairs and into the cockpit.

'Hayden, one last thing: do you think anyone saw us fly in?'

Hayden's lips tightened. 'Jim, I know it wasn't ideal but that was the best route I could—'

Jim held up a hand. 'I'm not questioning that. I'd just like to know if you think we were seen.'

He shrugged. 'It's likely, yes. There were farms down there, roads we had to cross. This craft isn't carrying any markings, so we could be taken for Venezuelan Air Force or Colombian Air Force. We just have to hope they weren't interested – or at least decided to mind their own business.' He opened his hands. 'Jim, if it was up to me, I'd just as soon leave and come back here, but the orders were to wait.'

Jim nodded. 'They want to keep our presence here quiet. I guess if you went back and made a return flight it would treble the risk of you getting spotted.'

Hayden shrugged and grimaced.

'Well it looks pretty isolated, so you should be safe enough. Keep a lookout all the same. You going to manage okay?'

Hayden shrugged. 'We have supplies for ten days and a couple of tents for sleeping outside.'

'I wouldn't light any fires. Smoke will rise above those trees.'

'Yeah, yeah, I know.'

'We'll rendezvous with you inside a week. If we're not here by then, don't wait any longer; get the hell out of here.'

Hayden asked the question with his eyebrows.

Jim nodded. 'Yes, I'm saying go without us.' He smiled and placed a hand on Hayden's shoulder. 'I know you're not in my chain of command but you can still consider that an order.'

'Good luck, Jim. You take care.'

'Yeah, you too.'

Jim went back to the others. 'Okay everyone, let's move out.'

8

The branches that had almost hidden the logging trail were slender enough to be tackled with mission knives; the thicker ones yielded to the application of a little brute force. With the entrance to the path now clear they got on board the Toyota and set off. Miguel drove steadily down the narrow trail, the four-wheel drive smacking smaller branches out of the way. The sky darkened and rain began to fall steadily, then more heavily, obscuring the view ahead with a veil of grey and making the trail, already littered with small branches and other detritus, muddy and slippery. They continued for a while, the rain drumming on the roof and the windscreen wipers slapping back and forth at double speed. Then Miguel slammed on the brakes, bringing them to a skiddy halt and throwing them forward into their seat belts. Jim, who was in the passenger seat, looked at him and Miguel pointed.

Through the sheets of rain Jim saw that a tree had fallen across the path.

'Shit.'

'We'd better take a look,' Miguel said.

'Yeah.'

Sally leaned forward from the back. 'You'll get soaked,' she said. 'Can't we wait till this stops?'

Jim shook his head. 'I don't know how long that'll be. This is their rainy season, so it may be set in for quite a while.' He thought for a moment. 'Look, Miguel can open the rear hatch from inside. We'll run round and shelter under it while we get the army uniforms out. Then we can use them as another layer over these clothes. We'll need the boots, too. You and Fernando stay in here for the moment. Okay, Miguel?'

Miguel nodded and pressed a button tucked away low on the side of the dashboard. There was a clunk as the rear hatch opened, accompanied by a sharp increase in the rushing sound of the rain as it lashed through the forest canopy. They opened the doors and ran around. When they'd pulled on the uniforms and boots they squelched up to the tree and examined it. Miguel followed the end of the trunk into the brush on one side and then the other, nodded to Jim and they hurried back inside the vehicle.

Jim heaved a breath. 'Well, Miguel, what do you think?'

'At least it's only the trunk on the path; the branches start over there on the left.' He pointed. 'I guess we have two choices. We could pick up plenty of dead branches and pack them both sides, make a kind of ramp up and down.'

'I don't like that idea. The ground is soft and the branches could sink in. Our clearance isn't that high. We could be dumped on the top of that trunk, balancing on the oil sump. Worse still, we could rip a hole in it. What's the other option?'

'We move it to the side.'

52

'What? No way! It's much too heavy to carry, even for the four of us.'

'Oh, for sure it's too heavy to carry. But maybe not too heavy to lift. If we line up a lot of branches on the ground they'll be all slippery with rain and mud. We could lift it on and then slide it out of the way.'

Jim bit his lip, then nodded. 'It's worth a try. If we can't move that thing off the path this mission has failed before it's even begun. And I don't want any sort of barrier left here. We could be in an all-fired hurry when we come back.'

Miguel said, 'Problem is, that tree has sunk a little into the mud already. We can never lift it like that. We need to unstick it first.'

'The jack? We've got run-flat tyres but they may have left it in with the tools. I'll check.'

Moments later Jim returned. 'I've got it. Okay, Sally and Fernando, you can put on your uniforms and boots now. We'll need your help.'

The four spread into the forest on either side, looking for substantial branches, bringing them back, and laying them at an angle to the fallen tree. It took them the best part of an hour, but now there was a kind of horizontal slipway leading off to one side. They paused to catch their breath. The rain had done nothing to relieve the clammy air, which was even stickier in two layers of clothing.

Jim set up the jack under the trunk, but as soon as he started to wind the handle it sank into the mud. They made a second search, stuffing smaller branches down the hole the jack had made. He tried again and the same thing happened. He straightened up, running his tongue over his lips. 'This isn't working.'

'If there were a few rocks around…' Fernando said.

'Come on, guys,' Sally said, 'it was better this time. Let's get some more wood and give it another try.'

It was just like Sally, Jim thought. Always ready to have a go.

They nodded and spread out, repeating the exercise. This time the jack held enough to begin to lift the trunk. Once it had sucked free at that end it became easier. Jim got a good length out of the mud and they lined up on one side of it.

Miguel said, 'We lift and when I shout we throw it forward onto the branches, okay?'

They nodded. For all his cherubic appearance Miguel was immensely strong, and they knew it. He took the centre and counted down.

'Three… two… one… lift!'

They strained, then had to drop it.

'Shit!'

'*Carajo!*'

Jim looked down and his shoulders drooped. The trunk had hammered the jack into the mud. To make things worse a cloud of mosquitoes had gathered. He batted at them, then blinked the rain out of his eyes and crouched down to dig out the jack.

Even Miguel was breathing heavily. He scanned along the length of the trunk. 'There is too much still in the mud,' he said. 'We need to jack up one end and put something underneath. Then do the same at the other end.'

Jim nodded and they went back to work. Fernando was already in the woodland and he came back, staggering under the weight of a partly rotten log he'd found where a tree had previously fallen.

'Hey, that's great, Fernando,' Miguel shouted,

They packed the hole under the jack and Jim raised the tree inch by inch until Fernando could push the log under it. Jim unwound the jack, letting the tree settle. There was a loud crunch and it sank a little, but held.

Jim switched to the other end of the tree and they went to work until the jack was sufficiently anchored and he raised that end, too.

'Right,' Jim said. 'Let's give it another go. Miguel?'

They took up their positions again and Miguel counted, 'Three… two… one… lift!'

For a moment nothing happened. As strong as all four of them were, the effort seemed beyond them, but they strained even harder and the tree moved. They lifted, their boots sinking into the mud, then Miguel shouted 'Now!' and they threw it forward onto their improvised slipway.

They paused for a few minutes, rotating their shoulders, brushing off hands chafed by the rough bark of the tree and recovering their breath.

'Well done,' Jim said, still gasping.

Miguel said, 'Now we push.'

Again he counted down for each push, and slowly the tree slid over the branches until it was lined up with the side of the trail.

They straightened up, sweat on their faces mingling with the rain and splashes of mud. Jim looked at them and laughed. 'We look even more disreputable than when we started out,' he said. 'There's plenty of water in the back. We'll take off the uniforms and wash the worst of the mud off hands and faces. We'll have to do this two at a time. Fernando and Sally, you go first.'

Perversely the rain seemed to have eased somewhat by the time they'd washed and got back into the vehicle. Miguel started the engine again and they skidded over the slipway and continued along the trail.

The uniforms had been soaking wet, and damp had seeped through into their civilian clothes, but the heat of their bodies and the air-conditioning that Miguel had put on full blast helped to dry them out and keep the windscreen from fogging up. Then light entered as the trees on either side parted and a road came into view.

'Whaddaya know?' Miguel said. 'Here's the two-track.'

'Dual carriageway,' Jim added, automatically.

'Is that what they call these in England?'

'It is.'

He grinned. 'And do you have horses pulling carriages along them?'

'You don't see many of those, Miguel. I guess it's just a throwback to the old days.'

'Cute, though.'

Miguel waited until no cars or trucks were in sight, then lurched quickly out onto the road and accelerated. Jim sank back into the seat. They were en route to Maracaibo – at last.

Once on the road they covered the ground quickly. At one point they went over a long bridge crossing high over a river, which showed them how impossible it would have been to try to walk the route without being seen. Signs of civilization began to appear: large boards, hand-painted with the portraits of local bigwigs, the occasional battered-looking shop.

Jim pointed to a small track leading off the main road. 'Let's park up there before it gets too busy. We need to hide the handguns.'

Miguel took the track, brought the vehicle to a halt, and turned off the engine. They got out and stowed the handguns in the space under the loading bay floor, where they joined the army uniforms and multirifles. Then they got back in, but this time Jim directed Fernando to the front passenger seat and sat with Sally in the back.

He said, 'Miguel, when we were studying the city maps you identified a car rental outlet, didn't you?'

'Sure did. A Budget place on Calle 76. I think we'll try that first.'

'Okay, get a medium-sized car, a few years old, local manufacture preferred. Rent it for four days, that should more than cover it. Fernando, you go with him, but don't show yourself inside the office. Then drive both the vehicles to a hotel further from the centre. Check in separately and phone me when you're there. If you spot a small eating place nearby all the better.'

'Okay, what about you and Sally?'

'I need to make contact with this cyber group in town. I'll go with Sally – a man and a woman will arouse less suspicion. I'll tell you when to drop us off and we'll walk from there. Okay, let's go.'

9

Jim and Sally chatted in Spanish as they walked through town. When Sally was recruited into the SAF she'd cleared the language hurdle easily as she was also fluent in French and German. She spoke classical Spanish but she'd been tutored by Miguel in the local accent. Jim tried to copy it, including the softer sound for 'j'.

'Don't worry about it, Jim,' she said. 'According to Miguel there's a variety of accents around the country. So long as it's Spanish we probably won't attract attention.'

Jim said nothing, but not attracting attention was at the top of his agenda right now. As far as he knew, the people on the streets around him were just ordinary folk going about their business, but you could never tell whether watchful eyes were among them, and they were here, unarmed, in a country where hatred for Americans had been stoked up to a very high temperature.

Fortunately the rain had ceased completely, although the roads and sidewalks were still wet and the air was heavy with humidity. Road signs on the way helped to orientate them as they made their way towards the rendezvous with the USCYBERCOM group.

Sally said, 'You know the induction, Jim, when you're driven around in a foreign city, hooded, and you have to know where you've been?'

Jim laughed. 'Wendell's idea, just in case we were kidnapped. I kept it on,'

'I thought I was going to flunk that part.'

'A lot of very good candidates did. And we had to recognize languages as well – even dialects if it was Spanish or Arabic.'

Sally said, 'I was okay with that. It was remembering the twists and turns, building up a picture in your mind and tracing it all on a map afterwards. That was tough. Has anyone ever had to make use of it?'

'Only one person that I know of. Holly.'

'Holly Cressington?'

'Yes, the Defense Secretary's daughter.'

'We were good friends but she never mentioned it.'

'It was after she was kidnapped in the Yemen. They drove her to a Palace and marched her through a maze of corridors to a cell. She knew exactly where she was the whole time. That paid off big time when she broke out.'

'Well, well. Thing is, it's remained with me, that ability. I can almost memorize a map once I've seen it.'

He smiled. 'Me too. So I guess we both know we're almost there.'

'Yup.'

'Seen anything suspicious so far? Anyone taking an undue interest in us?'

'No,' she said. 'And I have been watching out for it.'

'Same here. Well it's time to check if we really are being followed. Walk a little faster and start talking more animatedly, waving your arms around.'

'What are we arguing about?'

'Oh, I say you forgot to buy coffee, and you say if "If you don't like it *you* can do the shopping" – something like that. Don't raise your voice, though. When I give the signal we'll stop dead to do it some more and we'll have a quick check around. The usual mantra—'

They said it together: 'Turn your eyes, not your head.'

They argued for a bit then stopped and turned to each other and Jim took in the scene behind them. Was there any change in the pattern, someone hesitating?

'A few people back there,' he said.

'Looks okay, though.'

'I agree, but we'll make some turns now, just to be on the safe side.'

They diverted through some back streets and checked again, but no one was following them. A few minutes later they returned to the original route and arrived at their destination. It was a sizeable mansion with a grubby white frontage, perhaps the former home of a diplomat back in more normal times. Jim looked up and down the street but it was quiet here. He phoned the contact number he'd been given.

A voice said, *'Hola.'*

'Hola. ¿hablas inglés?'

'Yes, I speak English.'

'Sorry, I'm late. There was a holdup on the bridge.'

'Which bridge?'

'The Brooklyn Bridge.'

'Okay, wait there.'

A minute passed, then the door was opened by a man in his twenties. He was tall and rangy, his slim build accentuated by the close-fitting black T-shirt and jeans. He glanced at Sally and frowned. 'And you are…?'

'This is Lieutenant Sally Kent, one of my team. Colonel Jim Slater.' Jim extended a hand, which the man shook briefly. He said, 'Come on in.'

They entered a hallway. After the walk through town it seemed remarkably cool inside. He said, 'Before we go any further I need a password.'

'It's Hallowe'en,' Jim replied. 'With an apostrophe.'

'Okay, I'm Harry. Come on down.'

Further along the hallway a flight of stairs rose to the right but there was a door under the staircase, which Harry opened. It appeared to be a storage cupboard with brooms, a vacuum cleaner, dustpan and brush, and a box of polishes and cleaning agents. He pulled a phone from his pocket, entered a number and pointed it. A motor whirred and the entire floor slid to one side with all the equipment riding on the top of it. Stone steps led downwards.

Jim exchanged bemused glances with Sally.

'A small modification,' Harry explained. 'Where we're going used to be a wine cellar. Follow me.'

As they descended the steep stairs Jim heard a noise, looked up sharply, and saw the false floor sliding back into place.

10

They entered a large space with a curved, half-cylindrical ceiling. The air was cool and he thought he could catch the faintest hint of wine barrels, although nothing remained of the place's earlier use. At the far end there were rows of dusty shelves. At the front the space was occupied by two long benches loaded with computers, a line of monitors, and what looked to Jim like a rack of radio receivers and transmitters. In one corner there was a sink and some kitchen equipment, including a coffee maker. Three other men, very similar in age and lightly built like Harry, swivelled on their desk chairs and got to their feet to meet the newcomers.

Harry opened his hands. 'Welcome to the Cyber Unit. Just in time. I was beginning to think you weren't coming.'

'Only got the go-ahead last night. You're all USCYBERCOM?'

'Yes.'

'Which component?'

'Army.'

Jim relaxed a little. He felt more at home among US army combatants, and that's how these guys would be classified. As he looked at Harry and his colleagues, with their lively eyes and quick movements, they seemed to him more like young college graduates or Silicon Valley nerds than soldiers. Somehow, though, they'd got into this country undetected. How did they bring in all this equipment? He asked him.

Harry said, 'We didn't, it was here already. The place was set up as a listening post years ago. What I understand is that most of this,' he gestured at the equipment, 'was brought in when there was a US Embassy in Caracas. Someone thought the friendly regime wouldn't last and a unit like this one would come in handy. They were right on the money, weren't they?'

'If the equipment is that old won't it start needing maintenance and spares?'

'Oh yeah. Each returning crew posts a report of what's needed and the next crew takes it out. We've got qualifications in computing, software, electronics in general, so we fix things up before we start. Come and sit down.'

He led them to a table and chairs near the kitchen area. 'Coffee?'

Jim's cell phone buzzed. 'Excuse me,' he said, turning away.

Sally said, 'Coffee would be good. Black no sugar for both of us.'

Harry turned to one of the others. 'Justin, you want to brew up some coffee while I talk to these folks?'

Jim came back to them. 'Sorry about that. It was Miguel. Just wanted to tell me they've got a car. Now they're going to seek out a hotel. Is coffee on the way?'

'Yes,' Sally said, 'Black no sugar, that's right, isn't it?'

'It is. Well remembered.'

63

They sat down at the table. 'Right,' Harry said. 'What do you want to know?'

'Everything you've discovered so far,' Jim said. 'To start with, when's the envoy expected to land? We haven't even been told his name. We have to call him Mr X.'

'Same here. Mr X is expected the day after tomorrow. Private plane, to all appearances, but it's a military crew and they're well prepared for any funny business. The pilot will radio me when Mr X has disembarked.'

'Any idea what time?'

'All we've been told is around midday.'

Jim nodded. 'I gather the Venezuelan army is providing a military escort into town. Any idea what that'll look like?'

'Yeah, we hacked into their communications, so we know what's going on. Mr X will get into a small armoured vehicle with two soldiers. There'll be a similar vehicle in front and another one behind it, each with four soldiers.'

'And then?'

'They'll drive to the Mayor's residence – that's where the negotiations are taking place. The residence doesn't have high walls or fences but their army will be throwing a very strong cordon around it. In fact the street's already closed to traffic and pedestrians. We won't be able to get near it.'

Jim winced. 'That's awkward. Is there any other way of monitoring what's going on?'

'Only up to a point. We'd love to use drones but they're certain to pick them up on their vehicle radars. So we went out at night a week ago and put some miniature cameras up on the trees opposite. Not ideal but we should get some idea of what's happening. We checked the pictures at the time but we haven't turned them on since. The cameras are small and we don't want to drain the batteries by transmitting to here unless it's strictly necessary.'

Jim said, 'Okay, crucial thing is how Mr X is being handled on the way out. Politely? Roughly?'

'Sure we'll be looking out for all that.'

'If they treat him nicely and take him to the airport, all well and good; we'll pack up and go home. What we really need to know, Harry, is if they're hustling him and taking him to a prison. Where would they take him?'

'Buena Vista, almost certainly. It's the local prison and that's where they take all political opponents.'

'I've heard that place is very bad news.'

'You heard right.'

Justin came to the table with a tray of coffee. Harry said, 'Thanks, Justin. You guys having some yourselves?'

'You bet.'

Harry passed round the disposable cups of coffee. Jim tried it. Strong, but very tasty. For a while they just sipped the coffee.

'Thing is,' Harry said, putting down his cup, 'we may not be able to tell. They could treat him nicely and still drop him off at the prison. Or there could be a high wind and the cameras are shaking about too much, or leaves get in the way and we don't get a clear view. That's where you come in.'

Jim said, 'There's only four of us.'

'I know. Let me get a map.' He went to one of the benches, pulled open a drawer and returned with a map of Maracaibo, which he spread on the table. Jim and Sally stood to get a better view. Harry ran a fingertip over the map.

'This here's the Mayor's residence,' he said. 'When they come out the vehicles will have to go this way.' He traced a route. 'Now here's the crucial intersection. If they turn left here they're going to the airport; if they turn right, they're going to Buena Vista, simple as that.'

'Is that the only route to the prison?' Jim asked.

'It's the most direct route – no reason why they'd decide not to use it. You wouldn't want to be taking a convoy like that through a maze of side streets.'

'Okay, we'll deploy on the road to the right, somewhere beyond that intersection. Only we don't want to be hanging around too long or we'll attract attention.'

'I think we can help with that. There's a hoarding near the intersection with the usual painted picture – some government minister, I guess. One night a couple of us put on workmen's overalls and pretended to be working on the back of it. We installed a camera, high up. It should tell us which way they're turning.'

'That was risky.'

'Yeah, we did it at the quietest time of night but we were still shitting bricks.'

'You did that for us?'

'Not entirely. If you get picked up, we have the camera. And if the camera doesn't work we have you on the ground. One way or the other we should be able to tell Washington where they're taking him.'

'We're not planning to get picked up, but thanks; the camera was a good move.' Jim pointed to the map. 'Can I keep this?'

'Sure, we've got others.'

Jim took a fibrepoint from his pocket and circled the intersection. Then he folded the map up. As he was pocketing it he said:

'Will you be able to tell us when they leave the Mayor's residence?'

'Sure, we should be able to say that much at least. We'll tell you anything we see. Hang on, I'll give you the communicators.'

Harry went over to the benches and came back with four handheld devices.

'Now we rigged these up ourselves, so they're nothing fancy. We took most of the circuitry out of some throwaway cell phones and replaced it with our own. There won't be anything on the screen and there's no camera – all that's to extend the battery life. Two buttons: on, off. Doesn't matter if someone sees you using one, they'll think it's a cell. But these operate via satellites on a reserved frequency, encrypted. They'll monitor that frequency the whole time, whether they're on or off. If they're on we can talk to each other and all our exchanges will be relayed to Washington, so there's no need to do any actual reporting.'

Jim nodded, handed two to Sally and pocketed two himself. 'You have any questions, Sally?'

'No, I think you've covered everything.'

'Right. We'll get back and brief the others. Thanks, Harry.' He shook hands and waved to the others and Sally did the same.

'I'll show you out. Good luck.'

11

The moment Jim and Sally left the house they switched back into Spanish. There weren't many people around but in such a situation it was important not only to speak the local language but to act and feel like locals.

'We'll get a taxi,' he said, 'but not close to here, we could compromise the cyber group. I don't want to hail one in the street, either; I wouldn't know if we were being ripped off. We'll look for a proper taxi rank.'

'There'll probably be one at a Metro station,' Sally said. 'The line isn't all that far from here.'

They started to walk. After a few minutes Sally said, 'Just out of interest, Jim, why did you choose me for this assignment?'

'Why not? I needed capable people with good Spanish. You fitted the bill.'

She smiled. 'So would almost every soldier in the SAF.'

Jim shrugged. 'Okay. Look, I saw you go down in that action in Tanzania, saw the rounds hit your leg. I felt every damned one of them. You were in bad shape and you could have been invalided out of the army. But you stayed on.'

'The army's my career, Jim. I didn't want to leave all that behind.'

'Just the same, it took guts to focus on your rehabilitation the way you did. I thought it was high time you saw some real action again.'

'And this is real action?'

'Who knows? It could turn out that way.'

They walked in silence for a while, then Sally said quietly:

'We've never talked about that incident.'

'I didn't know you wanted to.' He glanced at her. 'Do you?'

'Well, yes, because there's so much I don't remember. I was chasing some insurgents, afraid they'd get away. Next thing I remember is a tremendous pain and after that it sort of goes blank.'

'Captain van der Loos ran up, hurled his body over you and sent both of you rolling down the slope and out of danger.'

'Wish I'd known. He must have saved my life.'

'May have saved your limb, too. He splinted your leg while I pumped you full of morphine. We got you to a local civilian hospital and when you'd been stabilized I had you transferred to a regional US military hospital in Germany.'

She shook her head. 'I'm sorry, it was stupid of me to run after those guys.'

He shrugged. 'You weren't to know they'd suddenly drop down and start shooting.'

'Did they get away?'

'Nope. Vince ranged a smart grenade over their heads and that, as they say, was that.'

His cell vibrated. He listened for a while then said, 'Fine. We're on our way.'

'That was Miguel,' he said, returning the phone to his pocket. 'They parked the Toyota and the rented vehicle at their hotel. There's a pizza parlour not far from there. They'll buy four, with coffees and water, then pick us up a block past the hotel. He gave me the street name.'

'Great, I could do serious damage to a pizza after the day we've had.'

Jim grinned. 'That tree was something else, wasn't it? Especially with the rain sheeting down. But only fun in retrospect.'

After they'd walked on for a while Sally said, 'Were you planning to check us into the same hotel as Miguel and Fernando?'

'Best to choose somewhere else. I don't know how frequent visitors are these days, but having four in the same hotel could attract attention. I'm sure we won't have a problem finding another one.' He glanced her way. 'It's okay, you can have your own room.'

She gave a short laugh. 'Jim, have you thought about how that would look?'

'What do you mean?'

'A woman checking into a hotel on her own? A bit conspicuous. And she could be on the game.'

'Oh hell, we're trying not to attract attention.'

'It's okay, we can manage with a twin room.'

'What if they only have double beds?'

'We can manage with that, too. Look, Jim, I can trust you. I told you, I was very friendly with Holly Cressington, still am. I know how close you two were, and how you drew the line about getting any closer.'

Jim looked at her in astonishment. 'She told you?'

'Not in so many words. Most of it I guessed and then she came clean. She found it very hard to say goodbye, Jim. And I think you found it hard, too.'

He took a deep breath. 'Hardest decision I ever had to make. Senior officers do not have relationships with junior officers, they just don't. There was no way it could progress while she was with the SAF.'

'But after what happened in the Yemen she left the service. She felt she didn't have a choice.'

'Yes. She wanted me to go with her. I couldn't, Sally. I'd have been miserable as hell, and I'd have made life miserable as hell for her, too.'

'I know. It's taken her a long time to get over it, but there we are. That's how I know I can trust you.' She turned to him and smiled. 'And if we're supposed to be posing as a couple while we're out here on the street this would be more convincing.' She linked her arm in his.

He gave her a quizzical look. 'Don't overdo it.'

They laughed.

No more was said until Jim spotted a Metro station. They caught a cab at the rank outside, and Jim gave the driver a destination two blocks from where they'd agreed to meet Fernando and Miguel.

*

The rented vehicle was parked in a quiet street opposite a disused warehouse. They climbed in the back

'What make is this, Fernando?' Jim said. 'I don't recognize it.'

'It's a Chery, a Chinese make. They have a factory in Brazil.'

'No local manufacturers?'

'Seems most of them flopped or moved out. Can't cope with the foreign exchange situation. This was the nearest I could get. They say it's quite popular.'

'It's fine. Do you have a full tank of gas?'

'Sure do, they supplied it that way. A full tank costs less than a penny here. Can you believe that?'

'Seems to me like everything is cheap,' Miguel said.

Jim said, 'Only for us. You compare it to what they earn and everything except gas is expensive. But at least it means they're getting some benefit from their oil.'

They handed round pizzas and paper cups of coffee. The four said little more while they were eating and drinking.

'What do you think of the pizza, Sal?' Miguel asked, turning from his seat in the front.

'Not bad, but not exactly *al forno*. I think it was more *al supermercato* and warmed up in a microwave.'

'Still, hits the spot.'

'Yeah, my spot's smaller than that,' Sally said. 'Anyone want another segment?' She paused. 'No takers?'

'I'll have it,' Fernando said, and she passed over the cardboard plate.

When everyone had finished Jim said, 'Okay, let's bring Fernando and Miguel up to speed.'

He and Sally handed them their communicators.

'Courtesy of the cyber unit. The link's via satellites on a reserved frequency and it's encrypted. Once we've deployed, all conversations between us have to be on these. Cyber and Washington will be listening to whatever we say, so be brief and to the point and then switch them off.'

They looked at the devices, registered the simple controls – just on/off – then pocketed them.

'Mr X arrives two days from now. The pilot will contact the cyber unit to let them know when he touches down and they'll pass the information to us. Mr X will disembark and the Venezuelan army will escort him to the Mayor's residence for the talks. Our cyber friends will tell us when he arrives.'

'How long you think the talks will last?' Fernando asked.

'If they're making progress it could take several hours. If they aren't it could all be over within half an hour. What's important is where they take him after that. Is it back to the airport or off to prison? Cyber has cameras up so they should know when he comes out. They may even be able to tell us how he's being handled but that's not certain and it could be unreliable. The crucial thing is the route the escort takes.'

Miguel said, 'There's only four of us. We can't be everywhere.'

'That's right. To start with I thought we'd have to tail the convoy, which would be very risky. Turns out to be simpler than that. First, if they're taking him to prison they'll almost certainly be heading for a jail called Buena Vista – that's where they take all their political opponents. The place has a bad reputation. If Mr X is going there the best he can expect is ill treatment. More likely they'll torture him until he's dead.'

Fernando said, 'Jesus, what a country!'

'Okay, second, there's a key intersection where they'll take a left for the airport but a right to the prison. The cyber group has set up a camera there, so we may get some warning about which way they've turned. That would be helpful but we can't rely on it. Tomorrow morning we're going to check out that street from the intersection to the prison. I'll tell you why in a minute.'

Miguel said 'Okay' and Fernando nodded.

'Tomorrow afternoon I want you, Miguel and Fernando, to time a drive from the Mayor's residence to a point along the road to the prison – in the morning we're going to decide where that point should be. You won't be able to get close to the Mayor's residence; the road's been closed off and it'll be swarming with soldiers. Just choose somewhere about the same distance.'

Fernando said, 'A military escort will drive faster than me. They'll be using flashing lights and sirens and moving people out of the way.'

'That's okay, we only need an estimate. The key thing is to leave us enough time to get into position without having to hover around, which people may notice. And basically, that's it. We'll be waiting somewhere along that route. If the convoy turns left at the intersection and takes Mr X to the airport we can go home. If it turns right and comes past us on its way to the prison our job is to report that to Washington. End of story. Those are our orders, and that's what the CIA asked for.'

'Since when we do what the fuck the CIA wants?' Fernando growled.

'It so happens I agree with you, Fernando,' Jim said. 'So we'll just call that Plan A. Let's consider the second scenario: the convoy turns right, towards the prison. According to CYBERCOM the escort will be three vehicles, small armoured jobs. Mr X will be in the middle one, with a lead vehicle in front and another one tailing behind. Four soldiers in the lead and tail vehicles, and two riding with Mr X. They'll have sidearms for sure, probably not rifles. That's three armoured vehicles and ten armed soldiers. And we're on the street, unarmed. Not great odds, right?'

There were murmurs of assent.

'So let me propose my Plan B.'

When Jim had finished outlining his plan they were all grinning.

'The odds are the same,' Jim said. 'It's still a high risk operation. Question is: are you up for it?'

The two in front nodded vigorously.

Jim said, 'Sally?'

'You bet.'

'Okay. Now look, if they've changed the arrangements and it's more than three vehicles it's back to Plan A. Those odds we can't handle. Understood?'

Again they nodded.

'Good. Fernando, Sally's going to another hotel with me. Can you drop us near to one? Nothing too up-market.'

'Sure, no problem.'

'We'll do our reconnaissance separately tomorrow. Grab something to eat at a café or somewhere during the day. In the evening we'll get together around this time and compare notes. Then we'll go over the operation again. Just a reminder: don't forget the shouts at the end. That's important. Anything else?'

Miguel said, 'If you're buying bottled water during the day I'd go for a brand. I wouldn't trust the local stuff.'

'Good point,' Sally said. 'What shall we have in the evening?'

'Coffee's good,' Fernando said.

'Yeah,' Miguel said. 'We'll get large ones again.'

Sally said, 'The takeaway's a good idea but could we have something different to pizzas? Isn't there some local food we could try?'

Fernando said, 'There are a few places. We'll take a look.'

Jim felt a surge of pride. In two days' time these three could be risking their lives against formidable odds but the only thing that concerned them was the food and drink they'd be ordering tomorrow evening.

12

Jim and Sally's hotel was comfortable enough. They managed to secure a room with twin beds and they used the en suite bathroom to change in. Next morning they breakfasted in the hotel restaurant. It was self-service, so they had coffees and something that looked like croissants but were actually stuffed, some with minced ham, others with a soft cheese. Then they walked a short distance to a quiet street where they'd arranged to meet Fernando and Miguel. The Chery was already parked there.

'Okay,' Jim said. 'This morning we'll stroll down the street from the intersection to the prison. Sally will come with me. Fernando and Miguel you tail us. We'll all be looking for the best place to be if the convoy comes down there the next day. When I spot that point I'll send out a message on the communicator the cyber unit gave us. It'll just look like I'm using my cell.'

They nodded.

'Remember, Washington will be listening in, so keep everything short. I'll simply say something like, "This looks like the best observation point". After that we'll spend some time looking for suitable places to hang out the next day while we're waiting. All right so far?'

Fernando nodded again. Miguel said, 'You want to meet up for lunch?'

'No, it's better if we're not seen together. In the afternoon, Fernando, you do your drive from the Mayor's residence, or thereabouts, to the observation point we just chose. Miguel, you go with him to do the timing and the navigation. It'll give us an idea of when to expect the convoy if it's coming our way.'

'You said the cyber guys set up a camera at the intersection,' Fernando said.

'They did, but we're on the ground in case it doesn't give them a suitable picture. Maybe the camera's not working or someone spotted it and took it down. Stuff can happen, so belt and braces, always belt and braces.'

'Belt and braces?' Miguel said.

'I understand that,' Sally said. 'Braces are what Brits call suspenders, aren't they?'

Jim nodded and Miguel's face lit up. 'Oh right. So if the belt fails the suspenders kick in and your pants stay up. I love it! Don't want to go into action with your butt showing.'

They laughed until Jim held up a hand. 'Okay, you've got it. We'll meet up here in the evening at 1900 hours. There's a place I noticed when we were walking over from the hotel. They seem to serve local dishes to take out.'

'What do you want?' Miguel asked.

'You choose.'

'Sally?'

'Same here. Surprise me.'

'Okay, let's go,' Jim said. 'Drop Sally and me off somewhere near the intersection. We'll be walking slowly and Sally will have her stick, so it shouldn't be hard to keep tabs on us.'

Fernando started the car and they moved off.

Ten minutes later Sally and Jim were walking down the road from the intersection, chatting in Spanish, with Sally exaggerating her limp. It was baking hot, so they'd chosen the right-hand sidewalk, where the buildings cast some shadow. Unfortunately that didn't make a lot of difference; Jim could already feel his shirt sticking to him and he saw that Sally's face was flushed.

A steady stream of cars passed in both directions.

'It's not Los Angeles,' Sally said, 'but there's plenty of traffic.'

Jim smiled at her. 'Couldn't be better as far as we're concerned. Not here, though. It's too wide. This stretch must be a fairly new road.'

Sally said, 'Maybe it joins an older section further down.'

'I hope so. We'll see. Now just hold it here a moment. Lean on your stick as if you're taking a breather.'

While they were, to all appearances, resting, Jim glanced up the road behind them. He saw Fernando and Miguel much further back on the opposite sidewalk, facing the oncoming cars and trucks.

'Good,' he said. 'They're with us.'

They continued on their way. Then Jim tensed, alarm bells ringing. Two men were coming towards them, both of them bearded and stocky. They stopped in front of Jim and Sally. One spoke in heavily accented Spanish.

'Please, can you tell us where is a bank?'

Jim did his best to look relaxed but he was ready to spring into action. This could be genuine, or a ruse to cover up a mugging, or something more serious than that.

From the way Sally leaned forward it looked like she was taking it as genuine.

There were two dangers now: she might show them her map, on which the intersection was circled, or she might gesture with her stick to show them the way, making a nonsense of her limp.

'Do you have a map?' she asked, using her Venezuelan-accented Spanish.

The man who'd spoken to them fished in a pocket of his lightweight jacket and brought one out. It was a tourist-style map with points of interest, including banks and exchange offices. She pointed to where they were and gave him directions, without using her stick. It wasn't clear whether he'd understood her, but he nodded vigorously, said a ponderous *'Muchas gracias'* and they walked on. Jim pivoted slightly to make sure they hadn't turned back but they were crossing the road. It seemed like it had been genuine after all.

He breathed out and smiled at Sally. 'You handled that well.'

'I was ready for any funny business, though.'

They continued on their way. 'Did you pin his accent?' Jim asked.

'Slavic. Russian probably. It was the way he pronounced the Spanish. I wonder what a couple of Russians are doing here.'

'Russia's one of the few countries that supports Venezuela, so perhaps they're encouraging tourists.'

'Yeah, maybe,' Sally said, 'but why Maracaibo? I'd have thought Caracas would be a more likely spot for tourists.'

'Maybe it has attractions we don't know about.'

'Cheap sex?'

'Could be.'

The street had narrowed, still two lanes but much tighter.

'This is more like it, Sally. This part of the street is older – you were right about that – you can see from the surfacing and the buildings.' He looked around, noting landmarks. 'How close are we to the jail, do you think?'

'A quarter of a mile, maybe.'

He nodded. 'Okay, we'll press on. I want to look for side streets.'

Fifty yards later Sally said, 'There's one, over on the left.'

'Let's take a look.'

They crossed carefully, noted the name of the street, and walked down it a short way.

'Looks ideal for Fernando. Let's get back to the main drag.'

He put a call through on his communicator. 'Miguel, Fernando, Can you see us? Good. This looks like the best observation point to me. Check out the side street.'

'Will do.'

He switched off the device before pocketing it and they continued down the road. There were several more side streets, narrower than the first. Then a sizeable crowd appeared ahead. The people were curiously silent.

'That's odd,' Sally said. 'We must be at Buena Vista now.'

As they got closer they could see that every member of the crowd was standing there silently, holding a placard with a picture and a name. The pictures were mostly of young men, but there were also some of women and older men.

'Jim, I think you should stay back here. I'm not a threat, a woman with a stick. I'll see what this is about.'

Jim watched as she limped over to a middle-aged woman and had a quiet conversation. She went on to an elderly man and another woman, then came back.

'It's heartbreaking, Jim,' she said quietly. 'The pictures are of *desaparecidos*, family members who've disappeared into that prison. They were arrested and imprisoned without trial and no one's had news of them since. They can't visit, they don't even know if they're alive or dead. The woman's son is eighteen. He was involved in a protest. The man also has a son of thirty-five; he may have been arrested at the same protest. The other woman's daughter is a journalist, aged twenty-seven. They're standing here to put pressure on the authorities to release their loved ones.'

'So this is a protest, too.'

'Yes, they're doing it peacefully and silently to avoid getting arrested themselves. From time to time the police move them on and they don't try to resist. But one by one they filter back.'

Jim shook his head.

'It's disgraceful, Jim. This is no democracy; it's an autocracy of the worst kind.' She sighed. 'I wish there was something we could do about it.'

'It's for another day, Sally.'

She nodded glumly.

'Come on, we need to find a suitable place where we can wait, and then we'll time the walk from there to that side street we showed Miguel earlier.'

*

At 1900 hours Jim and Sally joined Fernando and Miguel where they'd met that morning. They got into the back of the Chery.

Jim said, 'How did it go?'

Fernando said, 'That street you found? It's good. There's somewhere further back where I can park this car without blocking the road. Miguel will be in the Toyota.'

'I can park it on the pavement, not far from the intersection,' Miguel said.

'That's great, Miguel,' Jim said. 'And raise the two extra seats in the back of that vehicle tomorrow. We won't be needing the whole of the loading bay, and it could be useful.'

'Will do.'

'This afternoon we timed the journey from the Mayor's residence to that side street,' Fernando said. 'Should take a convoy about ten minutes. Took us a bit longer, but like I said, they'll be clearing traffic out of the way with sirens and lights and we were just going with the flow.'

'Okay, Sally and I found a good place to wait as well.' He paused, biting his lip. 'I wish to hell we could rehearse the moves.'

'Don't worry,' Fernando said. 'Miguel and me did it a few times. I reckon we've got it nailed. Shall we go get the takeaways?'

Jim smiled. 'Sure. And then we'll all grab some sleep. We've got a busy day ahead.'

13

At twenty-two minutes past eleven the military aircraft carrying Mr X was on the final approach to Maracaibo airport.

Jim and Sally were leaning on the wall at the back of some shops, facing a rubbish-strewn yard. The others were some distance away, Fernando in the rented Chery sedan in the side street and Miguel in the Toyota all-roader, which he'd parked near the intersection, just off the main road. All had been in place since ten o'clock that morning.

'It's hot again,' Sally sighed. They were sheltered from direct sun here but the air temperature was high. 'It could be worse, I suppose,' she added. 'It could be pouring with rain like the other day.'

Jim nodded distractedly. In his mind he was still stepping through Plan B in case they had to use it, but he couldn't think of anything he'd left out.

The temperature continued to rise. Jim passed the bottle of water to Sally and she took a swig. As she handed it back she said, 'If we do go to Plan B I wish I was doing something more useful. You did promise me some action, remember?'

'Sally, don't underestimate the task I've given you. We need that fourth person in reserve.'

She shrugged and they continued to wait. Their communicators buzzed together, making them jump. Jim grabbed his from his chinos and Sally dipped into a pocket of her dress for hers. They opened the line together.

'Harry here. Plane just landed.'

'Thanks, Harry,' Jim said. On this channel the less said the better. They clicked off the communicators and put them away again.

Jim checked his watch. It was eleven-thirty.

Sally said, 'How long will it take them to get to the Mayor's residence from the airport?'

'Twenty to thirty minutes. Probably nearer twenty.'

'Okay.'

At eight minutes to midday the phones buzzed again.

'Harry here. Three army vehicles just arrived at the Mayor's residence.'

'Copy that,' Jim said.

They continued to wait. One o'clock came and went. If the meeting was going well, Jim thought, it could be hours yet. His mouth was dry again and it was hard to resist the urge to keep drinking water. He glanced at Sally. Her face was flushed.

'You okay, Sal?'

'I guess so. Must be well up in the nineties. You'd expect to see a clear blue sky up there, but look at that overcast.'

Jim looked up and nodded. 'Sticky, too. North Carolina can be bad enough at this time of year, but this is off the scale. It'll be nice to get into an air-conditioned car.'

'I can hardly wait.'

'Shouldn't be much longer.'

At a quarter past one they got the message they were waiting for.

'Harry here. Just leaving. Same three vehicles. Couldn't see how they were handling him.'

'Okay.'

He straightened up, pushing himself off the wall. 'Not much over an hour. Doesn't look like they were negotiating very seriously, does it? Ten minutes from the Mayor's residence to the intersection. It'll take us eight minutes to get to our observation point, so let's go.'

They went out to the road and turned right along the sidewalk, taking it at the same pace they'd used when they timed it the previous day. This was dictated by Sally, who was pretending to bear her weight on her stick, while Jim walked between her and the road.

Eight minutes later they were in place, with Sally leaning on the stick as if resting. Jim tilted his head towards her and appeared to be speaking quietly. In reality he was saying nothing, and his thoughts were whirling.

Come on, Harry, tell us where the hell they are.

Five long minutes passed. Then their communicators buzzed. Harry sounded excited.

'Three army vehicles turned right. Repeat, right, towards the prison.'

'Hear that, everyone? Three army vehicles coming towards the prison.'

He clicked off. His repeat was the signal for all of them to turn off their communicators.

Because the situation had changed. They'd switched to Plan B.

It was game on.

*

Fernando came lurching out of the side street in the rented Chery, crossed over to the other side of the road, and passed close to them, driving fast. At almost the same moment the Toyota all-roader driven by Miguel appeared from the opposite direction. There was a squeal of tyres, Fernando slewed obliquely across the narrowest part of the road, and Miguel drove into him, hard enough to make a dent in the wing. They got out of their vehicles and came out arguing and waving their arms around.

'Here we go, Sally,' Jim said, 'stay sharp,' and he went over to them and joined in the apparent altercation.

He heard a roar of engines and looked up to see the flashing lights of the convoy. Other vehicles were mounting the pavement to get out of the way. The convoy screeched to a halt, blasting sirens and sounding their horns at Miguel's all-roader, which was now blocking the road. The air was pulsating with noise.

Jim walked toward the last of the three army vehicles, gesticulating and keeping half an eye on Fernando and Miguel who were going up to the first two. All three were trying to explain the hold-up with a lot of gestures but not speaking loudly. The passenger side window of the first vehicle whirred down. Without hesitation Miguel dipped into the back of his trouser waistband, lobbed in the goodnite, then ducked down to avoid the escaping gas. At precisely the same moment Hernandez lobbed his goodnite into the second vehicle.

Jim approached the third vehicle, passing close enough to the others to obscure what was happening behind him. He was apologizing profusely and waving his hands but the window didn't roll down. Instead the door opened and the soldier came out with a large semiautomatic pistol in his hand. He fired into the air, and the small crowd that had already gathered on the pavement shrank back. Then the man lowered the pistol and Jim, still gesturing helplessly, found himself staring into the barrel. There was a frozen moment, then the soldier jerked up and fell to the ground, spasming.

Jim whirled round to see Sally holding part of her stick in her left hand. In her right hand was the taser. She pulled out the leads embedded in the soldier's neck. The other occupants of the vehicle were already drawing their sidearms. Jim threw his goodnite inside, slammed the door, and they both ducked away.

All four then converged on the second vehicle. The occupants had already collapsed under the influence of the fast-acting anaesthetic gas. Miguel took a deep breath of air and opened the rear door. He grabbed the civilian, who'd slumped forward into his seat belt, quickly unbuckled the belt, pulled him out, and hauled him away, his heels dragging on the road.

'Fernando,' he shouted. 'Get the other side. There's a woman in there.'

'A woman?' Fernando took a breath, opened the door, and reappeared moments later with her over his shoulder. They hurried to their vehicles, bundled the unconscious man and woman into the back of the Chery and slammed the doors. Then, for the benefit of the bystanders, they shouted loudly:

'*¡Saludos del Hombre Gordo!*'

They jumped into their vehicles, backed them away from each other and drove off.

It was all over in less than two minutes.

14

They stopped outside the disused warehouse where they'd had the pizzas on the first day, got out of the cars and gathered by the Toyota.

Jim said, 'Great job, well done everyone.' Then, as Fernando opened the rear door of the rental car, he said, 'Why'd you take the woman?'

Miguel shrugged. 'Didn't look like a soldier to me. Look, you can see: she's young, no uniform, no sidearm, wearing trainers. I figured they were taking her to that jail with our Mr X.'

Fernando looked thoughtful. 'Maybe she's a translator.'

Miguel laughed. 'You think our people would send an envoy to negotiate who couldn't speak Spanish? Not even the CIA are that stupid!'

'The CIA aren't stupid at all,' Jim said quietly. 'They just tend to be careless with other people's lives.'

'Well,' Sally said. 'Are we taking her or not?'

Miguel opened his hands. 'If they find her before she wakes up they will take her to that jail.'

'We take her, she will see all of us when she wakes up,' Fernando growled. 'And she will know we are Americans. If she's with the government we'll have to kill her.'

Jim took a deep breath. 'She comes with us. I hear what you're saying, Fernando, but I agree with Miguel. I think they were carting her off to that prison. If I'm wrong I'll deal with it myself. Now let's get going, for God's sake. We've stirred up an ants' nest back there.'

Fernando shrugged and they hauled the two civilians out of the Chery and strapped them into the middle seats of the off-roader. As they did so Jim got a good look at the man, He was about five foot ten, lightly built, the face clearly the one in the photos they'd been given, although more lined.

They left the key in the driver's seat of the Chery but when they closed the doors the car gave a series of chimes to warn them. Fernando dipped inside quickly for the key and left it on the windscreen instead. Either the rental company would retrieve it or it would be stolen. Either way it wouldn't make any difference to them.

Miguel took the driver's seat in the all-roader with Jim next to him. Fernando and Sally scrambled into the auxiliary rear seats. They took off, heading for the road they'd used when they first came into the city. Jim turned to speak to Sally.

'Well, Sally,' he said. 'You saw a bit of action after all – and got me out of a tight spot.'

'See,' she said, smiling. 'I told you that stick was useful.'

'I'm glad you brought it. That was a 45-calibre the guy was holding and he looked like he had a mind to use it. So thanks.'

'My pleasure.'

Like the rest of them, Miguel had a good mental map and they were soon on the right road. Before long they were crossing the bridge over the wide river.

Sally said, 'These two are still out cold. How long will it last, Jim?'

'A good half-hour. I specified the long-acting goodnites when I drew them from the armoury. If we had to use them the idea was to give us a good lead on their army.'

'You anticipated this whole action?'

'Most of it, yes. We were told not to intervene, but I knew I couldn't stand by and watch that guy being taken to prison. It pays to think things through in advance.'

Sally looked at Fernando, smiled and shook her head.

Fernando checked his watch. 'It's not far off half an hour now.'

'Yeah, they'll be coming round soon.'

'We're almost at that forest track,' Miguel said. 'I'm going to slow down. I don't want to turn across the road while there are any other cars in sight.'

Jim nodded. 'Good idea.'

The entrance to the logging trail came up on the left. The road ahead was clear. Miguel glanced in the rear-view mirror then swung the all-roader across. The sky instantly disappeared as the trees closed over them and the vehicle began to buck and shimmy over the rough ground. A low moan came from the woman. Jim turned to look at their two passengers. The woman stirred, squeezed her eyes shut, blinked, then opened them wide. She looked all around her.

Jim said to her in Spanish, 'It's okay, you're with friends.'

She stared at him but said nothing. Next to her Mr X was also stirring. He winced and shook his head groggily.

The all-roader continued its jolting progress along the trail.

'Miguel,' Jim said. 'Stop well short of the clearing. Hayden and the others may be a bit jumpy, and if we don't identify ourselves first we may be a target for a fast-firing cannon.'

'Roger.'

They bounced and skidded over the raft they'd improvised to move the tree trunk to one side. A few minutes later Miguel drew to a halt. All four got out of the vehicle, leaving the civilians inside. They spread out as much as possible and crept forward. Brilliant sunlight filtered through the leaves ahead, where branches had already sprung back across the entrance to the trail.

Jim was slightly ahead of the others, so he saw it first. He dropped immediately, lying full length, and the others followed suit. His stomach seemed to have risen into the back of his throat and he could scarcely swallow.

The crew of the Rotofan – Hayden, Cliff, Kelly, and Rafael – were dead. They'd been propped up against the undercarriage of the Rotofan. Flies buzzed in a cloud over their heads and crawled on their faces. A dark stain had spread like a wide bib over the shirt of each one.

Miguel was now at Jim's elbow. 'Shit!' he said, and started forward, but Jim grabbed Miguel's waistband and hauled him back. Jim turned and saw to his consternation that the two civilians were standing behind them, gazing slack-jawed at the bodies.

'Get back,' he hissed at them. 'Everyone, back to the vehicle.'

They hurried back to the all-roader and gathered there. The two civilians were breathing hard, running their tongues over their lips, and the young woman's dark eyes were wide with terror. At least both of them were alert and steady on their feet. Those goodnites were designed to be used by police for crowd control. Once the anaesthetic gas wore off it had few after-effects.

Jim jabbed a thumb towards the clearing behind him. 'There's nothing we can do for them,' he said, 'but they may have been left on display like that for a reason. The killers could have booby-trapped the bodies or the Rotofan or mined the ground in front of them. They may even be out there waiting for us. We're not taking any chances.'

Miguel nodded. 'This is an isolated place, Jim. How do you think they found them?'

'We were obviously spotted flying in. Someone must have informed police or army or a local gang. Probably a local gang; police or army would have shot them. Miguel and Fernando, get your rifles from the Toyota and watch that direction.' He pointed towards the clearing. 'Sally, get your backpack and rifle.'

'Aren't we driving back to the road?'

'No, it's too dangerous now. These two are conscious so the soldiers in those vehicles will have come round, too. We've made them look foolish and incompetent, so they'll be mad as hell and keen to level the score. Before long there'll be Venezuelan army on every route out, road blocks, drones – it's too risky. If we were lifting off in the Rotofan it would have been fine, but as it is we'll have to walk.' He looked at the two civilians. 'All right?'

The woman said nothing.

Mr X said to Jim, 'Who exactly are you?'

Jim still didn't know who the young woman was, so he just beckoned to Mr X and led him a short distance away where they could speak out of earshot. 'I'm Colonel Jim Slater. This is a US Special Forces squad. Your hosts were taking you to a notorious prison, so we extracted you.'

For a moment he said nothing. Then he began to laugh softly.

'What are you laughing at?'

'Sorry, just that this wasn't supposed to happen.' Jim frowned, but he just added, 'I'll explain later.'

'All right, now you know who we are. Who are you? We know you only as Mr X.'

'I'm Maynard Dexter. You can call me Maynard or Dexter. Most people call me Dexter.'

Jim nodded. 'All right, Dexter, you can call me Jim.' Then he jerked his head and they returned to the vehicle.

Sally was standing there with a holstered pistol on her belt and a backpack dangling from one hand, her compact automatic rifle cradled under the other arm. Miguel and Dexter were watching the clearing, rifles levelled. At the back of the all-roader the loading bay was up, providing access to the compartment beneath. Jim took his own gear out and now all four of them were battle-ready.

Dexter said, 'I presume the plan was for that Rotofan to fly us back to the States.'

'Yes.'

'What they did to the crew, that was dreadful. Look, I don't want any more bloodshed on my account. Maybe it'd be best if I gave myself up.'

Jim opened his mouth to reply, but—

'It will not help.'

They whirled to face the speaker. The young woman had spoken for the first time, and in good English.

Jim frowned. 'What?'

She shrugged. 'It will not help because it is not you they're after. It is me.'

15

There was a shocked silence. Jim looked at the girl in astonishment.

She shrugged. 'I am from the Guárico organization.'

'The Fat Man cartel?' Jim said.

'Yes. I belonged to the Fat Man's harem. The army picked me up. I think they were planning to have fun with me – or give me to Los Feroces for them to have fun with me.'

A thought flashed through Jim's head.

We shouted '¡Saludos del Hombre Gordo!' 'Greetings from The Fat Man!' The idea was to give credit for the prisoner extraction to The Fat Man rather than the US. As it turned out that's even more credible than I anticipated. The cartel may well be keen to get her back.

'Let's have no more talk of giving yourselves up,' he said. 'Right now we need to get away from here and make it to the other rendezvous.'

'It's a fair distance to the coast,' Sally said. 'We've got water and emergency rations, but not for six, and not for as long as that.'

Jim winced and there was silence as he bent his head, looking at the ground and thinking about it. Then he straightened up. 'We've been gone just three days. The Rotofan crew were equipped for ten. There should still be ample supplies on board.'

Sally's eyes widened. 'Jim, they may have taken the supplies or booby-trapped them…'

'Yeah, I know. I'll do it. Sally, you're second-in-command. If I touch something nasty you'll take charge. You all have a map, you all know the coordinates and the password. Head off without me.'

Miguel said, 'Jim…'

But Jim shook his head. 'You two,' he pointed at Dexter and waggled the finger between him and the woman, then pointed to the all-roader. 'This could get dangerous. I want both of you inside the vehicle.'

They nodded and got in.

He turned back to his squad. 'First we need to make sure we're alone here. We'll spread out and do another circle around the clearing. Miguel and Fernando you go to the left. Sally with me, to the right. We're not taking any chances, either. You see a stranger, shoot them.'

They moved out. All had undergone jungle training and they went stealthily, staying low and putting their weight down gently and progressively at each step. It took fifteen minutes before they met halfway around.

'See anything?' Jim asked softly.

'No,' Fernando replied.

'Okay, complete the circuit.'

They passed each other and met up again at the entrance to the logging trail.

Jim put his rifle on the ground. He muttered, 'Okay, now for the Rotofan. You guys stay low. Here we go.'

He crept towards the craft, focusing his mind entirely on the task. His eyes flicked between the Rotofan, where someone could be waiting on board, and the ground, where he was looking for the slightest disturbance that might indicate a landmine or a fine trip wire that could detonate claymores. He'd done a lot of this when he was a Lieutenant in the SAS, clearing deserted mountain villages that could harbour terrorists. Those people had a nasty habit of leaving traps of every sort behind them.

The rank smell of the corpses wafted towards him as he approached. They must have been killed soon after the team had left. He averted his eyes from their faces and buried his nose in the crook of one elbow to take the edge off the stench.

The door of the Rotofan was open. Closer to the bodies he could hear the buzzing of the flies, and as he passed they lifted in a swarm, then resettled. He checked the steps and the ground below them carefully, looked around the open hatch for anything that shouldn't be there, a small device or a wire, but saw nothing. Taking a deep breath he put a foot on the first step and transferred his weight onto it. It creaked but nothing happened. He breathed out and climbed the rest of the steps, peered inside and looked up and down the fuselage. It was empty. There was a small kitchen area adjacent to the cockpit. The supplies were probably in there.

Placing his feet with care he checked all round the door to the kitchen area, then gently opened it. Nothing happened. He examined the shelves, starting at the top and working downwards. On the floor itself were two boxes. They could be the supplies or they could contain several pounds of Celonite. He swallowed, then drew one out, sliding it slowly across the floor. The flaps weren't sealed. He eased one open, saw tins and packets and jars. He opened the other flap. It was safe. He checked the second box in the same way. Just more supplies.

He wiped a sleeve across the sweat trickling down his forehead and began to breathe normally. Then he hefted one box. It was heavy but he wasn't aiming to make this journey twice so he rested it on his knee and tucked the other one under his arm. Then he straightened up and made his way, still with infinite care, down the steps, through the stench and the flies, and across to the logging trail. Fernando and Miguel came forward, took the boxes from him and put them down. They said nothing, but Fernando clapped him lightly on the shoulder. Clearly they were well aware of the huge risk he'd taken for them.

They divided the supplies between them, taking what they needed and putting them into the backpacks. Then Jim pulled a map from the outside pocket of his backpack and took a bearing with his wristwatch compass.

His back was to the clearing now, and he pointed into the forest on the left. 'We'll head off that way.'

Dexter and the woman walked up and joined the group. She glanced at Dexter's leather shoes. 'The ground here is rough. Those are not good for such a walk.'

Dexter shrugged. 'It's that or bare feet. I'll wear these.'

Jim said, 'Miguel, Fernando, Sally, take the uniforms too,' he said. 'We don't want to leave them here. The rendezvous is being managed by SEALs, and they may open fire if we reach it wearing civvies.'

They packed the uniforms, then hoisted the backpacks and picked up their rifles.

'Is there anything else left in the all-roader?' Jim asked. 'Anything that could identify us as Americans?'

Miguel said, 'Not really, Jim. There's nothing in the pockets. The modifications where the spare wheel went were a little special, but no one knows what we put in there. You want us to torch it?'

'I would, except the smoke would be a great signal for any pursuers, telling them exactly where to start their search. I'm assuming there's nothing incriminating in the Rotofan, either, but I'm not going back there to check.'

Sally grinned. 'Oh, really? Why not?'

He shot her a rueful smile. 'All right, everyone ready?'

Dexter said, 'You people are heavily loaded. I should take something.'

Fernando laughed. 'You think this is heavily loaded? You should see what we carry on our morning run!'

Miguel and Fernando led the way, choosing their route through the forest, ducking low branches or brushing them aside and hacking with mission knives when it couldn't be avoided. Sally and the young woman followed close behind them. Jim and Dexter fetched up the rear, and Jim turned at frequent intervals, scanning his rifle to check they weren't being followed. In the back of his mind Jim was still pondering what Dexter had said:

'This wasn't supposed to happen.'

He was right in one sense. Wendell had been quite specific in his instructions: *'Your brief is simply to report on what's happening, not to intervene.'* But how did Dexter know that? And how could it be wrong when they were about to incarcerate him in that prison?

16

For half an hour they hacked and ducked their way through the forest. Then a gap appeared between the trees where the low-growing vegetation was stunted or absent and they found themselves on a rough trail. They paused to look up and down it.

'What do you think, Jim?' Miguel asked.

'Could have been made by animals.'

'Or men,' Fernando said darkly.

'Maybe. Take it, we'll make quicker progress that way. But be on the lookout for trouble.'

They moved off again. The going was easier now, and Sally and the woman seemed to converse from time to time as they walked. Jim, still at the back with Dexter, noticed how easily the young woman moved. She was about the same height as Dexter, who was not far short of six foot, and she held herself tall. Her heavy, dark brown hair bounced loosely on her back.

After a while Dexter walked forward to join her and Sally came back and fell into step with Jim.

'After Maracaibo I thought it would be sweltering in here,' Sally said. 'It's hot and humid, but not nearly as bad as I expected.'

'We've known a lot worse, Sal,' Jim said. 'We're quite a bit higher up here than in the city and we're getting the benefit of any breezes coming in over the lake.' He lowered his voice. 'I saw you two talking,' he said quietly, pointing at the young woman. 'Learn anything useful?'

'Her name's Rosario Dorotea Villar. She says we can call her Rosa. She was abducted last year by the cartel. Apparently the Fat Man likes to collect attractive young women – for his own nightly pleasures, no one else's.'

'How many are there, for God's sake?'

'Six at the moment.'

He raised one eyebrow. 'This was last year and she hasn't tried to escape?'

'I asked her that. She said they were well guarded, so it wasn't easy. She saw an opportunity when he let her shop for clothes and underwear, but some army soldiers recognized her escort. They killed him and snatched her. When we'd been talking a while she switched to English. She speaks it very well.'

He nodded. 'Do you believe her story?'

Sally shrugged. 'Doesn't make a lot of difference whether I do or not. Fact is, government troops were taking her to that prison. We know what would have happened to her there. Unless…'

'Unless what?'

'Unless she's a plant.'

'A government agent?'

'Yes. She's attractive, bilingual. She'd be a good candidate for a spy.'

Jim thought for a moment. 'I can't see why they'd send a spy in a military convoy with Dexter. It seems they didn't have any further use for him, and the journey would be too short for her to learn much of value even if they did.'

'She could have been told to ask him questions during a torture session.'

He grimaced. 'I see.' For a few moments he was buried in thought. Then, 'You're right to be cautious, Sally, and she may not be everything she seems. But there's not much we can do about it, so let's take her at face value for the moment.'

Bright sunlight now penetrated the trees and dappled the path ahead. They'd reached the edge of the forest. They debouched into an open area that sloped down into a valley. Tall grass was interspersed with rocks and clumps of trees. On the other side the ground rose to a higher level.

Jim looked at the open sky. Now that they were out of the trees there'd be a decent satellite signal.

'Wait here,' he said. He walked a short distance away and used the communicator to put a secure call through to the USCYBERCOM group.

'Harry?'

'Yes.'

'Jim Slater here. I need you to get a message to General Harken in the DoD.'

'Okay. Go ahead.'

'Tell him our Rotofan crew was ambushed. They're all dead. We have to walk to the alternative rendezvous.'

'Jeez, that's tough.'

'Yeah. Look, we need to keep moving so I'll leave it with you.'

'Don't worry, Jim, I'll handle it. Good luck.'

He rejoined the others. Rosa pointed to a dip in the ridge opposite. 'We need to go down here and up over there.'

Jim's eyes narrowed. 'You seem to know this area well.'

'I should, I was brought up not far from here. I recognize the profile of those hills.'

'Well, we're not going that way,' Jim said.

She looked at him, an eyebrow arched. 'Why not?'

'The ground's too open. Look at it from the enemy's point of view. This area's far too big for them to search for us on foot. That means taking to the air with Rotofans if they've got them, helicopters if they have any that are still working, or drones. Drones are the most likely. They'll spot our Rotofan easily, and when they do they'll get troops in there and find the Toyota abandoned. So now they're searching a smaller area, but they'll still do it from the air. We need to take a route that keeps us under cover.' He pointed to a clump of trees. 'We'll make for those trees, then go quickly from those to the next ones, until we can get up to that dip in the ridge.'

'It's a long way round,' she said.

'Too bad, that's how we're going to do it.'

They set off down into the valley and made it into the first stand of trees. Then all the soldiers froze. Jim said, 'Don't move, anyone.'

Dexter said, 'What's up? I didn't hear anything.'

Sally said, 'We've been trained to hear a stick breaking at two hundred yards. Which is a lot quieter than the drone that's heading this way.'

They listened intently. Miguel said, 'Surveillance drone. Doesn't sound heavy enough for an attack drone.'

Jim nodded. 'I agree. Keep still. Movement is what could give us away.'

The buzz of the drone swelled, then began to die away. 'Okay,' Jim said. 'It looks like they were searching both sides of that highway we came up on and saw the Rotofan. That's narrowed things down for them. Go on, but be prepared to take cover again. It may come back.'

They moved through the trees. Rosa had dropped back to join Jim. There was a new sound in her voice. Interest? Curiosity? 'You're very smart,' she said.

'Keeps me alive,' he replied.

'Everyone calls you Jim. Can I call you Jim?'

'Sure. Sally says we can call you Rosa.'

'Yes.'

'Where did you learn to speak English, Rosa?'

'My father arranged for me to go to a good school, in Southern California.'

Jim turned his head sharply and looked at her. 'A girl from Venezuela? How the hell did he work that?'

She smiled. 'He has a lot of business contacts: Colombia, Mexico, Texas, California. They passed me from one to the next and gave me a new identity. My name became Rosa Theresa da Silva. I did well and went to the University of Southern California. Studied Economics and Business Management. I'd been away a long time so I came back to visit my father.' She shrugged and gave him a smile.

She was a striking young woman, he thought. Flawless complexion, fine bone structure, white teeth, long eyelashes, and eyes so dark they looked like big black pupils. Had she really been pounced on by the Fat Man's operatives? It wasn't all that hard to believe. He tore his gaze away and focused on the route ahead.

They'd come to the edge of that group of trees. Scanning the area all he could see was open ground in every direction. The shortest distance between them and the next decent patch of woodland was a good four hundred yards.

'Okay,' Jim said. 'Let's do this quickly.'

It wasn't easy to run through the tall grasses, and they had to really pick their feet up. That was no problem for the squad, who were used to jogging through terrain like this, and with her long legs Rosa could keep up with them, but Dexter, who was older and wearing ordinary shoes, was in difficulty, stumbling, tripping, and slipping and sliding all the way. Jim, who felt obliged to run with him, bit his lip in frustration.

They were about halfway across when he heard the sound he didn't want to hear.

The drone was coming back.

17

Jim could see the drone now, flying directly towards them. He shouted, 'Miguel, with me!'

He took Dexter's left elbow and Miguel, seeing the problem, took the other. They continued to run, lifting Dexter between them, his feet still walking but barely touching the ground. Jim glanced up. No way were they going to make it to the woodland cover before that drone was directly overhead. There was no choice.

'Sally, Fernando, take it out!'

Sally and Fernando dropped quickly to a firing position, resting an elbow on one knee. They targeted and ranged the drone and fired almost simultaneously. It exploded – no flash, no sound, just disintegrated. Fragments came spinning down. A faint echo of the shots came back to them.

They put Dexter back on his feet and he doubled over, breathing hard. He straightened up slowly and swallowed. 'Sorry,' he gasped.

Jim's eyes narrowed. There was a good deal further to go on this journey. Could Dexter cope with it, or were they pushing him beyond his endurance?

'How old are you, Dexter?' he asked.

'Fifty-two. But things have been very sedentary for me lately.'

'Can you make it to that cover? You can take your time now.'

He nodded and walked on with Miguel on one side and Jim on the other. They regrouped at the trees.

'Okay,' Jim said. 'Change of plan.'

They gathered round. 'Nice shooting, Sally, Fernando. But even if our pursuers didn't hear the shots they'll know we knocked out their drone. Now they've got a fix on where we are and they'll come looking for us. Question is: where are we going to be when they arrive?'

Rosa said, 'We were heading along the valley for that dip in the ridge.'

'Yes, and that's just where they'd expect us to go, so we have to do it differently.' He pointed. If it wasn't a mountain it wasn't far short of one. At its highest point it was wreathed in cloud.

'That way?' Rosa's eyes widened. 'That will be very, very difficult.'

'I know, but we've got time. Sally, Miguel, Fernando, I know you can handle it. Rosa?'

She shrugged. 'Sure, if that's what you want. It's better than getting captured by those animals.'

'Dexter?'

'I'm up for it. You've saved my life already, Jim, so I'll do as I'm told.'

Sally said, 'It's pretty open up there. Do you think they have another drone?'

Jim's lips set. 'That could be a problem…'

He looked up. Heavy clouds were gathering and the light faded rapidly. The air was suddenly chill. Moments later the rain started and increased to a roar, splashing off the rocks that were interspersed among the grasses and thrashing at the canopy of leaves above their heads. The downpour dropped a silvery curtain over the entire landscape.

'There's your answer,' Jim laughed. 'Timing couldn't have been better.'

Dexter and Rosa looked at him.

Sally said to them, 'He means if they do have more drones they can't operate in this, and even if they could they wouldn't see a damned thing. We need to take advantage of it.'

'Right, let's try to get up there before the rain stops.'

They set off, each taking their own path up the steep slope, eyes fixed on the few yards ahead of them, which was as far as they could see. Dexter had to make frequent stops to catch his breath. That was understandable: the grass and rocks were treacherous and the rain was turning the ground into a veritable sponge. Jim saw how the muddy water bulged and spilled over the tops of the man's shoes. Higher up, the ground became more stony; the grass sparser and the rocks more frequent. Here the falling rain gathered and flowed in streams, so the going was slippery and Dexter was finding it hard to get a purchase. He slid back on almost every step and Jim had to grab his arm to keep him upright. The others were well ahead of them by now, but Jim didn't push it and Dexter made no complaint.

It took a full hour before things began to level out. By now their clothes were soaked through and clinging to them. It was cold and up here the mist was so thick they could barely see a yard in front of them.

'We'd better go carefully,' Jim said. 'We seem to be on a ridge and we don't know what kind of drop there is on the other side. I'll take the lead. Miguel, can you look after Dexter?'

Miguel dropped back and Jim moved forward, feeling the slope of the ground under his feet. It wasn't steep here but it could still end in a cliff so he moved cautiously, descending at a shallow angle. He continued to make his way down, the others behind him, and then quite abruptly the mist cleared. He stopped, and looked through the falling rain down a slope that gradually eased into level ground. The slope was modest but it would be treacherous in these conditions, so they continued to take it slowly.

The rain continued unrelentingly for another hour. When it finally stopped they were walking across level terrain. Water streamed and puddled everywhere and the mud clung to their shoes and boots making every step heavier. The air, however, had a wonderful clarity and the view ahead was spectacular, rolling hills emerging from mist and grasses glittering under their burden of water droplets.

Miguel and Fernando were well in the lead now, with Sally behind them and Jim at the rear with Rosa and Dexter.

Jim took a deep breath. The air was fresh and cool with a grassy smell. He said to Rosa, 'You have a beautiful country.'

'Yes,' she said, 'when it is not raining.' She laced her fingers through her hair and slung it back in a shower of spray and they both laughed.

Miguel was waiting for them. He pointed ahead. 'Jim,' he said, 'there's some sort of rock formation up there. Maybe we can find a place to rest and dry out.'

'Okay, let's you and me take a look.'

The formation was about fifty feet high, and the ground around it was strewn with loose rocks of every size. They found a place where rocks had detached from the main mass of the formation and left a kind of cave, not all that deep but enough to provide some shelter. The rest of the group caught up with them.

'What we need now is a fire,' Fernando said.

Jim thought about it. Fernando was right. Their clothes were wet through, and as the exertion of the walk subsided they'd begin to shiver. A fire was the answer. Could they risk it? Smoke here would rise, but not freely; it would have to strike the overhang and curl over the front. It would be thinned out by the vegetation that clothed the slope above. In any case, looking around he could see a slight mist rising everywhere; the sun, warm now, was evaporating off the water. In this visibility a drone would have to be almost overhead to spot them.

'Okay. They may have given up on us by now but we can't depend on it. Keep listening out while we see if we can find anything dry to burn.'

They hunted down twigs and branches that had been sheltered to some extent, and stacked them together to make a good pile. Before long they had a fire blazing. Fernando and Miguel dragged and rolled some of the rocks, arranging them so that they could sit around it. They broke out some rations and handed them round with bottles of water. After that the men took off their shirts, which they held out to the heat. Dexter discarded his suit jacket and even took off his shoes so that he could dry his socks. There was no sound of a returning drone.

Although still very damp they were feeling more relaxed now. Jim got his map out and identified their position. He nodded, folded the map up, and returned it to his backpack. He said to Dexter, 'You ready to tell us now what went on back there?'

Dexter gave a one-sided grin. 'Yeah, why not? It's all top secret, but after the hand they dealt me I couldn't care less.' He shifted slightly to make himself more comfortable.

'Venezuela's economy is in dire straits, has been for years,' he began. 'It doesn't take an economist to see why: mismanagement, extreme politics, sanctions resulting from rigged elections and human rights abuses, you name it. So their brilliant government has now arrived at a radical solution. Anyone here heard of the Cuban missile crisis?'

Jim said, 'Come on, Dexter, that must be nearly a hundred years ago.' The others were just shaking their heads.

'That's right, it is, but it's still the closest we ever came to all-out nuclear war.' He circled a pointing finger around the circle. 'Those who do not study history are forced to relive it. And you may not know it, but you are reliving it right now.'

He must have noticed the blank expressions, so he continued:

'All right, what was the Cuban missile crisis? It started with US deployment of missile bases in Turkey. That set Russia's nerves jangling so they made a countermove of their own, an agreement with Cuba that allowed them to construct nuclear missile sites on the island. When the US found out, they quickly set up a naval blockade to prevent the Russians completing the installation. The Russian fleet was already on its way, loaded with missiles. Now we had a highly dangerous stand-off. The US President, John F. Kennedy, was determined not to allow missile sites to be constructed on their doorstep but Russia's leader, Nikita Kruschev, was notoriously capricious, and no one knew which way he'd jump. The whole world held its breath as the two super-powers faced up to one another.'

Miguel leaned forward. 'What happened?' he asked.

'There were several tense days but fortunately both leaders knew full well what the consequences of nuclear war would be. Russia finally backed down. They turned their ships around and agreed to dismantle the existing sites in exchange for America doing the same in Turkey. And everyone heaved a sigh of relief.'

Jim was waiting. 'What has this got to do with Venezuela?'

'I'll tell you. For some years Russia has been in an expansionist mood. They want the old Soviet Union back, don't they? So we have the Crimea, Georgia, South Ossetia, and Abkhazia. The world complained bitterly, imposed sanctions, but otherwise did nothing. Now the Bear has turned his greedy little eyes on the Baltic states. That's different, because the Baltic states are part of the alliance. So the US reinforced the borders with a chain of medium-range missiles to guarantee their security. That's annoyed the hell out of the Russians.'

He raised a forefinger. 'So, to the point. The US has learned that Venezuela has agreed to let them erect medium-range missile sites on an isolated stretch of coast north-east of Maracaibo.'

Miguel muttered, 'Holy shit!'

.

18

The fire settled, disgorging a shower of sparks, but all eyes were on Dexter.

He gave them a rueful smile. 'Holy shit indeed.'

Rosa said, 'When I was in the city I overheard some foreigners in a café. I'm sure they were speaking Russian. That would explain it.'

Sally said, 'Jim and I encountered a couple of guys when we were carrying out our reconnaissance. They asked the way in Spanish but I was pretty sure they were Russians.'

'Yes,' Dexter said, 'they've already started to excavate underground silos for the missiles and an air defence system, so they have engineers and advisers in Maracaibo right now. Venezuela's government is delighted. It provides work for local people, the visitors are spending freely in shops, restaurants, cafés, and supermarkets, and as part of the deal Russia is pumping money into the country, most of which will no doubt find its way into the pockets of the administration and the Los Feroces cartel. Best of all, it puts their fingers right up the nose of the US.'

'That's not a new threat, though, is it?' Jim said. 'Russia already has ICBMs capable of hitting American cities.'

'True, but the missiles could just be the start. They could follow up with a large garrison of Russian paratroops, a couple of big transport aircraft and a squadron of fighters on hand at Maracaibo airport, and a naval force in the Gulf. At least that's the way I see it, and I expect Washington is thinking along the same lines.'

Fernando growled, 'President Nagel won't sit still for that.'

Dexter smiled at him. 'Ah, but what can she do? This Russia is not the Soviet Union that Kennedy was dealing with – these people will be a lot harder to face down. The US can't offer to withdraw the missiles from the Baltic because they'd be back-tracking on their treaty obligations. So I was given the job of taking a tempting package of offers to Venezuela: ending of sanctions, commitment to importing certain goods, investment, and so on. All this in return for agreeing to putting a halt to the construction of the missile sites.'

'Why you?' Jim asked.

'I've done a lot of business in Central and South America, including Venezuela, and I know the country. Some years ago, during a brief thawing of relations, the US reopened its Embassy in Caracas and as I had a lot of experience here they appointed me as an Attaché. It didn't last, of course. When this government was elected they threw all of us out and closed it down.'

'Sending you here doesn't make any sense,' Jim said. 'Aguilar's administration is violently anti-American. The chances of them responding to an offer like that are no better than the proverbial snowball in hell. Surely you realized that?'

'I was aware of it, obviously, but I wasn't in a good position to refuse – I'll explain later. But you're right, of course: when I arrived I was not treated courteously and I had to wait for half an hour before they'd even see me. Finally I was ushered into a room with several people at the table, including a couple of government ministers. I was ready to present them with a written agreement but all they wanted was a verbal summary of the offer. The whole time they were listening they were exchanging half-smiles and sceptical looks. Their response was to read out a long prepared statement from President Aguilar, and I had to sit through this diatribe for maybe another half-hour.' He gave them a wan smile and shook his head. 'At the end they thanked me for coming and said I would now be treated to some Venezuelan hospitality. I could guess what they meant by that. They shoved me into a vehicle and bundled Rosa in with me. We were no doubt heading for Buena Vista when you rescued us.'

'So the diplomacy failed,' Miguel said.

'On the contrary, it worked exactly as intended, I was just a little slow to realize it. You see, everyone would like to see a regime change in this country: the people certainly would, and the US and fifty or more other countries around the world recognize Juan-Luis Delgado as the rightful winner of the last election so they'd welcome it, too.' He shrugged. 'None of that helps. You can't interfere in the internal dealings of a sovereign state – not without justification. I was to be the sacrificial lamb who furnished the justification. I'm sure your observers have already informed Washington that I was being taken to prison, and I'm equally sure that US forces were already assembled within striking distance. By now they will have received the go-ahead. Their task will be a full-scale invasion aimed at toppling the government. Once Aguilar is ousted and Delgado is instated, they'll withdraw.'

Sally blew out a breath and exchanged looks with Jim, whose mouth had tightened.

It would have been nice to know that, wouldn't it? he thought. *It's typical of the way things work. Folk in Washington sitting behind big desks stamp 'TOP SECRET' all over the file and us poor bastards do the heavy lifting in ignorance.*

At one level he could understand it. They weren't told too much in case they were captured.

I'm not blaming Wendell for this. It's not his fault. He's just a conduit for operations like this and he has to do what he's told, same as us.

Miguel said, 'I guess this whole scheme was masterminded by the CIA.'

Dexter nodded. 'Almost certainly.'

'Goddamned CIA,' Fernando growled.

'Even for them,' Jim said, 'it's a bit of a stretch to use a former US Attaché as a pawn in their game. President Nagel couldn't have been happy with that.'

'I don't suppose she was, but her approval wasn't quite as difficult to secure as you might think. You see, I would be dead right now if I hadn't agreed to be the envoy. To do this they extracted me from prison. And I was on Death Row.'

19

Barely a wisp of smoke escaped from the fire now, but the group was still bathed in warmth from the embers, the glow from which deepened the gathering darkness beyond. Silence had settled like a blanket, on them and on the whole landscape.

Sally said slowly, 'You… you're a convicted murderer?'

'Yes.'

Miguel said, 'But you're innocent, right?'

'Wrong, I'm afraid. Guilty as charged. But don't be alarmed. I'm not a serial killer or anything like that.'

This was received with a mixture of puzzled frowns and uneasy smiles.

'You want to tell us what happened?' Jim asked.

Dexter shrugged. 'Well I've told you this much so you may as well hear the rest.' He took a deep breath. 'I said I did a lot of business in South America. I tried to persuade my wife to come with me on those trips. She never wanted to. She didn't even visit when I was the Attaché in Venezuela. After the Embassy shut down I returned to my commercial role, working hard, travelling long distances, seeing a lot of people, and I successfully secured a number of sizeable contracts. The company should have been thriving, but somehow we never seemed to turn a decent profit. The last time I returned to the States I thought I'd try to find out why. Late one night I opened the office and went through the books, page by page.'

He looked around the group, then went on. 'It took a while but I identified the problem all right. My long-time business partner, Jason, had been siphoning money out of the company and into his off-shore accounts. There were also a lot of items identified as "client incentives". That attracted my attention because never in my life have I bribed clients to secure an order. When I dug deeper I found he was buying expensive jewellery: a bracelet, a necklace, earrings, a brooch. And as the English say, the penny finally dropped. I realized why my wife never wanted to come with me on trips. I confronted her, of course, and she admitted she'd been having an affair with Jason for years, and she wanted a divorce so she could marry him.'

His voice had gone hard.

'So it wasn't enough that Jason was stealing the money I'd worked so hard to earn for us. He was fucking my wife as well.'

'So you killed him,' Miguel said.

'Oh, he deserved to die, but I don't know if I actually meant to kill him. All the same I loaded a revolver and put it in my pocket when I went to see him. He was all smiles, trying to brush everything aside, and when I remonstrated with him he laughed and called me a gullible fool. I pinned him against the wall and shoved the barrel of the pistol under his chin. It was good to see the terror in his eyes.

Unfortunately I'd already gone too far by then and I couldn't stop.' He closed his eyes. 'I pulled the trigger.'

Someone exhaled a long breath. No one spoke. Then Dexter said:

'I propped him up, sitting against the wall, wiped the revolver and placed it in his hand to make it look like suicide. I knew my wife would find out he was dead and she'd put two and two together, so I told her we'd had an argument and he pulled a gun on me and in the struggle it went off.'

Dexter smiled. 'It might have worked, too, got me manslaughter. Unfortunately I was totally new to this sort of thing. I'd forgotten about the shell casing, which was still in the revolver, and the other five rounds. All had my fingerprints on them, and mine only.' He shrugged. 'It probably took them all of five minutes to find out the revolver was registered to me. Open and shut case. I'd gone to my business partner with a gun in my pocket and shot him. My lawyer pleaded a crime of passion, but the prosecution argued that it wasn't an impulsive act but a carefully premeditated murder. That's Murder One. They don't believe in long prison sentences these days, so I went straight to Death Row.'

The only light that illuminated Dexter and the intent faces of the listeners now was a fitful reddish glow from the embers.

'What about your wife?' Sally asked.

He shrugged dismissively. 'She sued for divorce the moment I was arrested. That was okay, I didn't contest it, wouldn't have wanted to for a moment; I had no doubt she'd been a knowing party to the whole deception. Still I had some satisfaction in court, watching my defense attorney shred her and her deceased lover to pieces. And neither she – nor anyone else – can get their hands on Jason's money, the money he stole from the company that I earned and he salted away overseas.'

'Your company, what happens to that?' Miguel asked.

'No idea,' Dexter said, with a laugh. 'I can hardly try to wind it up now, can I? I'm supposed to be dead!'

Jim nodded. 'Now I understand what you said about things being sedentary for a while. How long did you spend on Death Row?'

'Just under two years. It reached the stage where all appeals had failed and the date of the execution had been set. That was when I was approached by someone from the Department of Justice. He presented me with a choice. Stay in prison and be executed in two weeks' time, or accept the role of a Special Envoy to Venezuela to negotiate a deal. No details at that stage, just the merest outline. Oh, and he gave me an incentive. If I succeeded in the negotiations, I'd get a Presidential pardon.' He opened his hands. 'So now you know.'

'That was one hell of a choice,' Miguel said.

'It was,' Jim agreed, 'but really a choice between a nice peaceful exit under anaesthetic and being tortured to death in a Venezuelan prison. You must have known that.'

'Yes, and I thought long and hard about it. Finally I agreed, for two reasons. I'd been on Death Row for almost two long years. Every avenue of appeal had been exhausted and now I was waiting for execution. When you're faced with the certainty of death, a chance of staying alive – even a small one – is better than none at all.'

'I can understand that,' Jim said. 'What was the other reason?'

'I don't have delusions of grandeur, Jim, but I have a proven record as a good negotiator, in both my business and diplomatic roles. It seemed to me that I had an outside chance of being the person who avoided a Third World War.'

The group went quiet again. Someone sighed.

The silence was broken by Miguel.

'You didn't realize you were the bait in a CIA trap?'

Dexter gave him a rueful smile. 'I started to work it out when they were reading me that polemic from Aguilar. By then, of course, it was too late. The CIA were banking on Aguilar and his chums behaving true to type, and they did.'

Jim said, 'No wonder we were told on no account to intervene.'

Dexter raised his eyebrows. 'Really? They said that? So you disobeyed orders?'

'Let's say I acted on my own initiative. It's not the first time I've done it.'

'If there were witnesses to the rescue you could find yourself in serious trouble.'

Miguel said, 'We shouted "¡Saludos del Hombre Gordo!" Greetings from the The Fat Man! It was to make them think we were the The Fat Man cartel, not the US.'

Rosa's mouth opened as if she were about to say something, then she closed it again and shook her head.

Jim looked around him. 'We'll bivvy here for the night. It's not a bad spot and we're protected from the rear. There isn't enough room to erect tents inside the cave and I don't want them outside because they'd be visible from the air.

We've got our sleeping bags and we can keep our rifles within reach. What shall we do about Dexter and Rosa?'

Sally said, 'Wrap them in the tents? It should keep them warm.' She shrugged. 'We don't have anything else.'

'Good idea. Then sentries on three-hour stints. Sally, you go to 2100 hours, Miguel 2100 to midnight, I'll take midnight to 0300 and Fernando 0300 to 0600. It'll be getting light then, and we'll push on.'

20

General Wendell Harken pressed a button on his desk to speak to his PA.

'Anna, I need a car, immediately.'

By the time Wendell was downstairs the Army sedan was waiting for him.

The driver opened a rear door for him.

'Where to, sir?'

'White House.'

*

Wendell was conducted through strict security checks in the West Wing then taken down to the basement. He was met there by the Situation Room's Senior Duty Officer.

'General Harken,' Wendell said. 'I'm responding to a CRITIC call.'

'Very good, General. May I just check your I.D.?'

The officer passed the I.D. over a handheld reader, then checked the name against a list and handed it back. 'Please come with me.'

Wendell followed him to the main conference room, where the SDO pushed the door open for him and stepped aside. Wendell went in and nodded to the five people sitting in black leather armchairs around the long table: Admiral Mike Randall, Director of the National Security Agency; Hunter Freeman, Director of National Intelligence; Joe Templeton, Director of the CIA; Bob Cressington, Secretary of State for Defense; and General George Wagner, Chief of Staff of the Army. The CSA's tunic was so stiff with medal ribbons that Wendell wondered – as he sometimes had before – whether he could bend to tie a shoelace.

'Wendell,' the CSA said with a warm smile.

'George.'

The others nodded. Wendell took a seat and waited. This was the operational group, the people who not only 'needed to know' but needed to make it happen. It had met several times before, initially without him; he was included once he had an SAF team in the field. Everyone here had a direct role in the operation with the possible exception of Hunter Freeman, Director of National Intelligence. In the normal course of things Joe Templeton, Director of the CIA, would report to Hunter so it would have been discourteous to exclude him, but Wendell had yet to hear him make a contribution. The door opened and they were joined by the White House Chief of Staff, Carol Anders.

'Thanks for coming, gentlemen,' she said. 'The President will be with us very shortly. She's anxious to be updated on the situation in Venezuela.'

They waited in silence. This gave Wendell the opportunity to reflect on the contrast between the sober suits of the three political administrators and the riot of colour presented by the beribboned tunics of the military men. For him nothing could have better illustrated the essence of this operation.

He thought about the woman they were waiting for. Wendell had had dealings with Harriet Nagel when she was a senator and a presidential candidate. She'd been a popular President, both nationally and internationally, based on her intelligent grasp of issues, her willingness to listen, and a knack for understanding the political or personal problems of those she spoke to. Now she was coming to the end of her second term. This operation in Venezuela could make or mar her legacy and she would be acutely aware of it.

Barely a minute later she hurried in. She wore a pea-green collarless jacket over a white blouse and her hair was neatly brushed, but there was little sign of her usual relaxed manner. She looked quickly round the table and as she sat down she said, 'Right, who's going to start?'

The CSA leaned forward. 'I can start, Madam President. The operation's in progress as we speak. We've landed marines on the coast at locations north of Caracas and north of Maracaibo. Their objective will be to secure the airports and stop all outgoing flights. We'll install our own people in the control towers to divert incoming air traffic.'

The President spoke. 'I understand the need to do that at Caracas. What's the point of doing it at Maracaibo as well?'

'It's to stop their allies – let's be specific, the Russians – shipping in military personnel and equipment to resist the invasion.'

'Good,' she said. 'Go on.'

'101st Airborne has already landed paratroops around Caracas. They've set up road blocks on all exits from the city.' He looked at the President. 'That's important, ma'am, to prevent President Aguilar and his entourage from running away.'

She nodded.

'Once we have control of the airports we'll land a Leviathan at Maracaibo and two at the Simón Bolivar International Airport – that's the main airport serving Caracas. They'll unload troops, troop carriers, light utility vehicles, and tanks, and we'll converge on the capital. Meanwhile the marines will take control of the television stations.'

'How much opposition are you expecting?' the President asked.

'Only token, ma'am. The idea is to demonstrate overwhelming force. We think they'll capitulate in short order. Then, as we agreed, we'll force President Aguilar to call an election, one he can't rig this time.'

'All right, it seems to be going according to plan. But I'm told there's a problem.'

Joe Templeton said, 'Yes, ma'am. Aguilar has dealt with any potential opposition by having the leaders assassinated or imprisoned. Unless we can mount a credible candidate he'll be re-elected, and we'll be back where we started. The only one who has any hope of defeating him is Juan-Luis Delgado. He actually won the last election – the one Aguilar misreported – and we and fifty-four other countries want to see him rightfully installed as President. It's vitally important that he comes out of hiding and starts campaigning as soon as the election is called.'

President Nagel sucked in a deep breath. 'Well? So what's the problem?'

He swallowed. 'We can't contact him.'

'What?'

'During and after the last election Aguilar imprisoned some of Delgado's most vocal supporters on trumped-up charges. There's every reason to believe they were tortured to death. That's why Delgado went into hiding.'

Joe looked at the CSA, who said, 'Our cyber unit out there has been monitoring communications continuously since Delgado went to ground. He's had nothing incoming or outgoing, encrypted or otherwise. It's prevented Aguilar's snoopers from locating him. Unfortunately it's also made it impossible for us as well.'

'Have we no idea at all where he is?' the President asked.

'Not really. Shortly after the last election he was sighted in the north-west of the country. That's all.'

'Bob,' she said to the Defense Secretary. 'You had a special forces team out there, didn't you?'

'Yes, ma'am. Four members of the Special Assignment Force. They sent back valuable intelligence.'

'Where are they now?'

Bob gestured to Wendell. 'General Harken should answer that.'

Wendell said, 'Madam President, a military Rotofan flew them to a place not too far from Maracaibo and waited for them there. The four should have come back the same way but when they reached the Rotofan they found the crew had been killed. Fortunately I'd arranged a secondary rendezvous for them on the coast. That's where they're headed at the moment.'

The President said, 'Who's leading this group?'

'In view of the importance of the mission the CO of the SAF took charge,' Wendell said. 'Colonel Jim Slater.'

A murmur went round the table and a rueful grin crossed the CSA's face. 'Bit of a wild card, that one.'

Wendell frowned. 'I wouldn't say wild, George. Unconventional, certainly. But the SAF is nearly always tasked with unconventional missions, so he's ideal in that post. And if you look at his record, he's pulled off some pretty remarkable coups in recent years.'

The President said, 'I know Colonel Slater and I'd say he's the perfect man to find Delgado for us. He's resourceful, and – although he'd deny it – he can be quite diplomatic when he needs to be. General Harken, are you in contact with him?'

Wendell said, 'Currently, no, ma'am, and I'm not sure if it's possible in a secure way. The only communicator is the one he's been given by the USCYBERCOM unit in Maracaibo. Even if he still has it, it works on a different frequency to anything else, and it's encrypted. We'd have to contact the cyber unit and transfer the call to him that way. I don't know if it can be done. What do you think, George?'

The CSA sucked his lip. 'Those guys are pretty smart. I think they might just be able to cobble something together. To route you through they'd have to receive your hot line, transcribe, encrypt and retransmit on the new frequency. I can ask them.'

'How long would it take to do all that?' Wendell asked.

'I don't know. If it can be done at all it's going to take a full day – at the very least.'

They looked back at the President. She said, 'Go ahead. Tell them to work day and night. We have to get a message through to Colonel Slater. We need Delgado out and campaigning as soon as the election's called. Keep me posted.'

They all rose as she got to her feet and left the conference room.

21

It was the end of the last watch, but there was no need for Fernando to go round shaking anyone; light in the eastern sky and a burst of bird song had roused them from sleep even before the sun appeared above the mountains. Sally, Miguel, and Jim drew themselves out of their lightweight metallized-foam sleeping bags and stood to stretch and rub sore backs. Then they extracted Dexter and Rosa, who were tightly wrapped in the tents. Sally took her army uniform out of her backpack and rubbed the still damp shirt over her face. The others saw what she was doing and followed suit.

Rosa said, 'I didn't think I'd sleep but I did.'

'Me too,' Dexter said. 'But I was pretty beat.' He rubbed his arms. 'It's damned cold out here.'

Fernando said, 'When the sun comes up maybe you will think this was better.'

Dexter smiled ruefully. 'You could be right.'

They sat down on the rocks and handed out some rations and water.

Jim's communicator buzzed. He got up and walked a short distance away before he made the connection.

'Jim Slater.'

'Colonel, it's Harry.'

'Yes, Harry?'

'I have General Harken on the line for you. I'm going to port you through. We made a bit of a lash-up here so I hope this works.'

There was a loud click then Wendell's voice, indistinct but recognizable despite a slight echo.

'Jim, where are you right now?'

'Where? We're on our way to the second rendezvous. Didn't you get the message?'

'Yes, I got it. Look, don't leave the country yet. Without going into too much detail President Aguilar will be calling an election soon.'

What a surprise.

'It's essential,' Wendell went on, 'that his main opposition candidate enters the race.'

'You're talking about Juan-Luis Delgado.'

'That's right. We want you to locate him and tell him to start preparing his campaign.'

Jim's eyebrows shot up. He couldn't hold back a derisive laugh.

'Who's "we", Wendell?'

He heard an intake of breath. There was a pause, then Wendell said quietly:

'Don't shoot the messenger, Jim.'

'Okay, okay, I'm sorry. It would be nice to know where all this comes from, that's all.'

'You know I can't answer that. Let's just say it's a highly-placed group close to the White House.'

'And is this highly-placed group aware that Delgado has gone to ground? Even Aguilar hasn't been able to get his hands on him, and he's had all the time since the last election.'

'Yes, they're aware of that.'

'Well if he couldn't do it, how the hell how am I supposed to?'

'You'll find a way. President Nagel's depending on you for this, Jim.'

So that was it: the pressure was coming right from the top.

'Do we have any idea at all where he might be?'

'He was last sighted in the north-west of the country.'

'Oh, wonderful.' He blew out a breath. 'Okay, okay, I'll do what I can.'

As Jim ended the call his eyes settled on Rosa, who was talking animatedly with Sally. He remembered something Aidan Summersby had said when he was having lunch with the journalist.

'Delgado's alive all right, but no one knows where he is. Some say he's in hiding with the Guárico Cartel. No one knows where they operate from either.'

No one? Not quite. Rosa knows.

Jim walked back to the group. Sally, Fernando and Miguel were already putting away the sleeping bags and tents.

Sally murmured, 'Problems, Jim?'

'Nothing to worry about.'

Dexter got to his feet. 'Well, I've enjoyed your company for long enough. I'm afraid I'll have to leave you this morning.'

They all stopped what they were doing and looked at him.

'What?' Miguel said. 'Why?'

'Look, you're all heading back to the States. If I dropped in on the scene over there it would be disastrous for both of us. You, because it would mean you'd disobeyed orders. Me, because the whole CIA plan would collapse. American forces have probably landed already, and if I'm alive they won't have the slightest justification for being here. I'd have to be eliminated instantly, and the CIA would no doubt waste no time in obliging.'

'What will you do?' Rosa asked.

'Simple: I won't appear – ever. The Venezuelans will be too embarrassed to admit that I was taken out from under their noses, and so far as Washington's concerned I'm in a Venezuelan prison and their military action was justified. People go into that prison all the time and disappear, so even if US soldiers raid the prison and don't find me they'll assume I've gone the same way.'

Jim frowned, 'What are you saying?'

'I have contacts – I even have some assets – in Colombia and I can make it to the border. I'll stay there under an assumed name and enjoy the rest of my life in nice quiet retirement.'

'You'll never make it into Colombia,' Rosa said. 'There are bandits everywhere along the border. They want money to allow you to cross. You have money?'

'No, the soldiers took it all.'

'Then they will kill you. Look, my home is not far from the border. I can get someone to take you across. I want to go home, so it would be better for me, too.'

'Where's your home, Rosa?' Jim asked casually.

'It's in the north-west.'

That fits nicely.

'Two civilians, on their own, unarmed, in this place?' Miguel said. 'I don't think so.'

Fernando said, 'We should all go with them.'

Jim said, 'Rosa, Dexter: would you excuse us for a moment?' He beckoned to his squad and they walked a short distance away.

'Look,' Jim said. 'I'd say our alternative rendezvous is about fifty miles from here as the crow flies. That's a big ask for someone in Dexter's physical condition and, like he said, they'd kill him if he materialized Stateside. Rosa's proposal is a good one. Clearly they can't travel alone but it's out of our way. If we tried to get to the rendezvous from there we'd have to work along the coast, which is heavily populated. Managing it unseen would be nigh on impossible. So we'll compromise. I'll go with them and you three go straight to the rendezvous.'

Fernando said, 'Just you? No, Jim, we should all—'

Jim held up a hand. 'It's not up for discussion, Fernando. You'll find it quite hard enough getting to the rendezvous undetected from here, let alone trying to do it through that coastal area. Sally, you'll take Miguel and Fernando with you and rendezvous with the SEALs. We can all leave together but when your route diverges from ours you go your own way.'

Sally exchanged looks with Fernando and Miguel, then turned to Jim. 'How are you going to get back?'

'I'll manage.'

They joined Rosa and Dexter. 'Okay, it's decided. Sally, Miguel and Fernando will continue to the rendezvous. I'll come with you two.'

Dexter said, 'Jim, I wouldn't want to—'

'No arguments, please, Dexter. This is how we're doing it.'

Dexter shrugged. 'All right. Thanks.'

'Rosa,' Jim said. 'Do you want to look at a map?'

'Yes, okay. I think I know where we are, but it will be worth to check.'

Jim sat on one of the rocks and unfolded the map across his knees. Rosa bent over and traced a slim finger over it. Her face was very close to his and he could feel her breath on his cheek. 'All right,' she said softly, and pointed to a valley. 'We have to go up there.' She straightened up, placing a hand on his shoulder with a light squeeze. It was a casual enough gesture, but to him it felt like anything but.

He refolded the map, got to his feet, and turned to face her. Her dark eyes rested on him and he held her gaze.

The team hoisted backpacks. Fernando kicked around the ashes until he'd left no sign of the previous evening's fire. Miguel moved one or two rocks to make it look more random. Then they set off, Jim leading the way with Sally and Rosa.

Sally pointed to a clump of trees. 'You want to move under cover again?'

Jim surveyed the view ahead and pursed his lips. 'I think it'll be safe enough to walk in the open now, and we'll make faster progress that way.'

They walked for an hour, then took a rest for Dexter's sake. The level ground continued ahead of them but to the right the terrain rose higher.

Sally checked her watch compass. 'We need to take the high route.'

Rosa said, 'We go straight ahead.'

'Okay,' Sally said, 'we'll leave you here.'

The three shook hands with Rosa and Dexter.

'Jim,' Sally said. 'When we get there what shall I tell them happened to you?'

'Tell them all four of our Rotofan crew were murdered. Say we were making our way to the alternative rendezvous but we thought whoever killed them was following us. I split away from you as a diversion. It's a pretty standard tactic.'

'Okay.' She frowned and looked at him steadily. 'I hope you make it back all right. Good luck.'

'You too,' Jim said.

He watched for a few moments, feeling a slight pang of loss as they set off towards the hills.

Then he got to his feet and looked at Dexter. 'Ready?'

Dexter pushed himself off the ground and took a deep breath. 'Ready as I'll ever be.'

.

22

The route towards the coast that Sally, Fernando, and Miguel
had chosen began with a series of gentle ascents and
descents. They were in good spirits; the going wasn't
challenging and they were making excellent progress. After
about ten miles they embarked on a steeper ascent, taking a
line along the side of a mountain. Ahead of them a blanket
of cloud concealed the top, spilling over it and thinning on
its descent, an eerie sight, like a waterfall frozen by a still
camera. Minutes later they were inside it. It was a replay of
the experience during the earlier part of the trek, when Jim
was leading them. Although it wasn't raining this time the
mist was thick and penetrating, and very soon they were
soaked to the skin. Visibility was next to zero, so Sally took
the lead, feeling her way carefully and testing the slippery
rocks before placing her feet. They continued to climb, then
the ground levelled out and they slowly began the descent on
the other side. Quite suddenly the mist cleared and the view
opened up in front of them.

They were looking out over the Gulf of Venezuela. The
mountain sloped away below them and about half a mile

away a road extended to both left and right as far as they could see. There were no vehicles on it.

'That's the coastal highway,' Sally said. 'I wonder why there's no traffic.'

'Maybe they've put up road blocks,' Fernando said.

'Yeah,' Miguel said, 'but even with road blocks they'd let stuff through after they've checked the driver and passengers.'

'True.'

'Well something's coming now,' Miguel said, pointing to the right.

'Down!' Sally said, making the hand signal at the same time. They dropped to the ground, instinctively adopting the prone firing position, rifles extended in front of them.

Fernando turned his head to look at Sally. 'What is the problem?'

'There's not a single vehicle on that highway and all of a sudden we see one. Says to me it can only be police or Venezuelan army. In this country I'd bet on Venezuelan army. And if we can see them they can probably see us.'

Without changing his position Miguel shucked off his rucksack and fumbled in a side pocket. He came out with a monocular, held it out to show the others, then put it to his eye. He scanned and focused for a few moments, then said, 'Dead right, Sal. It's army all right. A covered jeep of some sort. I haven't seen a model like that before.'

'Okay, they're still patrolling. Perhaps they've guessed we're going to the coast.'

The vehicle passed without slowing down. When it had receded into the distance Sally stood up.

'Right,' she said. 'Obviously we can't go down this way. It's much too exposed – wherever we were we'd be in full view of the road. We'll have to travel inland. So it's back over the ridge, guys.'

Fernando and Miguel exchanged glances, and they began to climb back up to the ridge.

They were about half-way there when they heard it.

'Drone!' They said it together.

'Quick,' Sally shouted. 'Get up into the cloud!'

*

It was mid-afternoon when Rosa announced that they were now very close to her home. Dexter sighed and sat down on the trunk of a fallen tree. He looked all in, very far from the smart, suited diplomat they had extracted from the armoured vehicle the previous day. The jacket was long gone, the shirt sweat-stained and rumpled, the trousers muddy. Jim hated to think about the state of his feet inside those shoes and damp socks.

Rosa pointed ahead of them. 'There is a rough track ahead,' she said. 'It is best if you both wait there. I will go in and make the arrangements. Dexter, when you see a vehicle coming along that track from the left there will be a man driving and I will be with him. I will get out and you will get in. He will take you across the border to Maicao. Can you manage from there?'

'Yes.'

Jim started to take off his backpack. 'You'll need money—'

She said, 'I will give him pesos. They will be more useful than bolivares.'

'What about paying bandits or border guards?'

Her lips lifted in a sardonic smile. 'The man I will send knows how to deal with them.'

With the end now in sight Dexter seemed to acquire a fresh infusion of energy. He got up and they walked as far as the track. Rosa left them there and went down it to the left.

Jim and Dexter waited in silence. Half an hour went by. Dexter's mouth twitched. 'I hate to say this, Jim, but that could be the last we see of her.'

*

The buzz of the drone's rotors was getting louder as the three of them made it onto the cloud-covered ridge. They stood there, getting their breath back. Sweat on their faces coalesced with water droplets from the mist, which were also clinging to their hair and eyelashes, beading the rifles, and sinking into their clothes.

'And Jim thought we were out of danger,' Fernando said.

'Be reasonable,' Sally said. 'He couldn't know there'd be patrols and drones along that coast road.' She listened carefully. 'The drone's gone now. We'd better head for the other side of this ridge.'

Still enveloped by the cloud they made the same cautious progress up to the highest point, and then began the slow descent. Again Sally led the way. Was it her imagination, or was the mist thicker than before? She couldn't even see as far as her feet, but used them to feel the slope of the ground on every step.

Behind her there was a grunt, then a rattle of stones and a cry.

Fernando shouted 'Miguel!'

Sally turned and grabbed his sleeve, just preventing him from going down the steep slope after his friend. She called, 'Miguel? Are you okay?'

A faint voice floated up to them, 'I can't get up.'

She ran her tongue over her lips. A series of nightmare scenarios and courses of action raced through her mind: Miguel with a broken ankle, a broken leg, or worse! They couldn't leave him here – if he was found they'd torture and kill him and their whole operation would be exposed. But how could they carry him the remaining distance across terrain like this?

23

Sally took a deep breath. *One thing at a time.*

'Fernando, we're not risking injury ourselves. We'll continue down until we get out of this damned cloud. At least we'll have a clear view then.'

He grunted his assent.

'Hang on, Miguel,' she called. 'We're coming.'

They continued their painfully slow progress down the mountainside until finally the cloud thinned, then substantially cleared. Puffs of mist drifted across their view as they looked across the slope.

'Can you see him?' she said.

Fernando shook his head. 'No. Damned mist.'

She pointed. 'Let's head that way.'

They walked across the slippery slope to where Miguel might be, scanning ahead all the time. Then Fernando pointed.

'There he is!'

She could see movement ahead. They closed the distance quickly.

Miguel's fall had been interrupted by a large prickly bush, and he was lying almost upside-down in it. He was struggling to get up, but his efforts were resisted by the weight of his backpack and the clawing branches of the bush.

'Stay still,' she said to Miguel. 'I'll just check you over before we try to move you.'

She felt her way around one ankle, the knee, moving both very gently. Then she did the other side.

'You don't seem to have broken anything. Arms okay?'

'Yeah. I slid most of the way.'

She jerked her head at Fernando, who went around to take his right arm while she took the left. 'One, two, three…'

They had to pull hard, but it was enough. Miguel's feet touched the ground and he straightened up, wobbling as he adjusted to the sloping ground. One sleeve of his shirt was torn, the skin underneath grazed and scratched, and there were more grazes on the side of his face and forehead. His hands were skinned where he'd evidently tried to arrest his slide down the slope. He dusted them off, wincing.

'Thanks.'

Sally breathed a sigh of relief.

Fernando tilted his head to one side. 'Trust you to look for a quick way down.'

Miguel's lips twisted in a rueful smile. 'Trod on a rock and it rolled away under my foot.'

She frowned. 'Where's your rifle?'

'Aw, shit. Must have let it go along the way.'

Fernando looked at her. 'Can we leave it? It will hard to find up here.'

'We have to try. It's a recognizable US weapon, so it'll give us away if someone comes across it. Miguel, stay here and sort yourself out.'

The mist began to thicken again as Sally and Fernando made their way back up the steep slope.

She stopped. 'This is hopeless. I can't see a damned thing.'

'You know,' Fernando said. 'The rifle could have slid past him. It might be down below.'

'Good point. Let's hope so. We'll all go down the steepest way and keep our eyes open.'

They returned to Miguel and told him what was planned. He responded by coming out with the monocular again and scanning below them.

He pointed. 'I think that's it, down there.'

They made their way towards it. The rifle was lodged against a low outcrop. Miguel picked it up and looked it over.

'Seems okay. Won't know until I fire it.'

'Let's hope you don't have to,' she said. 'Okay, now we need to go parallel to the coast so what's our best option?'

Miguel wiped a sleeve over his eyes, then deployed the monocular again.

'Some of those fields are pretty waterlogged,' he said, sweeping it around. 'Jesus, look at those puddles –I think they could grow rice down there.' He handed it to Sally.

She scanned the landscape from side to side. 'Must be getting the run-off from the mountains.' She sighed. 'No way of avoiding it, though, so we're in for a muddy time.' She handed the monocular back to Miguel. 'Nice little gadget. I must get me one of those.'

He tucked it into the deepest pocket of his chinos. 'It's farmland, and where there are farms there are people,' he said.

'I know. We'll head down to that last patch of woodland below us and camp for the night. Reveille at 0500 hours so we can set off before dawn. That way we can make some progress before we're in danger of being spotted.'

'Unless there are drones around,' Fernando said.

'Christ, there's nothing we can do about drones. If you see one just smile and wave and hope it doesn't register the rifles.'

Fernando lifted the straps of his rucksack off his soaking shirt, wriggled his shoulders, and let the straps go back. 'How far before we get out of the farmland, Sally?'

'The fields seem to peter out on the other side of this plain, and there's some higher, scrubby looking terrain beyond that. We'll aim to reach that as fast as we can. You okay, Miguel?'

'Yeah, I'll manage. But what about roads?' Miguel said. 'If there are farmers with stuff to sell they'll have access to that highway.'

'Yeah. We'll deal with that one when we come to it. Let's go.'

Fernando led the way down. Over his shoulder he said, 'No chance of a fire this time, eh, Sally?'

''Fraid not. Even if the sun comes out we won't see much of it in the woodland. We'll have to sleep the best we can in wet clothes.'

'Lovely,' Miguel said. 'Do they have bears in Venezuela?'

Sally laughed. 'I don't think so. But with the amount of water down there we might get the odd capybara.'

'Or a caiman,' Miguel said.

'Oh my God, not a caiman.'

*

In the Gulf of Venezuela an inflatable rubber dingy, technically a Combat Rubber Raiding Craft, pulled into the side of a US Navy patrol ship that was waiting at anchor. A Navy SEAL climbed out and was greeted by his replacement.

'Anything?' the replacement asked.

'Nothing,' Petty Officer Bart Newsome said. 'Fucking waste of time. I'm going to see the Lieutenant.'

'Good luck with that. I'd better go, though.'

'Sure. Have fun.'

While the SEAL clambered into the dingy and started the outboard motor Newsome was on his way to see the mission leader, Lieutenant Bill Avery. He found him below.

Avery looked up. 'Yes, Bart?' The service used first names in private.

'Just came off the rendezvous, Bill. Not a sign of them. How much longer do we have to wait here?'

Avery frowned. 'Our orders were to wait until told to pull out, Bart. That hasn't changed.'

'For Christ's sake how long does it take to drive from Maracaibo here? A couple of hours? It's two days! They're not coming – are they? – and someone's just forgotten we're stuck out here.'

Avery took a breath and his mouth set. He got to his feet, and pointed at the coastline, visible through the porthole. 'That's Venezuela out there. I'm not pulling out, not while there's the remotest chance it would leave a special forces team stranded in that goddamned country. Army and Navy special forces work together, support each other. If you think

149

differently you're in the wrong service. Do I make myself clear?'

Newsome swallowed. 'Sorry, Bill. Guess I was out of line. Just fed up spending hours and hours out there waiting for folk who never show.'

'The waiting's just as much part of the job as the action, Bart. Get used to it.'

Newsome nodded and left quickly.

Avery remained standing, looking thoughtfully at the door Newsome had closed behind him.

You're right about one thing, though. We can't hang around here for ever. I'd better contact WARCOM.

*

Jim and Dexter continued to wait for Rosa to reappear.

Ten minutes later they heard the sound of an engine and the crunch of tyres on the rough track. A four-wheel drive vehicle appeared and stopped. Dexter went over to it. Rosa got out and Jim saw her give him some money. He bowed and, rather gallantly, Jim thought, kissed her on both cheeks. Then he got into the vehicle and it drove off.

Rosa came over. 'My people are very protective of me, Jim. It would be more safe if you gave me your rifle and automatic now. I don't want anyone to think I am coming back at the point of a gun.'

His eyes narrowed, then he reluctantly handed her the weapons. She tucked the automatic into her waistband and cradled the rifle. The way she did it suggested that handling firearms was by no means new to her.

They walked together down the track and approached what appeared to be a farm: large buildings on three sides, extending into an incomplete fourth side that left an opening wide enough to drive a vehicle through. As they went in Jim tensed. Two armed men were standing in front of a sentry box just inside the entrance.

One smiled. In Spanish he said to Rosa, 'It's good to have you back, *jefa.*'

Jim frowned and looked from one to the other.

Did he say jefa*? That means 'boss'. Maybe I misheard.*

'Thank you, Jaime,' she replied in Spanish. 'It's good to be back.' She waved a hand casually at Jim. 'This man is with me.'

They gave him a cautious nod, but he noticed the way their hands tightened on their automatic rifles.

And then, apparently as an afterthought, she handed the man Jim's rifle and semiautomatic. 'Jaime, could you put these in the armoury for me? Label them "Jim".'

'Sure, no problem.'

Armoury?

She looked over her shoulder at Jim. 'You won't need those here. You can have them back when you leave.'

She seemed to be walking even taller than before. Jim took in the open courtyard, the large buildings, the sentries. 'This is your home?' he said, staring at her. She smiled.

'Yes. Welcome to the headquarters of our organization, the Guárico Cartel.'

He blinked. 'The Fat Man cartel?'

'You are out of date, Jim. The Fat Man died a year ago. I am the leader of this organization now. The Fat Man was Antonio Martinez Villar. He was my father.'

24

Jim's jaw dropped, then he felt a flash of anger. 'Rosa, what the hell have you got me into?'

'Relax, Jim,' Rosa said, smiling. 'You are among friends. Come, we have walked a long way and we should have something to eat and drink. And I want you to meet José.'

Jim's thoughts were whirling. He was in a lot deeper than he'd expected, and he didn't need telling that his life was in the balance. The danger wouldn't come from Rosa. Aguilar's people must have known they had the head of the Guárico Cartel in their hands. What they would have done to her to extract the location of the Cartel – and possibly of Delgado – didn't bear thinking about. That's what she was facing as they were taking her to Buena Vista jail and she'd be grateful that he'd intervened.

No, it's not Rosa I have to worry about, it's the people around her. Mobsters like these are notoriously suspicious. Their instinct will be to regard me as an intruder and deal with me accordingly. I'll have to watch my back.

Rosa led the way into the building. The interior was like no farm Jim had ever seen. As they walked along a corridor, light from the low sun streamed through windows on the left.

It slanted across a carpeted floor and up a wall hung at intervals with large, strikingly modern paintings in the South American style. She entered what seemed to be a private dining room. A man was standing there, waiting for them.

Rosa said, 'This is José Manuel Herrera. José this is Jim.'

'Jim Slater,' Jim said, extending a hand.

José shook his hand, studying him with watchful dark eyes. He had an aquiline nose and a growth of hair on his face that was more than a stubble but less than a beard.

Rosa said, 'José was my father's closest associate and advisor, you might call him his "lieutenant". And now he is *my* lieutenant.'

José said, '*¿Hablas español?*'

Jim nodded. '*Sí.*'

José continued in Spanish, 'I have ordered a late lunch for you both. I myself have eaten. I will come back when you are finished.'

Jim said, '*Muchas gracias.*'

Rosa led the way to a table laid with a cloth, cutlery, and glasses and gestured for him to sit down. She took the chair opposite him.

'Okay, what's happened to Dexter?' he said brusquely.

'Don't worry about Dexter,' she said. 'I felt sorry for him. He had a very bad experience. For years his partner and his wife were deceiving him, then he was for many months in prison waiting to be executed. And the CIA used him, Jim.'

'I know.'

'I thought he deserved a break. Hugo will take him across the border, like I promised. And I gave him enough money to take a bus wherever in Colombia he wishes to go.'

Jim nodded slowly. After what she'd told him earlier he still wasn't sure how much of this he could believe.

'And what you told me about yourself, back there?' he said. 'I guess that was a little short of the truth.'

She laughed. 'Only some of it. My father did like to have beautiful young women and yes, there were six, but of course I was not one of them.'

'Your education…?'

'All true. And now, naturally, I am making good use of my business knowledge and experience. You see, Jim, we must move with the times. We are a powerful organization with substantial resources. I am taking the first steps to move us away from the traditional paths and into legitimate business enterprises.'

'What, no more drugs, protection money, prostitution?'

She grimaced. 'We were never much into prostitution. Drugs, yes, people trafficking, yes, and some protection rackets. It will take time to dismantle all this and we must survive as we are developing other avenues, no? But I am patient. Ah, here is the lunch.'

A white-coated elderly woman approached with a tray. Her movements were slow and deliberate as she bent down and placed the tray on the table. She smiled at Rosa and there was a brief exchange in Spanish.

The woman took a plate from the tray and placed it in front of Rosa. She did the same for Jim. On the plates were what looked like small pitas filled with beans, cheese, tomato, and egg. The woman hesitated, a wrinkled hand poised over the tray.

'*Cerveza? Café?*'

Jim looked at the tray. He'd been caught that way once before, but the bottles, misted with condensation, were unopened. No chance of someone doctoring his drink this time.

He said, *'Cerveza, por favor.'*

She opened a bottle and placed it in front of him without pouring.

'Rosa?' she asked.

'Igualmente.'

She opened a bottle for Rosa, too.

When she'd withdrawn Rosa said, 'Teresa has known me since I was a little girl. She's slow now but I wouldn't dream of making her retire.' She gestured to the plate. 'These are *arepas*. They are made with corn flour. I hope you like them.'

It was a welcome change from emergency rations, and the beer was refreshing. When they'd finished Rosa sat back, engaging him with her dark eyes, a secret smile on her face. Now that she was back on home territory her whole presence was more commanding.

'You know, Jim, we were never properly introduced, but let me guess. All four of you are Americans, of course. You rescued us from that convoy, just four of you against three vehicles full of armed soldiers. Did you kill anyone?'

'No.'

She clapped her hands in delight. 'You see, Dexter was right. They would be far too embarrassed to own up about how they lost us. But if you could do all that you are not ordinary soldiers. I would say you're special forces.'

'Correct. US Army Special Assignment Force.' It was safe enough to say it. This woman had even more to lose by revealing what she knew than he did.

'And because you are very smart, and think strategically, and because you gave orders to the others you have to be at least a Captain. Perhaps a Major.'

'Colonel.'

Her eyes widened. '*¿Realmente?* I'm honoured! Rescued by a Special Forces Colonel, no less. So at last we have been introduced properly. It is a pleasure to meet you, Colonel Jim Slater.'

'Are you mocking me?'

The playfulness vanished. 'No, Jim, no.' She gazed earnestly at him and covered his hand with hers. 'I would never do that.'

The door opened and José came in. She withdrew her hand quickly.

That's interesting. Would José have been jealous if he'd seen it?

She gestured to a chair and they switched to Spanish.

'So,' José said to Rosa. 'Are you ready now to tell me what happened to you and Eduardo?'

'Yes, but first we have to tell Jim how the situation was here. It's okay, you can trust him.'

José gave Jim a penetrating look, then shrugged. 'Okay.'

Rosa said, 'When my father became ill the responsibility for running this place fell very much on José, but also on the other lieutenant, Óscar Pablo Guzmán. Óscar had been with him even longer than José, and he expected to take over the business when my father died. He was very angry when my father left it to me, and even more when he heard of my long-term plans for entering legitimate business. Óscar and José had grown up with the traditional activities, but José saw the need to change and Óscar did not. Óscar left and took twelve of our people with him. He set up on his own and he's recruited others from our organization around the country. Now he has – what, José, thirty?'

'Perhaps more.'

'And he wants to take us over.'

José said, 'We have observers and we fly drones over their camp, so we know what is happening. There is no question, they are preparing to attack. About a week ago it looked like they were ready. They have the numbers and they have the equipment, so it would be a hard fight. I didn't want Rosa to be here if things went badly. And we had made a solemn promise to Antonio Martinez to protect his daughter. I am not sure that Óscar cares much about promises.'

'José sent me off with Edouardo,' Rosa said. 'The plan was for Edouardo to drive me to a safe place. Before we could get there we were stopped by an army patrol.' She turned her head. 'It was just bad luck that they stopped us, José. And even more bad luck that one of them recognized me. So they arrested me. They left Edouardo in the vehicle…' She paused, her throat catching. 'And they threw a grenade into it.' She put her hand over her eyes. 'Poor Eduardo.'

José's jaw was twitching. He slammed his fist down on the table. 'Bastards!' he said. 'Animals!'

There was a short silence before she continued.

'I was a big catch, so they drove me to the Palacio de Miraflores and showed me off to President Aguilar. He said, "Take her to Buena Vista. Find out what she knows, then do what you like with her." He said to let Javier Arellano know as well.' She turned to Jim. 'He's the head of the Los Feroces cartel. Aguilar thought Javier's people would also like to have a piece of me.'

José murmured, 'My God!'

She went on, 'There was an army escort outside taking a man to Buena Vista, so they pushed me in with him. As it happened it was the best thing that could have happened.' She was speaking to José now, but indicating Jim with an open hand. 'Jim was on the route with three other soldiers. Just four of them, José, unarmed – you were unarmed, weren't you, Jim?'

'More or less.'

'And there were about ten soldiers in three armoured vehicles. I don't know how they did it without killing anyone but somehow they got me out with the man and took us with them.' She opened her hands. 'And that's it. Their car took us part of the way and we walked the rest across country.'

José looked at Jim, one eyebrow raised. If he thought Rosa's account was, at best, an exaggeration he was courteous enough not to say so. He simply said, 'You did well. Thank you. Where are your colleagues?'

'They're heading for a secret rendezvous. I accompanied Rosa, in case of trouble.' He wasn't going to say anything about Dexter.

'He saved my life, José. Not just my life, he saved me from torture and degradation. So he is our honoured guest.'

José nodded briskly. 'We will speak again tomorrow.'

He got up and left the room.

25

Rosa had her own suite of rooms in one wing of the building, and her staff had prepared a separate guest bedroom in that wing for Jim. He saw that they'd left him a change of trousers, shirt and underwear, which couldn't have been more welcome. He had a shave and a shower and dressed in the clean clothes. Then he paced the room, sizing up his current situation and trying to plan his next move. It wasn't particularly safe for him to remain here, and an impending attack from this guy Óscar wasn't going to make it any safer. On the other hand staying here would give him a chance to learn whether they were harbouring Juan-Luis Delgado or knew where he could be found…

There was a knock at the door,. When he opened it Teresa was standing there. She spoke quietly, eyes lowered, but he caught something about dinner. She led him to a large dining room rather like an army mess, where there were about two dozen other staff, men and women. As Jim came in there were a lot of curious looks. Being this tall probably wasn't that unusual around here; having straw-blond hair probably was. A few of the younger women, he noticed, were very beautiful. Rosa was already at a table, waiting for him. José didn't join them, and despite the obvious interest no one apart from Rosa spoke to him throughout the meal.

When dinner was over he went back to his room and undressed. As he had no night clothes in his backpack he got into bed as he was. The tension and exertion of the past two days ebbed away from him like an outgoing tide and he was soon asleep.

Jim slept like a cat, so although he didn't hear the door open he sensed a presence in the room. His eyes flicked wide open, and he threw back the covers to free his legs, prepared now to strike instantly or roll away from a blow. It was pitch dark.

A low familiar voice said, 'Jim, it's me, Rosa.'

She crept into bed and sat astride him. He felt the heat of her skin as it met his. Then she began to glide slowly back and forth on him.

'Rosa…'

'Shhh.'

She rode herself into him, soft sighs escaping from her, and he responded more and more. Then she reached down and he felt the cool wetness as he slid inside her. She set up a slow rhythm, contracting on each stroke. He'd had many wild nights with women but none had ever extracted the exquisite currents now spreading through his loins. He grasped her hips and thrust upwards into her with the same rhythm, following her lead. The currents flowed, the sensations grew, and in a frozen, suspended moment there were only currents and sensations and he exploded into her. He collapsed back, panting. She lifted gently, leaned forward, and kissed him, ran her tongue over his lips, and whispered 'Thank you.' Her weight disappeared and moments later he heard the door open and close softly.

He lay there, still breathing hard, his heart pounding. The tingling needles of sensation subsided quickly but the heat throughout his body lingered. He felt drained and deliciously drowsy. He ran his tongue over his lips and thought he could still taste her on them.

Why had she come to him? Was it a one-off, her way of thanking him for saving her from Aguilar's thugs? Or was it to satisfy an urge that both of them had felt?

Perhaps this was the way she enslaved her admirers. If so it was very persuasive. Had she done the same with José? His protectiveness of her could be based on more than his promise to her father and it would be as well to bear that in mind. To make things worse, José had unwittingly put her in harm's way, whereas his own contribution had been to rescue her. Had he become a serious obstacle, an intruder on an existing relationship?

Holly – Bob Cressington's daughter – once told him he had an instinct for survival. Perhaps it wasn't uncommon in someone who'd faced danger as many times as he had. Deciding on safe strategies was a conscious process, but it did seem like there was something else, a kind of twitching of invisible antennae that signified warning. And those antennae were twitching right now as he thought about José. His experience had told him not to take too much notice of situations that seemed peaceful and harmonious, because there could often be unseen issues beneath the surface. Could it be that José was as angry as Óscar had been when the Fat Man left the cartel to Rosa? Perhaps both harboured ambitions to be in charge here, possibly reinstating something like the Fat Man's harem. Maybe José hadn't put her in the car with Eduardo to protect her; maybe he'd told Eduardo to take her somewhere remote and kill her. Rosa seemed very confident of José's loyalty but he was not so sure. She may have had two lucky escapes the previous day, not just one.

His last thoughts before he eventually let sleep overtake him were that he would have to be very, very careful.

26

In the morning Jim found Rosa in the private dining room. Her fingers described a graceful arc as she indicated the chair opposite her. She looked so collected, so completely in charge, it was as if the person who drove him to ecstasy the night before was someone else, someone quite different from the corporate head of this organization. He couldn't resist the temptation to knock her off her perch.

'I enjoyed last night,' he said.

She slowly closed and opened her eyes and gave him a small smile. 'I thought you would. I did, too.'

'Where did you...' He decided he was being childish. 'Sorry, it's not polite to ask.'

'You are curious about how I learned to do it the way I do.' She seemed completely unfazed by the conversation. Far from being knocked off her perch she was very comfortably on it.

'Well... yes.'

She smiled. 'I told you my father had young ladies to entertain him. He was a very large man, that is true: four hundred pounds, maybe more. He would have crushed any woman he climbed on top of, and it wasn't easy for him to move anyway. So they rode him like cowgirls. I was friendly with them and when I was about eighteen one taught me all her tricks. It suits me that way. As you are perhaps beginning to see, I like to be in charge.'

He nodded. He wasn't used to being dominated, but there were certainly compensations. What he couldn't ask her was whether the same favours had been extended to José.

'What happened to those girls after your father died?'

'They didn't want to leave here, so they requested a change of role. They would stay with the organization but they wanted to be trained as operatives. So we trained them. They're quite good. Not physically strong, of course, but good shots.'

That, he thought, explained the striking young women he'd noticed in the mess the previous evening.

Rosa engaged him with those mesmerizing eyes. 'So, would you like me to come to you again tonight?'

'You're assuming I'll still be here.'

She smiled. 'Oh, I think you will still be here.'

Would he be? Was he a willing captive? Despite some misgivings he no longer felt anything like the same urgency about tracking down Delgado. Trying to do it on his own would be completely futile anyway and he was putting his money on his current situation leading him there.

Was that foolhardy? He didn't think so. Back in Washington Aidan Somersby had said the Guárico cartel wanted Delgado as President. Of course they did: defeat of Aguilar would turn the Los Feroces mob out on its ear, and that would create opportunities for this cartel. With Rosa's plans to take them in a legitimate direction it would make perfect sense to ally themselves with the Presidential contender. If she was thinking that far ahead she could have been in touch with Delgado already.

Teresa came and served them with *perico*: scrambled eggs mixed with tomatoes, onions and green peppers. They drank coffee with it. When they'd finished he poured more coffee for them both.

The door opened and José entered. He sat down next to Rosa and they all switched to Spanish.

'*Café?*' she asked him.

He nodded and she poured the extra cup that Teresa had laid.

'I have news,' he said. 'Our observers in Caracas tell us that American marines and paratroops and Rotofans landed yesterday near the city. They are advancing on the capital and they are well equipped. I think they aim to overthrow the government.'

Rosa and Jim caught each other's eyes. Evidently Dexter's rescue had not been disclosed and the CIA's devious plan was working as anticipated.

Rosa turned to José. 'This is wonderful. They will instate Delgado, and he knows of our support. We will be in a strong position, especially with our new goals. There will be projects and programmes and we can be a part of all of it.'

José nodded. 'You have picked the perfect moment, Rosa.'

'But what about Óscar?'

'I am glad you are safe, but I am sorry you have come back.'

Rosa frowned. 'Óscar is still preparing…?'

'An attack is imminent. We are sure now that it will be in the next few days.'

'Oh.' There was a moment of silence. Then she said, 'Jim, I think this will concern you, too.'

'Me? Look, I'm not part of—'

'For two reasons,' she said, speaking over him. 'First, don't you think it would be a shame, after your heroic rescue of me, if I now fell into the hands of a rival cartel? You know I could expect the same treatment from them as from the prison guards and Los Feroces in Caracas. And this just when we are on the brink of a new relationship with the government.'

He grimaced, then said, 'And second?'

'Second, wouldn't you like to get back at the people who killed your Rotofan crew?'

He felt his face go slack. 'How can you know that?'

'Your Rotofan landed in territory now controlled by Óscar. Even if his gang didn't see it themselves it would have been reported to them very quickly by anyone who did, because he would certainly reward them. And cutting throats is Óscar's chosen method of dealing with his enemies.'

'It's true,' José said. 'He took great pleasure in cutting throats. Always he grabbed the hair and started below the left ear. It was his trademark.'

Rosa said, 'He was probably there himself, with a handful of his followers.'

'Are you sure?'

'Oh, quite sure. Didn't you see how I reacted when I saw them?'

'You were shocked, understandably. It was a pretty gruesome sight.'

'Yes, but that wasn't all – I thought they could still be there in the forest, hiding, waiting for us. I wanted to get out of that place as quickly as possible. To make things worse, when you and Sally and Miguel and Fernando went around the clearing you left us alone, unarmed.'

Jim winced. 'That was an oversight. I'm sorry.'

'Well, it was a relief that you found no one.'

'I worked with Óscar for years,' José said. 'Drugs and violence, that's all he understands. Rosa has a new vision. If he took over here it would be a return to the old ways. There would be much bloodshed.'

'Is there a serious risk that he will defeat you?' Jim asked.

'Yes, there is. He has numbers now, and he is well equipped.'

Rosa said, 'Jim, you're a Special Forces Colonel. You could help us.'

'Is that why you brought me here?' His tone was sharper than he meant it to be.

She smiled. 'I didn't bring you. I hoped you would come – in fact I expected you to come. I am a good judge of character. I saw the way you put yourself at risk before your team. You didn't order anyone else to go out to that Rotofan, you did it yourself. You led the way when we were in the mist at the top of that mountain. So if somebody had to accompany me across dangerous country, I thought you would be the one to do it.'

Jim grunted.

'Well, now you are here. Will you help us?'

In Jim's mind there was an image of Hayden and the others, blood gushing from their cut throats. They didn't deserve that. It would be good to avenge their murders.

'All right.'

José said, 'We should meet again, and I would like to bring two of my most trusted people. In here, perhaps, in one hour?'

'*Bueno*,' Jim and Rosa said it together.

When José had left, Rosa switched back to English. 'Thank you, Jim. Actually there's another reason why I feel you should do this, but I didn't like to say it in front of José, and that's why I am speaking in English now. As a cartel we have cells all over the country but this is the nerve centre so it has to remain secret. From the air it just looks like another farm. You haven't seen it but at the back there is even a tractor and other equipment. But anyone who has been here knows where we are. José is aware of this more than anyone because he is very protective of the cartel. He is quite prepared to kill to make sure our location is not revealed.'

'Is that why your father's harem girls opted to stay here?'

'I'm sure it was. They knew the score. Do you see now why I had one of my people take Dexter to Colombia before he could discover who I was and where I lived? If he had come with us he would not have left here alive.'

Jim frowned. 'Are you saying I won't leave here alive?'

'It could be a problem. Listen, Jim, you saved me from those animals in Maracaibo. I will never forget that. I will help you as much as I can. And you have made it much easier by agreeing to help us.'

He got to his feet. 'Okay, I understand. I'll see you here in an hour.'

27

Back in his room Jim sat on the bed and thought about his situation. Rosa had offered a convincing argument. Having saved her from meeting a nasty end in Buena Vista, it would be unforgivable to leave her now to the mercy of Óscar and his cronies. And if it was Óscar who killed Hayden and his crew – and he had no reason to doubt it – this would be a chance to level the score.

Even if he wanted to flee it would make no sense. For one thing he could say goodbye to his chances of finding Delgado. For another, he'd be alone, unarmed, with a pocketful of worthless currency, trying to find a border crossing in a hostile and lawless country. And if Rosa was planning to make a repeat appearance that night she would see that he'd gone missing, raise the alarm, and José would come after him with a posse of his men. No, he was trapped, and he knew it.

Staying was hardly a more attractive proposition. José had said Óscar had numbers and he was well equipped. What state of preparation were they in here? How large was the force they could muster and how good were the personnel? It was one thing to go into battle with his SAF soldiers, who were skilled and experienced and utterly reliable; quite another to contemplate doing it with a bunch of people who were probably acquainted only with gang warfare. One thing was clear: if anyone in this building was going to survive the forthcoming confrontation they'd need a damned good battle plan.

When he returned to the private dining room Rosa and José were already there, and two younger men had joined them. José introduced them as Gustavo and Ismael. Both were clean-shaven. Ismael was the more heavily built of the two. His flat nose and tilted eyes were suggestive of first people ancestry. Gustavo had more Mediterranean looks: a full head of dark curly hair, brown eyes with long eyelashes, and smooth, coffee-coloured skin. In Spanish once again, Rosa introduced Jim as 'Colonel Jim Slater of the US Special Forces' and they raised their eyebrows.

Ismael said, mainly to Rosa, 'We thought US Special Forces would be hunting us down, not helping us.'

She answered, 'Óscar and his breakaway people killed his friends. He is as anxious to defeat them as we are.'

They nodded, apparently satisfied with the explanation.

'Let's get started,' Rosa said. 'Jim?'

Jim addressed José. 'I need to know the strength of the enemy. You said you have observers on the ground. Are they reliable?'

'Yes, very reliable. But also they have placed some cameras and we fly drones from time to time. Everything fits. Óscar and his gang are getting ready.'

'And you say they are well equipped.'

'Yes, they have weapons and several armoured vehicles. Not tanks, smaller ones for carrying soldiers.'

'They're probably a larger version of the ones I saw in Maracaibo. The armour's good against bullets but not much else. How many soldiers do they have?'

'Óscar has been recruiting people from other cells. We think thirty-five, but new ones have been arriving. By now it could be forty, maybe even more.'

'And how many do we have here? Battle-ready, I mean.'

'Twenty-two.'

Jim straightened up sharply. 'Twenty-two?'

Rosa said, 'This is mainly an administrative centre, Jim.'

He blew out a breath. 'So, twenty-two. Does that include you and Rosa?'

'Me, for sure. Rosa, no.'

Rosa said, 'I can handle a rifle. You should count me too.'

'Your father said—'

'My father would want to see me protecting the organization he built up.'

He shrugged. 'Okay, twenty-three.'

Jim's lips set. He was just as much at risk here as Rosa and the rest of them, and by the sounds of it they would be facing a fighting force that was not only well-equipped but possibly twice as large. Óscar must be feeling pretty confident of success.

'You're seriously outnumbered,' he said. 'I don't like those odds. What armaments do you have?'

'The usual. Assault rifles, multirifles with smart grenades for the under-barrels, hand grenades…'

'RPGs?'

There was a quick exchange in English and Spanish. The phrase *granadas propulsadas por cohetes* emerged and José nodded.

'*Sí.*'

'Attack drones?'

'No, only surveillance.'

'Okay,' Jim said. 'What's your plan?'

'We are in a strong defensive position,' José said. 'The entrance is narrow and we can take out anyone who tries to come through. We have firing positions in the buildings and they overlook the road.' He looked around the table and shrugged. 'That's about it.'

Jim shook his head. 'In a situation like this I put myself in the position of the attacker. Your—'

He spoke to Rosa in English. 'What's fortress or stronghold in Spanish?'

'*Fortaleza.*'

'Thank you.' He continued in Spanish, 'Your stronghold could become a death trap. If I was Óscar I'd toss in grenades, mortars, incendiary devices, even gas bombs if I had them. This building could be in flames or become uninhabitable very quickly. Your people would go running out through that narrow entrance and they would be mown down like…skittles?'

'*Bolos,*' Rosa supplied.

'*Sí, bolos,*' Jim said.

José opened his hands. 'So what can we do that is better?'

'Attack is the best form of defence, but with those numbers you also need a very strong element of surprise. When Óscar makes a move, how long before he gets here?'

'There is a road – not a good road, narrow and muddy, but good enough for his armoured vehicles and the rest of his men on foot. It will take about an hour.'

'Good, plenty of time. Is that the only way he can come?'

'*Sí.*'

'And as it's narrow the vehicles will be in single file.'

'*Sí.*'

'Can your observers tell you how long the convoy is and what is at the end of it?'

'Sure I can ask them to tell me that.'

'That's all we need to know. Have you got a map of this area?'

Gustavo came out with a map and they stood while he opened it on the table and traced his finger along a path. He said, 'Here is the way they will come.'

Jim examined it for a moment and then looked up. 'Okay. José, can we speak for a moment?'

He took José to one side and spoke quietly. 'Look, I told you how I would attack if I was in Óscar's position. But I am not Óscar. I am hoping he will think just like you, that we will defend this place with everything we have. So we must surprise him. Are you one hundred per cent sure that everyone in this building can be trusted? You have observers with Óscar. Maybe he has observers with you.'

José pursed his lips. 'I believe they can all be trusted. But…' He shrugged.

'What about those two?'

'Oh, Gustavo and Ismael can be trusted, of this I am absolutely sure.'

'Very well. I suggest the five of us go outside now and we will decide where each of your combatants will be when

173

Óscar arrives. But we will put them there only when we know he is on his way. And after that no one must be allowed to communicate with a phone or anything else.'

He nodded. 'I will warn them.'

'Okay. Let's go.'

28

She came to him again that night.

The moon was bright and blue-white light entered through the uncurtained windows. As she shed a filmy robe he glimpsed the outline of her naked shoulder, the tip of a breast, the swell of a hip. She had a beautiful body and now she laid it full-length on him and pressed her open mouth to his.

She started still more slowly this time, and as the intensity increased they seemed to scale even greater heights together. Afterwards she lay against him, a little to the side, her face nuzzled into his neck and the flat of her hand on his chest. Finally she sighed and gathered herself together. The mattress lifted and moments later the room door closed softly behind her.

He would have liked her to stay all night, but this was a game in which she set the rules. He wondered about her air of secrecy. Did she find it more exciting that way or was she anxious not to be discovered? His thoughts touched briefly on José but he put them aside.

He reached for his watch and checked the time. It was shortly after two in the morning. As he replaced it the moonlight faded, leaving the room in impenetrable darkness. An irregular tapping at the window started up and quickly turned to an incessant drumming; it was raining hard. Óscar would want good visibility – he wouldn't risk coming here in pouring rain. If this continued it could be a day or two yet before he launched an offensive. Jim allowed himself a small smile. Now that he'd decided to help Rosa and her organization fight off the attack there was even less reason to be in a hurry, especially with nights like this to look forward to.

*

Breakfast was in the private dining room again. This time it was Rosa who referred to the night before. Again he was transfixed by those dark eyes.

'You are good for me, Jim,' she said.

'Um, you're good for me too, Rosa,' was all he could manage to say.

Teresa served *cachitos*, a kind of filled croissant, much fresher and flakier than the ones he and Sally had chosen in the Maracaibo hotel.

'It's still raining heavily,' Rosa said. 'Do you think Óscar will attack in this weather?'

'No, he's unlikely to attack when visibility's so poor. And if the trails around here are anything like the ones we encountered when we were walking I'd say the road has become very, very muddy. It won't stop him, but it could slow him up.'

Later that morning José took him round the armoury and he inspected the weapons. They looked to be in good condition, clean and well-oiled. There was plenty of ammunition.

'When was the last time these were used?' he asked.

'Some were fired a few months ago. We had a problem with a small cartel trying to steal some of our business. But I tell my people always to put away the weapons in perfect condition.'

'All right. Look, we won't use the drones. They're sure to be spotted and it would better to let them think they're surprising us.'

'Okay.'

As they left the armoury a thought occurred to him. 'Do you have a gymnasium here?'

José shook his head.

It seemed that fitness wasn't a high priority in this administrative HQ. Well, it would make little difference in the forthcoming encounter. The outcome would be decided in the first few minutes and during that time no one would move an inch.

*

At lunchtime it was still raining hard, but Jim told José that everyone needed to stay on high alert all the same.

He was beginning to miss his normal early-morning run, but from what Rosa had told him it would be dangerous to leave the compound, more so in the present circumstances. Instead he decided to investigate the firing positions José had mentioned.

He mounted the steps to the upper floor and went along the corridor. The windows on his left overlooked the courtyard and could be useful if anyone succeeded in getting through the narrow entrance. He tested one and it opened easily. The rooms on his right faced the front of the building, those at the far end of the corridor were the closest to the entrance and he went down there. He tried a door and it opened. The room was empty. There were no windows but there was a narrow shutter on the wall opposite the door. He hinged it back to reveal a vertical slot in the wall, like an arrow slit in a mediæval English castle. Looking down he could see a stretch of the road outside. This could be used for covering fire, but the field of view wasn't good enough for aimed shots. He tried the next room and the next. It was the same for every room except the last, the one furthest from the entrance. Here there was a ladder leading to a trap door in the ceiling. He climbed up the ladder and pushed the trap door open.

He was instantly deluged with rain. He lifted his face to the sky and laughed, getting it in his mouth. It was refreshing, even though the temperature and humidity seemed to be as high as ever. He wiped his eyes, then clambered out and looked around. The roofs were tiled, rising at a shallow angle front and back and ending in a ridge. They were gleaming with water, which was coursing down into the gutters. The gurgle of the water as it drained away was barely audible above the rushing of the rain but he ignored the downpour and crawled up to the ridge. He found that he could lie on the slope of the roof there with a good view along the muddy road. It was hard to see through the moving sheets of rain but he could just make out a bend where the path vanished behind trees. That was where Óscar's little army would appear – if it got that far. He gave it some thought, then lowered himself carefully down the slippery roof, stepped onto the ladder, and closed the trap door before descending to the floor.

Back in his room he stripped off his soaking wet clothes, which were the ones he'd worn the previous day. Fresh clothes had again been left on a chair, but first he had a vigorous workout, followed by a shower. When he looked out of the window it was still raining, but not as heavily. He judged it was now too late for Óscar to mount an attack anyway.

*

In the evening he had dinner with Rosa and José in the large dining room. Since everyone knew by now that there would soon be a serious battle with the breakaway faction the atmosphere might have been subdued, but far from it: the room buzzed with lively conversation. This became even more animated when the main course was served: beef with rice, black beans, and fried slices of plantain. Rosa told Jim she'd asked the chef to make it for him, because *Pabellon Criollo* was close to being the Venezuelan national dish. Dessert was *quesillo*, which tasted like crème caramel. On a diet like this it wasn't hard to see how Rosa's father had become the Fat Man. He would have to be careful not to follow that example.

'Rosa, José,' he said, after they'd had coffee. 'I'd like to meet some of the men and women, the ones who'll be involved in the fighting when Óscar's people attack.'

'That would be a good idea,' Rosa said, 'don't you agree, José?'

José shrugged. 'Yes, everyone has finished, so let us do it now.'

José and Jim got up and toured the room and Jim shook a lot of hands. In this context being introduced as a US Special Forces soldier didn't do any harm at all, in fact that was his intention. Before long these people would be taking orders from him.

He now found himself looking forward to the night ahead. A couple of scorching glances from Rosa's dark eyes told him she felt the same way.

*

When Rosa left his room in the early hours of the morning Jim lay in bed, letting his pulse and breathing subside. There was, he reflected, a new tenderness in her lovemaking tonight. He wasn't sure how he felt about that. He knew he wasn't in love with her – enraptured, yes, but in love, no. At some point, and assuming he survived whatever happened in the next day or so, he would have to leave this place. If she was becoming attached to him that could be even more of a problem than it already was.

But why worry about that now? There was little he could do or say. The focus had to remain on the impending attack, and that wouldn't come until the weather cleared up.

He stiffened. Something had changed in the room but he couldn't put his finger on it. He sat up, straining to see or hear a hint of something, anything. Then moonlight filtered through the window, and with it came the realization.

The clouds have cleared. The rain's stopped. That's it.
Óscar will attack today.

29

The day dawned clear, with no sign of the rain returning and even a little sun filtering through the usual overcast. Jim had an early breakfast with Rosa and José. They ate sparingly and spoke little. Jim could guess what was in their minds: they were no doubt wondering what the day ahead held in store, and whether they'd still be alive at the end of it..

Jim's thoughts ran along more pragmatic lines. The size of Óscar's breakaway cartel wasn't his major concern; he'd faced worse odds before. But there was a big difference between going into action with a highly-trained, highly-disciplined force like the SAF, and with the rag-tag, potentially volatile bunch he had at his disposal today. The success of this operation depended on holding fire until exactly the right moment. It would take just one trigger-happy individual to start shooting too early and the whole element of surprise would be lost. Óscar would promptly deploy to both sides of the track, and their small band would be in an encounter they couldn't possibly win. That needed to be rammed home to them.

The other thing that concerned him was where in the convoy Óscar would be, because if he managed to get away he could start this all over again. Besides, Jim had his own reasons for wanting to see that man taken down.

At a knock at the door all three looked up sharply and slammed down their coffee cups. Gustavo came in. He clearly had news and wasn't sure who he should deliver it to. His eyes settled on José.

'Message from the observers, José,' he said. 'Óscar's people are getting ready to move.'

'Okay,' José said. 'Assemble everyone in the courtyard.'

When Jim went down to the courtyard he saw that their combatants had gathered there. Most of them carried multirifles, the rest carried RPGs in launchers.

Jim stepped forward to address them. Thanks to the introductions of the previous evening they knew who – and what – he was. 'In a few minutes José, Gustavo, Ismael, and I will show each of you the position you are to take. Do not move after that. There must be no shooting until the end of the convoy passes Gustavo and Ismael. Is that understood?' He scanned the faces in front of them. 'This is vitally important. When Gustavo fires a flare over the heads of the attackers it is the signal for those of you with launchers to send in the RPGs. Wait for that signal. You will be engaging at close quarters so keep under cover when the RPGs go in. Then open fire. No wild raking. It could put your comrades in danger and you will quickly run out of ammunition without time to reload. Aimed shots. Understand? Set your rifles to fire groups of three. Do it now.' A series of clicks sounded as they changed the rifle settings. 'Good. Everything depends on surprising them, so no talking and no smoking. Are there any questions?'

Someone raised a hand. 'Are we on both sides of the track?'

'No, one side only. Otherwise you will be killing each other.'

There was a murmur of laughter. Another hand went up. 'Why don't we have smart grenades in the underbarrels?'

'For the same reason. Those grenades are antipersonnel weapons and they are effective over a large range. If you explode one above the enemy you will be a target as well. Anything else?'

There were no more questions. He held up a finger and spoke slowly, with emphasis. 'Remember, wait for the signal. Óscar's people outnumber you. If you do not wait you will not survive this attack.' He stepped back and nodded to José.

José said, 'Do what the Colonel says. There is one more thing. Anyone seen using a cell or other device could be a traitor working for Óscar. Shoot him or her immediately, whoever it is. I mean that.'

They glanced uneasily at each other.

'Now you will come with us and we will show you your positions. We expect their convoy to arrive in less than an hour.'

He picked out a woman and one of the older men. 'You will remain behind in the courtyard, guarding the entrance. Rosa, you too.'

Rosa blinked. 'What are you saying? I will be with the ambush—'

'No, Rosa, you are needed here.'

'But…'

Jim laid a hand gently on her shoulder. 'Rosa, José is right. You could easily be hit by a stray bullet down there, and as the head of this cartel you should not expose yourself to unnecessary risk.'

Her lips met tightly, but she didn't object.

José placed the three where they could be effective without putting themselves in the line of fire. Then he came back and they walked the rest of their force about half a mile down the route along which Óscar would have to make his approach. By the time they'd rounded the bend that Jim had viewed from the roof it had become little more than a muddy trail. At the point they'd surveyed two days before there were trees encroaching on either side. Jim, José, Gustavo and Ismael each took five of the men and women and assigned them to the positions agreed previously, most at ground level, some up in the trees.

When that was done José said to Jim, 'Where are you going to be?'

Jim had anticipated this question. The last thing he wanted was to be caught up in a firefight where José was anywhere nearby.

'My position here is a little delicate, José. I'd prefer to be here with you, but I can't take an active part in what people will see as a war between rival cartels. I can still be useful, though. If this ambush doesn't work, or if some of Óscar's men get away and come running towards your headquarters, the people you're leaving behind are your last line of defence. I'll go up on the roof of the buildings at the front. I have these,' he lifted a pair of powerful binoculars that he'd drawn from the armoury with his own multirifle. 'I'll see what's happening and take out anyone running up before they get there.'

'Okay,' José said.

Jim extended a hand. 'Good luck, José.'

He walked back to the headquarters building and went up the stairs to the top corridor, opened the end door and ascended the ladder to the roof. His multirifle was fully loaded, including a smart grenade in the underbarrel launcher; up here, unlike in the ambush, it could be useful.

Now it was just a matter of waiting.

*

As the morning progressed the air cleared, the sun rose higher, and the temperature began to soar. Up there on the roof the tiles, shining at first with the rain of the last few days, quickly dried off and reflected their heat back at him. He wiped a sleeve over his forehead and raised the binoculars again. He scanned them back and forth above the trees in case he could see any rising smoke from vehicle exhausts but there was nothing. Nearly an hour had passed. He could feel the adrenaline coursing through him, the surge that always came with impending action. He welcomed it, knowing that it sharpened his awareness and reflexes.

The minutes continued to tick by. It was over two hours now since José's observers had reported movement from Óscar's camp, so where the hell were they? Perhaps it was a false alarm or a practice run. That would be bad for the morale of the soldiers down below, who would have to go through a repeat performance of all this. And if there were any traitors among them the advantage of surprise would be completely and utterly lost. He glanced at his watch again but continued to wait. The heat was making him drowsy and he shook his head, then used a technique he'd employed in similar waiting situations, focusing on each sense in turn, not just vision, but sound, smell – even touch, because it was possible that an approaching convoy could set off vibrations in the building.

In the event it was a sound that alerted him, a faint sound but a familiar one, a double whine. His eyes opened wide and he snatched up the binoculars. It was a Rotofan.

Holy shit!

Those aircraft were hugely costly and they didn't come off the shelf. Jim had no doubt at all that it was the Rotofan that Hayden had piloted, the one his own squad had flown in on. Óscar must have found someone who could fly it. On each side of that craft there was a cannon capable of firing six thousand rounds per minute. They would rip the trees to shreds and massacre the waiting soldiers in advance of the convoy. Then it would continue to fly over the headquarters building, raking it with fire, killing Rosa and the other two guarding the entrance. Exposed as he was on the roof, it only had to pass over him for a single second and his body would be riddled with a hundred bullets.

It was an absolute disaster.

30

Things had been pretty evenly balanced before. Óscar had the advantage of numbers; Rosa's crew had the advantage of surprise. Now it was Óscar who'd sprung the surprise, and it had tilted the odds firmly in his favour.

Jim's brain was in overdrive. Would the people he'd deployed in the ambush take pot shots at the Rotofan? It was military grade, and unlike some earlier models they'd used in the 22 SAS, the US version was armoured. Trying to bring it down with rifle fire would be no better than using pea shooters. If some idiot did take a shot he'd betray their presence and sign their death warrants. On the other hand if they kept their heads down there was a good chance the dense foliage would conceal them. Whoever was sitting behind those cannons wouldn't be expecting to see a target out there on the trail. If Óscar thought José was going to defend the headquarters like a fortress then the gunners would be preparing to open fire when they reached the compound. It mustn't get that far. But how to stop it?

Think, Jim, think!

The Rotofan was flying straight and level, and in this attitude the engine pods were almost horizontal. The engines! If he could explode his smart grenade in front of one pod the fragments would enter the engine and wreck it. That would be enough. Even in the hands of an experienced pilot those craft became next to impossible to handle with only one engine. He raised the multirifle and set the cross-wires of the telescopic sight on the Rotofan to get the range, which was closing rapidly. Then he set the proximity fuse on the smart grenade. He wanted it to explode in front of the target, not on contact. He ranged again.

His lips were dry. He hadn't had a chance to retest the sights on his rifle, so he had no idea if they were still accurate. To make things worse it was the most difficult shot he'd ever attempted with any weapon. He had just one grenade and if he got it wrong they would lose this battle, and all that would be left of him would be a bloody heap of rags on the roof.

He centred the cross-wires and kept adjusting the range. The Rotofan was a little over half a mile away, approaching the point where José and his people were deployed. It would be good to bring the Rotofan down now, before it reached them, but he'd struggle to make a shot at that range even with a fully adjusted sniper rifle let alone a grenade launcher.

The Rotofan made a slight change of course. It was no longer following the trail, it was coming straight for the compound. That confirmed it: they were working on the fortress assumption.

He swallowed. He was now facing that lethal machine head-on.

He continued to range it, debating the trajectory. There'd have to be a slight allowance for the fall of the grenade on the way to its target so he'd aim a little above it. He could only hope his guesswork was good. The Rotofan was flying low, so being up here on the roof gave him a better angle than if he'd been on the ground. And the grenade was an anti-personnel weapon so the cloud of fragments would be large. If he ranged it properly it would have time to spread in front of the Rotofan. If...

It continued to come on. Five hundred yards,... four hundred... three hundred...

Close enough. He fired.

One second later there was a brilliant flash and something out there expanded like a great white octopus, sending long tentacles in every direction. The sound of the explosion reached him at the precise moment the Rotofan flew into it.

There was a loud stuttering and the Rotofan shuddered and tilted.

Jim muttered, 'Sweet Jesus, I didn't get one engine – I think I got both.'

He raised the binoculars, saw the engine pods rotating to vertical, the pilot making a futile attempt to hold them aloft, but the craft pitched over and dived steadily down towards the forest maybe half a mile away. It disappeared from view and there was a strange silence. Then a ball of flame rose out of the trees casting a brilliant light over the forest. As it mushroomed into the air it changed from white to yellow to red and faded into a thick black cloud of smoke. The sound followed: a sickening *crump*.

He nodded grimly and muttered to himself, 'That's for Hayden, you bastards.'

The impact had thrown up quite a fireball. It was lucky it had rained so much recently. If the forest had been dry the whole area would have become an inferno.

The air was suddenly filled with the explosions of RPGs and the staccato sounds of gunfire. He'd been watching the Rotofan go down and he hadn't seen a signal flare. He bit his lip. Had the men taken the explosion of his grenade as Gustavo's signal and opened up too soon? If so, most of Óscar's people would retreat to safety and regroup. When they mounted a second attack there would be no element of surprise. He waited, rifle at the ready.

The firing continued for several minutes, then became sporadic and stopped altogether. He waited, watching the trail to see who would emerge first. A quarter of an hour passed, then he spotted movement and quickly raised his rifle. Five men had come around the bend and were heading for the compound with their hands held high. Behind them were four of José's men, rifles levelled from the waist.

Jim slid back down the roof, went through the trap door and down the ladder, and took the corridor and the stairs at a run.

'Stay there for a moment,' he called to Rosa as he ran across the courtyard and out through the entrance.

One of the four men shouted to the prisoners to halt and came over to him.

'José said to tell you that it's all over. We wiped them out.'

Jim felt the tension seeping out of him. 'Remind me, your name is…?

'Armando, Colonel. José wants their base completely wiped out, too. He sent one of the prisoners back there with about fifteen of our people.'

Jim's lips tightened. It was a reminder that the notorious brutality of these cartels wasn't far beneath the surface. It would be a long time before Rosa could change all that.

'Did you get Óscar?' he asked.

'I don't know. José and some others are searching the bodies now.'

Rosa came out with the man and woman who'd been on duty with her. 'Success?' she asked.

Before Jim could reply Armando said, 'Total success, boss.'

'Any casualties?'

'I haven't seen any.'

One of the prisoners spoke up. 'Óscar forced us to join him, boss. He threatened to shoot us if we went back. But now it's all over and we want to join you again.'

Armando strode over and slapped him hard across the face. 'Shut your mouth! You are not fit to address our leader. You will wait and see what José has to say.'

Rosa took one of Jim's hands in hers and squeezed it. 'Jim, this is such a relief. You have done us a great service.'

Seeing her eyes flick to the road he drew back and turned to see José walking towards them, his rifle hoisted over one shoulder.

He came up and clapped Jim on the shoulder. 'It worked perfectly. But I was worried about that Rotofan. Who took it out?'

'I did,' Jim said.

José's eyes widened. Jim went on:

'That was the same Rotofan I flew here on, the military version, and it had a fast-firing cannon on each side.'

José blinked, his mouth open. 'Those things are… we would have been…'

'Precisely.'

'How did you do it?'

'I put a smart grenade in front of the engines.'

'From this distance?' He shook his head in wonder. '¡Dios mío! You're Special Forces all right.'

'Did you find Óscar?'

'Yes, he was in the lead armoured car. A grenade took it out. I think he was killed instantly.' He scowled. 'Pity, I'd have liked to have had a little time with him.'

Armando pointed to the prisoners. 'These guys surrendered, José. What do you want to do with them?'

The vocal one again insisted they wanted to come back to the cartel, that they'd served Óscar against their will.

José said, 'We need people to help clear the bodies. We will take them back.'

Armando said to the prisoners, 'Right, you heard him. Move.'

Jim watched the retreating group, this time with José, Armando, and the three others behind them. They disappeared around the bend of the road.

Rosa was radiant. 'Tonight we will celebrate our victory! Special food, special wine!'

A burst of automatic rifle fire came from around the bend.

They met each other's eyes. Now there would be five more bodies to clear.

*

Jim was well satisfied with the way things had gone. Their defeat of Óscar and his nasty friends had protected Rosa and he'd settled the score for the killing of Hayden and his crew. Best of all he'd won the trust of this cartel. The question was: were they in touch with Delgado? He was rather banking on that. He was in a better position than before, but he'd still have to spot his opportunity.

That evening they had a magnificent three-course meal: a thick chicken soup with vegetables, followed by a spicy beef dish, and a three-layer sponge cake coated with coconut flakes, which Rosa called *Bien Me Sab*. There was beer and wine. At one point Rosa got to her feet, tapped a glass for silence, and said:

'A toast to Colonel Jim Slater, whose strategy today won the battle for us!'

There was applause and much banging on tables. Jim found it embarrassing. He suspected that most of them had drunk so much they would have raised a glass to Mickey Mouse.

The meal went on for a long time and the drinking for even longer. José left early. Rosa's face was flushed with excitement and with the wine. They exchanged frequent glances and Jim thought she looked lovelier than he'd ever seen her. Towards midnight the party began to break up. When they were out of sight of the others, Rosa spoke into his ear. 'Tonight you will sleep with me.' She took his hand and hurried him back to her room.

It was lavishly decorated with floor-to-ceiling purple drapes, a thick purple carpet, a dressing table, and a large, circular bed, turned back to expose pale lavender sheets. Without a word they undressed and slipped under the covers. She cupped his face in her hands and pressed her lips to his.

'How can I thank you enough, Jim? What can I do to please you?'

Jim swallowed hard. 'No complaints about what you did before.'

'Very well. And then you will stay here with me and we will try some other things in case there is something you like even better. I warn you: there will not be much sleeping tonight.'

And there wasn't.

31

It had taken Sally, Fernando, and Miguel three days to reach the coast. It wasn't so much the terrain, although it was tough in places, it was the need to stay out of sight. This obliged them to make numerous diversions around towns, farms, and other inhabited areas, and where there were roads to cross they had to do it at deserted times. Eventually, wet, tired, and muddy, they changed into their army uniforms, which were just as damp and muddy, and made the final approach to the designated rendezvous.

Sally looked around. 'These are the coordinates Jim gave me.'

'I can't see any boats,' Fernando said. 'Do you think they've gone without us?'

They scanned the bay. Fernando was right; there was nothing in sight.

She bit her lip. 'I guess if they're here they don't want to be in full view. I wonder what—'

A figure rose from the long grass. He was pointing an assault rifle at them.

Sally caught her breath.

'¡Deténgase ahí!'

'*¡Amigos!*' she replied.

'*¿Contraseña?*'

'Hallowe'en.' She added in English, 'With an apostrophe.'

He lowered the rifle and she breathed a sigh of relief. The Navy SEAL had been invisible in his taupe uniform and helmet.

'You took your sweet time,' he said.

Sally bridled. 'You try crossing fifty miles of this country on foot without being spotted.'

He laughed. 'Okay, okay, come with me.'

As they walked he opened a pouch on his belt and took out a radio transmitter. He spoke into it, then replaced it. 'The ship's on its way,' he said. 'We've been staking out this spot for days.'

'Well thanks for that, but I'd like to bet you were more comfortable than we were.'

He took in their bedraggled appearance and gave a grudging nod.

They descended into a cove and waited.

'Petty Officer Tony Davison,' he said to her.

'Lieutenant Sally Kent,' she said. 'This is Sergeant Miguel Garzón and Corporal Fernando Boudon.'

Miguel and Fernando nodded to him. Miguel grinned. 'Your Spanish accent is lousy.'

'Thanks, you can give me some lessons while we're on board. There'll be plenty of time – if you're not seasick.'

'*Touché!*' Sally said, laughing.

'Were you part of the force that landed at Caracas?' Davison asked.

Sally blinked. 'The US invaded?'

'Sure did. Big force, marines, paratroops, the lot. Right now they're taking over the President's palace, government buildings, and television stations.'

'Well, well,' Sally said. Then, thinking quickly, she answered his earlier question by adding, 'No, we were kind of an advance party.'

She thought about the timing.

We're asked to observe a US Envoy we know only as Mr X. We tell Washington he's being taken to Buena Vista and within days the US mount a full-scale invasion. Is that a coincidence? Is it hell! It takes time to set up something on that scale. Dexter was right: they must have been in position already, waiting for the go-ahead.

A US Navy patrol ship rounded the coast, sailed into the bay, and anchored. The crew lowered an inflatable dinghy.

'Let's go,' Davison said, and they scrambled down to the shoreline.

The sound of an outboard motor reverberated across the water and the dinghy raced towards them. It stopped about twenty yards out.

'You're going to get your feet wet,' Davison said. He added, with a glance at Sally, 'I'll carry you if you like.'

She fixed him with a look. 'Thanks, but after what we've been through I don't think we'll be worrying too much about wet feet.'

They waded out to the dinghy, rifles held high, and the crew helped them over the side. The outboard motor roared and they bounced over the waves to the waiting ship.

Nets had already been lowered for them. The four slung their rifles and clambered up.

'Come below,' Davison said to Sally. 'You guys can dry yourselves off there. Hungry?'

'We sure are.'

'Okay. I'll organize something. And I'll get the three of you some dry socks.'

'Now that would be wonderful.'

There was a friendly, and on occasion not so friendly, rivalry between the special forces. An amphibious assignment like this clearly called for a combined operation with the SEALs and in Sally's limited experience that had always worked well. Things were more prickly with Delta Force, who still liked to think of themselves as the elite outfit of the three. Which of course they weren't.

When they'd changed into the dry socks and some deck shoes Davison had brought with him, and had eaten a small – but very welcome – snack of sandwiches and hot coffee, Sally went up on deck and stood at the rail. She'd undone the regulation bun and her hair, now hanging loose, blew behind her in the wind.

She wasn't enthusiastic about boats. On a mission such as this she much preferred to be lifted in and out by air, especially on the way out, when you wanted to be quickly beyond the range of potential pursuers. Not that much could overtake this vessel at the speed it was going. She stood with knees slightly bent to absorb the repeated shocks as it hit the waves. Still, it was better to be out on deck with a horizon to look at, even though it was rising and falling to an alarming extent.

Above the sound of the sea smacking repeatedly against the hull came the clatter of footsteps on the companionway and a tall SEAL joined her at the rail. A powerful pair of binoculars dangled from a strap around his neck.

'Is a SEAL Lieutenant allowed to speak to an SAF Lieutenant?' he asked, raising his voice above the wind.

'Depends what he's going to say.'

He laughed and extended a hand. 'Bill Avery.'

She shook it lightly. 'Sally Kent.' It gave her a chance to look at him. Clean-shaven, kind brown eyes, white teeth – an all-American boy. Back at college she remembered, with a tinge of embarrassment, she'd been one of the cheerleaders for their football team. She'd had a bit of a crush on a quarterback who looked a bit like this guy. He seemed very young to be in charge of this mission. 'Where are we going, Bill?' she asked.

'Puerto Rico. There's an aircraft at the base waiting to take you to the mainland.'

'Great.'

'I was told we were only at this rendezvous as a backup. What happened?'

'We had to leave in a hurry with the Venezuelan army hot on our heels. We were supposed to exfil in the Rotofan that brought us in. That was the plan, but when we got to it we found the crew with their throats cut, all four of them.'

'My God!'

She nodded. 'Not one of us can fly those things, so we had to head here. We couldn't use our vehicle either because they were bound to set up road blocks so we went on foot.'

'Ah, we were wondering about the delay but that explains it. You had a lot of country to cross.'

'Yeah, we've seen quite enough of it.'

The ship pitched into a large wave and Sally staggered a little.

Bill seemed unperturbed. 'I was told to expect four,' he said.

Sally gripped the rail harder and nodded. 'We knew they were trying to catch up with us – they had drones out – so Colonel Slater split off on his own to create a diversion. It seemed to work. I just hope he's okay.'

'How's he going to get back?'

'He was heading north-west. Maybe he'll cross into Colombia and fly back from Maicao.'

'Okay. Look, I said I'd update your General Harken if I saw you, so I'll do that right away.'

He came back ten minutes later. 'All done.'

She lifted her face, then flinched as it was stung by flying spray. 'Wind seems to be getting up even more.'

'I'm not surprised, there's a hurricane on the way.'

Sally's face fell and she turned to the Lieutenant. 'How bad?'

'Category 3 already, and it'll probably gain strength as it nears the coast.'

'Are we in its path?'

'Hard to say because it's still swinging around. But with a system that size we'll be somewhere in it. We're aiming to make port before it hits. That's why we've put on some speed. I guess you were hoping to get back to Fort Piper today.'

Sally bit her lip. 'I was – if we can fly out.'

'Your pilots will have a more up-to-date forecast by then. With luck you might just make it.'

Sally turned back from him to view the sea, which had turned a slate grey, the waves tipped with foam. She narrowed her eyes, wiped away the strands of hair which had blown across her face, and pointed. 'What's that out there?'

Avery lifted the binoculars, searched for a while, then gasped. 'I can't believe it! A small fishing-boat! What the hell's it doing out here? It won't last two minutes when that hurricane hits.'

'If there's anyone still on board we'd better pick them up.'

He grimaced, and Sally sensed that the need to make port was passing through his mind. But so was the maritime code. He nodded and went forward. Moments later the engine note changed and the ship changed course.

In twenty minutes they were closing on the struggling fishing-boat, which was rocking violently, the mast swinging through wide angles from side to side. Bill Avery came back and stood at the rail with Sally, looking down on the boat. There was a man on the deck waving to them. His face was cadaverously thin and covered in a dark stubble. The wind blew a cloud of spray over him, which sank immediately through skimpy cotton clothing. He ignored it, just continued to wave and shout into the wind, '¡Ayúdanos! ¡Necesitamos combustible!'

'Jesus!' Lieutenant Avery said. 'They're out of fuel, but that's not going to help them even if we had any.'

They pulled alongside slowly, the engines grumbling and then stopping altogether. The loss of sound was replaced by the dull thudding together of the two hulls. A skinny woman came out of the cockpit, her feet planted wide. There was a baby in her arms and a young boy hanging onto her skirt.

Avery shouted in Spanish, 'You must all come on board. There is a strong hurricane coming.'

The man shook his head uncertainly. '*¡Necesitamos combustible!*'

Avery shouted, 'It is a strong hurricane. Your boat will sink to the bottom of the sea and you and your family will drown. Save your lives and come aboard.'

The response was a moistening of the lips, then a reluctant nod.

The rail of the ship was about ten feet higher than the gunwale of the fishing vessel, rising and falling as each swell passed first under the ship then under the fishing-boat. Avery shouted to the crew, 'Net!'

They hung the net over the side. One of the SEALs climbed down, banging against the hull with the rocking of the ship, then jumped into the fishing vessel. He gestured, urging the thin man to climb up but he shook his head. Instead he returned to the cockpit and came out carrying a couple of battered suitcases. He set them down on the rocking deck and indicated the cases, the woman, the child, and the baby, drawing a circle with his fingers. The SEAL thumped his own chest to indicate that he'd look after them, put a hand on the man's shoulder and pushed him gently towards the net. He stepped up on the gunwale, grabbed the net, and clambered up, his sinewy arms hauling with remarkable strength. One of the crew members reached down and helped him in.

Meanwhile the SEAL was trying to persuade the woman to climb up after him, but she wouldn't let go of the baby. At this point another SEAL climbed down. He was just about the tallest man Sally had ever seen. Without a word he picked up the suitcases, stepped onto the gunwale and passed them into waiting hands above. Then, using hand signals, he explained that he would do the same with the baby. At first the woman recoiled, but after additional noises of reassurance she handed over the baby and he stood on the gunwale again and passed it up to the men above.

Now the tall SEAL went to the young child, kneeled down and waved him to climb on his shoulders. The child drew back and hid his face in his mother's skirt. The lieutenant shouted down, and the woman took the child and placed him on the tall one's back, his arms around the man's neck. He promptly grabbed the net and climbed on board. The air was full of noise, the lamentations of the thin man about the loss of his boat, the baby crying lustily and the child howling for its mother. The only silent one was the woman, who seemed too shocked to say anything, her wide eyes large over sunken cheeks. The remaining SEAL got her to climb onto his back, then clambered up the net and onto the deck.

Avery delivered a series of instructions. When his men had led the family safely below decks he went forward. The engines roared, the hulls rubbed briefly as the ship turned, and they were under way again.

Sally went below to see what was happening to the family. Some of the crew had put blankets around the shoulders of the man and woman and they were saying they would bring food and water, but they were speaking in English. Sally stepped up and translated it all into fluent Spanish, much to the relief of the crew.

The steps clanged and Lieutenant Avery joined them. He had a brief conversation with the family and came back to Sally.

'They're from Maracaibo. I think they were heading for one of the Dutch Caribbean islands but they ran out of fuel. They've been drifting ever since, haven't eaten for two days. I'm surprised they even got this far in that rustbucket.' He checked his watch. 'We didn't lose too much time. We may still make it.'

One of the crew appeared with bottles of water and a plate of sandwiches, which the man, woman, and young boy fell upon eagerly.

The ship droned on, slapping through the waves, the jolts and the motion as bad as ever. When the family had eaten Sally sat down with them and asked why they had left Maracaibo.

The thin man clasped bony hands together, rocking them up and down for emphasis. 'I am a fisherman,' he said. 'Like my father and my grandfather before me. One time there is much fish in Lake Maracaibo, enough to feed a family and sell in the market. Not now. It is the oil. There are pipelines under Lake Maracaibo but no one maintains them. So they leak and the oil spills into the lake, year after year after year. Nobody cares. Now the whole lake is polluted. My nets come in, they are black and slimy with oil. If there are fish in the nets they are dead. Every day the bolivare buys less. The money we have saved is gone, finished. So now we have no food, no money.' His eyes filled with tears. 'I cannot feed my family. We have no choice. We have to leave.'

Sally said, 'Many people have escaped across the border into Colombia.'

'This is true. But for this you need money, for the Border Guards and for the *bandidos,* and we have no money.' He gestured at his wife, 'Maria and I, we decide, we will try by boat. If we die it is better to drown than to starve to death.'

Lieutenant Avery came up. 'How are we doing here?'

'They've had something to eat, at least. What are you going to do with them when we reach Puerto Rico?'

'Don't worry, there's a procedure for it.'

'They're penniless and starving, Bill.' she said. 'You wonder how people can be allowed to become so destitute. Their government seems to have turned its back on them.'

'And the world's turned its back on Venezuela.' Avery's lips tightened. 'There's nothing you and I can do about it, Sally.'

'Oh, I wouldn't say that,' she murmured to herself. 'Seems to me like maybe we just did.'

32

General Wendell Harken was waiting in the main conference room for the President, as were the others in the White House Situation Room. The big screens on the end wall, intended at other times for participants taking part digitally, were blank. Red figures on the clock in the corner gave the three times: 0800 for local time, 0800 for the time where the President was, and 1200 for UTC, Coordinated Universal Time. The black leather armchairs on either side of the long mahogany table were occupied by the same people as before, all responding to a CRITIC call.

President Harriet Nagel hurried in with the White House Chief of Staff, Carol Anders. The President went straight to her chair at the end of the table. As she was sitting down she said, 'Right, where're we at?'

General George Wagner, Army Chief of Staff leaned forward. 'The military operation has gone completely according to plan, Madam President. We have control of the airports in Caracas and Maracaibo and our own flights are the only ones coming in and going out. The Leviathons unloaded personnel and materiel at both airports and the army has secured the capital. The marines have taken over the television stations.'

'Did you encounter any opposition?'

'Not significant opposition, ma'am, at least initially. We took them totally by surprise, and all the main military objectives were achieved very quickly. After that things became a little more tricky. The main problem was at the Palace. There was quite a firefight there, so we sent in attack drones. That settled the problem outside the Palace but we encountered heavy resistance inside.'

'Casualties?'

'Overall, three killed, eight wounded.' He must have seen her wince because he added, 'Those figures are pretty light for an operation on this scale, ma'am.'

'All right, go on.'

'Once we'd taken the Palace we parked tanks in the grounds and around the area, mainly as a show of strength. Then Colonel Weaver went in to see President Aguilar.' He added. 'Colonel Philip Weaver was the officer in command of the whole operation, ma'am.'

'And…?'

'As instructed, he gave the man an ultimatum. Either we deliver him to the Hague charged with crimes against humanity or he calls an election. As we expected, he agreed to call the election. He also agreed to deliver the short speech we gave him to read in a broadcast to the nation.' The CSA took a cell from his pocket and scrolled quickly. 'The English version of the operative part goes like this:

"As you know, our economy has suffered badly from the sanctions applied by a number of countries, countries with whom we would normally trade profitably. They maintain that there were irregularities in the previous election. In the interests of our country I am therefore calling a new election, which will be conducted under international supervision and so seen to be fair and free." '

The President sniffed. 'I know we agreed on this but the man's a murderer. He should be under arrest.'

'It was a compromise,' the CSA said. 'We didn't want to look punitive. This way it just seems like we're facilitating a new election.'

'What's this about international supervision?' the President asked.

'It's us. We've recruited very experienced inspectors, ones who know all the tricks, including the ones Aguilar employs – stuffing ballot boxes, tampering with the figures, and so on.'

'We should get inspectors from other countries, too, countries with experience: the UK, France, Germany. I'll speak to their heads of government.'

'Good idea, ma'am.'

'So has the speech gone out?'

'Yes it has. It was transmitted every half hour for the following forty-eight hours, so it was seen in homes, cafés, restaurants, everywhere. There's also been a mail shot and distribution of leaflets and posters.'

'What about Delgado?'

The CSA looked at Joe Templeton, the CIA's Director.

Templeton shifted uncomfortably. 'We had expected Delgado to come out of hiding at this stage,' he said. 'He hasn't.'

The President's eyes widened. 'Why on earth not?'

Templeton said, 'He's not reachable by normal communications, so it's possible he's missed the election announcements. But there's another possibility. President Aguilar is a notoriously devious operator. Delgado may think the latest election announcement is a ruse to draw him into the public eye again so they can have him arrested or assassinated.'

'I thought Colonel Slater's team was going to contact him,' the President said.

They all looked at Wendell.

'Three members of the SAF squad reached the secondary rendezvous on the coast yesterday, and they were successfully picked up by the Navy SEALs. It was one of the SEALs who gave me this update as they sailed.'

'What were they doing there? I thought you'd asked Colonel Slater to track down Delgado.'

'Yes, ma'am, and with USCYBERCOM's help I did. He's evidently decided to go in search of Señor Delgado alone.'

'Is that wise?'

Wendell grimaced. 'It's hard for us to know what the situation is on the ground. He may have decided that it would be less conspicuous if he worked alone.'

'But no news yet.'

'No, ma'am. Señor Delgado has managed to keep out of harm's way since the last election, and he's managed that by staying well hidden. Finding him will be no easy task.'

'But finding him is absolutely crucial. See what the Colonel is up to now, will you?'

33

The communicator woke Jim from a deep, warm slumber. He opened one eye, unsure what the buzzing was or even where he was. Realization gradually seeped in and the fog cleared. He disengaged himself gently from Rosa, who'd been sleeping with her arm across his chest, and a drowsy murmur escaped from her. He crossed the room, felt around in the trousers that were lying on a chair, and drew out the device. He pressed the receive button.

'Slater.' His voice sounded low and husky from interrupted sleep.

'Colonel, it's Harry.'

'Harry…?' Jim blinked, still trying to clear his head. 'Oh, right, Harry. Go ahead.'

'I have General Harken on the line for you again.'

Jim looked at Rosa, who was now watching him. This call could look very suspicious to her.

What the hell, she already knows what's going on. And this could give me the opportunity I've been waiting for.

He took the communicator over to the bed, covered the mic, and mouthed, 'Pentagon.' Then he put his finger to his lips and held the device away from his ear so that she could listen in.

'Jim?'

Wendell again sounded like he was standing in an echo chamber, but it was clear enough.

'Wendell, glad you called. Any news of the three I sent to the second rendezvous?'

'Don't worry, Jim, they're safe. The SEALs picked them up and took them to Puerto Rico. They were delayed there by a hurricane but they'll be flying back shortly. Where are you right now?'

Right now? I'm in bed with a beautiful young woman. And it's been quite a night.

'Er, I'm in a pretty hot spot…' he glanced at Rosa, whose lips tweaked in a mischievous smile, '…that's to say, I'm in the right sort of area.'

Wendell said, 'You know we landed troops in Venezuela?'

'I heard a rumour along those lines.'

'Well your rumour's correct. We took over the airports in Maracaibo and Caracas and the main television stations. The capital's in our hands, and that includes the Miraflores Palace – that's the President's residence. President Aguilar has had to declare a fresh election. We'll be bringing in expert inspectors to supervise the arrangements and make sure there's no tampering.'

It was unusual to hear Wendell speaking so rapidly. Jim felt the man must be under a lot of pressure. Jim replied in a leisurely way, hoping to calm him down.

'That's good.'

'Yes, Jim, but now we have a serious problem. Everyone wants a change of regime and Delgado is the opposition candidate of choice – in fact, thanks to Aguilar, he's about the only opposition candidate left. The new election's being advertised on television, with handbills, the lot, but he still hasn't come out of hiding. We think he's afraid. If he's seen the broadcasts about an election he may be thinking it's all a con and the moment he makes an appearance Aguilar will do as he always has when he's faced opposition: have him assassinated – or put in jail, which in this case amounts to the same thing.'

Jim nodded. 'I see. That's tricky.'

'It's worse than tricky! If Aguilar gets re-elected this whole operation will have been for nothing. And we took casualties, Jim.'

Jim's face fell. 'We did?'

'Yes, three killed, eight wounded. I'd hate to feel it was an empty sacrifice.'

'So would I. And don't forget the four crew in our Rotofan.'

'Yes, them too. So it's more important than ever to find Delgado.'

Jim glanced at Rosa and was glad to see that she was following the conversation intently. He went on:

'That's all very well but… Look, let's just assume I can locate him. How am I supposed to persuade him I'm US Army and not one of Aguilar's spooks? The only I.D. I have is the fake Venezuelan one your outfit gave me.'

There was a short silence. 'Best to get him to phone the Pentagon. Have him ask to be put through to Bob or me. I can get them to expedite any call from Delgado.'

Jim inhaled deeply. He was wide awake now and in his mind he was already planning the moves for getting Delgado – and Rosa – on board. 'Okay, I can only try. But he'll need protection.'

'There are thousands of US troops in the country, Jim. I can make sure they free up a platoon or two for protection.'

'If Delgado needs a protection detail I don't want any old bunch of army grunts on it, I want my own people. They're trained in surveillance and countersurveillance. And we need a senior person in charge. Tommy Geiger would be the perfect man for that. He's just the right rank and he's been itching for a field operation ever since that grenade injured his leg.'

'Is he fit enough?'

'For something like this, sure. Could you get him to put a suitable platoon on standby? If Delgado phones you or Bob you'll know I've located him and you can give Tommy the go-ahead. They need to arrive at the airport that serves Maicao – that'll be nearer than Caracas or Maracaibo. I want them fully armed, and not just rifles: I want surveillance and attack drones, and missiles in case they get attacked from the air. And they'll need to bring four good armoured vehicles with off-road capabilities. There aren't too many roads around here, and most of them aren't much better than logging trails.'

Even over this line Jim recognized the dryness in Wendell's tone. 'I can do all that, Jim, but Maicao's in Colombia. I can foresee problems landing a US Army contingent there and expecting them to be waved through immigration and allowed to cross the border into Venezuela.'

Jim bit his lip. 'Ah.' There was a long silence, then he said, 'Wait a minute, we have trade agreements with Colombia, don't we? Didn't they include measures to control the drug trade?'

'Yes…'

'So you could have the soldiers oufitted and the vehicles painted with the Drug Enforcement logos.'

He heard a long intake of breath. 'Yes…I suppose that could work. All right, I can go pretty high with this, so they'll make it a priority. If they work flat out it'll take them a day to get the vehicles and uniforms ready, but that's not too bad. Your platoon should be ready to move the day after tomorrow.'

'Okay, when they land here they can contact me via the cyber group, like you just did, and we'll make arrangements to meet somewhere. And that cyber group needs to keep busy, too, intercepting any mischief Aguilar and his cronies may be cooking up, both before and during the election.'

'I'll tell them.'

'Who's in overall charge of the invasion force, Wendell?'

'Colonel Philip Weaver. He's a good man.'

'Right, we need him on side, too. Once my guys are in that coastal region between Maracaibo and Caracas I want him to give them full support, help with crowd control at any rallies, that sort of thing.'

'I'll speak to him myself.'

'Good.' Jim sighed. 'You know, none of this is going to be the slightest use if I can't find the man. Jesus, Wendell, of all the—'

'I know. Jim. Do your best. Good luck.'

The line went dead.

Jim switched off the communicator and put it down. He looked at Rosa. If there ever was a time to find out whether she knew where Delgado was, it was right now.

'Did you get that?' he asked.

'Most of it.'

He ran his hands through his hair. 'This guy Delgado's tucked himself away somewhere where no one can get to him. That doesn't seem to register with Washington. They want him to start campaigning. "Dig him out for us – would you, Jim? – you can have all of five minutes." Dear God!'

She frowned. 'I don't want Aguilar to be re-elected. Nobody does.'

'I know, but—'

'Jim, Aguilar has called the election but that will not stop him from trying to kill the one man who can defeat him. Are you sure you can keep Delgado safe?'

'My people have trained for this sort of thing and they'll be well equipped. He couldn't have better protection if he was the President of the United States.'

She gave him a small smile. 'Well, you helped us to defeat Óscar. Perhaps it is time we helped you.'

At last!

'How?'

'I told you Delgado has our support. My father made that clear to him. They met a number of times, and I was there myself more than once. He said to Delgado, "Juan-Luis, when you become President we can be your right hand. You will have the Venezuelan army, but we're better than that. They will cost you, we won't. And we don't behave like those pigs Los Feroces. You can depend on us." Out of these meetings they became friends. And not just them. José and

Óscar were also present at that time.' She held up a finger. 'Óscar is dead, but I think José may know where Delgado is hiding.'

'Could he take me to him?'

'After breakfast we will ask him.'

'Good. Well, I think we should get dressed, don't you?'

She reached out her arms and he lifted her slender body to him, feeling the soft pressure of her breasts against his chest. They kissed gently at first, then more urgently, and after that getting dressed acquired a lower priority.

At breakfast Teresa served them with *mandocas*, a kind of doughnut dressed with *quesco blanco* cheese. Jim had little appetite, and confined himself to just a nibble and black coffee. José seemed to be the solution to his mission impossible, perhaps the only solution, but he had serious misgivings about making such a trip alone with him. José wasn't a man he could trust.

José joined them as they finished breakfast. Rosa poured a coffee for him. Then she leaned towards José, lowered her voice, and began to speak rapidly in Spanish. Jim could hear the authority in her voice, but he could barely hang on to the conversation. Isolated words leaped out at him: *'Aguilar… régimen…gobierno…Delgado…ocultación…'* At one point she gestured at Jim, and he guessed she was telling him about the protection he could offer. José's small dark eyes swivelled constantly between Rosa and Jim.

There was a short silence.

José sat back, his eyes slightly hooded now, looking at Jim. 'I can take you there,' he said.

34

An hour later Jim was just about to leave when the door to his room opened. Rosa came in and stood in front of him. He could sense the pain in her voice, and in the way her lips quivered as she choked back tears. She took his hands.

'You will take care, won't you, Jim?' she said.

'Of course. And you must be careful, too, Rosa.'

'I will be all right. Gustavo and Ismael will make sure I am safe. Jim…'

'Yes?'

'Will I ever see you again?'

He looked at her. He was aware, as no doubt she was, that the countercurrents of life were pulling them apart. He gave her a sad smile. 'Who knows? But Rosa, whatever happens, these few days I've spent here with you, I'll never forget them and I'll never forget you.'

She dipped her head. He put his arms around her and she held onto him fiercely. Then the embrace relaxed, their arms dropped, and he left the room quickly.

José was waiting by an all-roader in the courtyard.

So, José, are you still worried because I know where this headquarters is? Would you be even more worried if you

knew that I'd already used my wristwatch to read and record
the geographical coordinates of this place?

Jim strolled over. He said, 'My rifle and pistol?'

José pointed. 'In the trunk. It is better if you look unarmed.'

By putting them in the trunk out of Jim's reach José had done nothing to reassure him, but Jim decided it would be insulting to check; he didn't want to make things any worse. He got into the passenger seat. José walked over to speak to the two sentries and while he was doing that Jim swiftly opened the glove compartment. It was the obvious place to look and sure enough he found a small snub-nosed revolver there: a Taurus Protector. He hesitated for a moment, but that instinct for self-preservation took over. Holding it by the grip, he slipped the catch with his thumb and used third and fourth fingers to push the cylinder out. He tipped the five 0.357 Magnum cartridges into his hand, pocketed the rounds, and locked the cylinder back in. Looking up he saw that José was already returning to the car. He hunched forward, pretending to have a coughing fit, stuffed the revolver back in the glove compartment and coughed loudly again to cover the sound of it slamming shut. José opened the driver's side door and got behind the wheel. He nodded to Jim and started the engine.

They moved out of the entrance, past the two sentries, and onto the muddy trail that they called a road, where he turned left. That was the direction in which the earlier vehicle had gone with Dexter, so it felt right so far. The track had been grooved by other vehicles on earlier journeys and the all-roader lurched and staggered as they drove. Early morning sun had raised a slight mist, giving the forest a haunted fairytale look. The trees leaned their upper torsos over the road, threatening to march across a feeble clearance like this the moment humankind's back was turned. Along the narrower stretches branches flailed at the windows, but José made no attempt to moderate his speed. Neither of them said anything.

Half an hour later the vehicle made a shallow descent into a valley. The rain had made it even muddier here than elsewhere. Ahead of them the trail rose again but at this point the all-roader's wheels spun, the engine over-revved, and the vehicle shimmied from side to side. José stopped immediately and muttered a curse. He turned to Jim.

'We are stuck. You will have to get out and push.'

'Okay.'

It was a feeble ruse, Jim thought, as he opened the door. This vehicle could easily handle it and José hadn't even tried backing off a little and going forward in a higher gear. Still, he went through the motions, closing the door and going to the back, while keeping José in his peripheral vision. He saw him dive to the glove locker and he came out pointing the pistol. Jim pretended to be surprised.

'Sorry, Jim. You got too close to us and too close to Rosa. You have to go.'

'José, think about what you're doing… '

But José extended the pistol, his left hand supporting the right, the barrel pointing at Jim's chest. His finger tightened on the trigger.

Again Jim said, 'José… '

There was a loud click as the hammer fell on an empty chamber. José's face fell and he looked down at the revolver. That was all Jim was waiting for. His speed and long legs had caught out many an opponent on the mat, but this was no gym and he didn't pull the heel strike. It landed squarely in José's stomach and he jack-knifed, staggered backwards into a tree and fell forward. Jim was on him in a flash, pinning him down. He applied a classic choke hold, reaching his left arm around the man's neck and using his right arm behind the head to compress José's throat and vital vessels against the edge of his hand. José flailed but he couldn't move or breathe and the pressure was restricting the blood supply to his head. The instructor who'd shown Jim this hold had demonstrated it on him, so he knew José's head would already be swimming. He held the pressure a little longer before easing off a touch and pulling him upwards, painfully hyperextending the man's spine.

'Now listen to me, José,' he said. 'Are you listening to me?'

The only answer was a strangled noise.

'You tried to kill me. I'm entitled to kill you instead. Right now. Is that what I should do, José?'

A sound like 'Ng…' came from José.

'Seems to me I have to make a choice. One, I kill you, which will be very, very easy. Then I take all the bolivares and pesos which are in that interesting belt you put on today and I drive to the border. I bribe my way through, drive to Maicao, and get the hell out of here. That's option one. Are you still listening?'

He jerked his left hand harder into José's throat for emphasis, and José grunted in protest.

'And then there's option two. I don't kill you. You drive me to Delgado as you promised Rosa and me that you would, and you don't try anything stupid like this again. You decide.

With option one I leave the country, Delgado stays in hiding, Aguilar is re-elected and all of your plans go to hell. With option two, I meet Delgado and I bring in a platoon of my men and women – every one of them as lethal as I am – and they protect him throughout the campaign. He is elected President, it's Los Feroces that goes to hell, and the Guárico Cartel is in with the new government. Your country has a future and Rosa's dreams come true.'

He jerked his left arm again. 'Which is it to be, José? Rosa's dreams or your petty suspicions and jealousy?'

He eased off the pressure and José gasped and swallowed.

'I'm waiting, José.'

The voice was hoarse and choking. 'I will take you to Delgado.'

'Do you swear that you won't try to kill me again?'

'Yes, I swear.'

Jim shouted, 'Say it!'

'I swear I won't try to kill you again, I swear it on my mother's life.'

'Not on your mother's life, she could be dead already for all I know.'

He swallowed again. 'I swear it on my own life. May God strike me dead if I harm you.'

Jim paused, withdrew his arms and shoved him away. He got to his feet and, while he was waiting for José to recover, picked up the pistol and threw it into the forest.

Slowly José pushed himself into a sitting position and spent a long time massaging his throat and gasping.

Finally he got to his feet and staggered to the open driver's door of the vehicle.

The engine was still running.

35

The muddy trails led to tracks that were more passable and after a while they came to a surfaced road. They travelled on this for about half an hour then suddenly swung off. For a moment Jim thought they were plunging directly into forest but an opening was there, just obscured by slender branches. José drove on down a path that was clipped back on each side but overarched by trees. A hundred yards later he stopped the car. The path continued ahead, but there was no indication of what it led to – or didn't lead to.

'We are here,' he said.

'Where?' Jim snapped. 'I don't see anything.'

'The house is at the end of this path. But first we will meet sentries. It is better if we go on foot now.'

'All right, José, you're going ahead of me, and be careful what you say. You introduce me as Colonel Jim Slater of US Special Forces.'

'Okay, okay. Look, I'm sorry. I made a mistake. It won't happen again.'

They got out and walked down the path. Two men came out from nowhere and waited, rifles levelled. José held his hands high and Jim did the same. For the second time that day he found himself staring into the barrel of a gun. This time it was a Kalashnikov AK74, probably Czech-made. When it came to armaments the Czechs weren't too fussy about who they sold to.

José said to one of the sentries, 'Please tell Señor Delgado that his friend José Manuel Herrera is here.'

The sentry jerked the rifle briefly towards Jim. 'And him?'

'He is Colonel Jim Slater of US Special Forces. He is also a friend.'

'I.D.'

José handed his over. The sentry examined it and handed it back. Then he took Jim's and looked up sharply. 'This isn't—'

José said, 'He is working here under cover. But he has helped us a great deal.'

'We will see. First we search you.'

They patted both of them down. Jim heard a rattle and realized with a grimace that he still had five 0.357 cartridges in his pocket. The sentry made him take them out. His eyebrows asked the question.

'You can have them,' Jim said in Spanish with a casual wave. 'I had to disarm a man and I forgot they were there.' He avoided José's eyes as he said it.

The sentry's eyes narrowed, but he pocketed the rounds. Then he took out a phone and there was a brief conversation. He looked up and said to José, 'You say we can trust this man?'

'You can trust him with your life.'

'Okay, you follow me.'

They walked further down the path and a stone-built house came into view. This, too, was surrounded and overhung by trees, and there appeared to be some sort of roof garden, because Jim could see small bushes and the fronds of ferns projecting from it. Neither the path nor this house would be easy to spot from the air, which was no doubt the general idea. They climbed the steps to the front door, entered the house, and turned down a high-ceilinged corridor, one sentry in front of them, the other behind. The sentry in front knocked on a door and in response to an '*Entrar*' from inside they opened it into a spacious room. Jim hadn't expected to see a study or library or office like this in such an ordinary-looking house. The walls were lined with bookshelves and an ornate rug covered most of the floor. Light from tall windows fell across a desk in the middle of the room. Someone was sitting behind it.

The man rose. He was tall and slender. His hair was dark and wavy, touched with grey at the temples, but the face was youthful and unlined, the wide mouth stretched in a welcoming smile. Jim recognized that face instantly from the media photographs he'd seen in the past. A few hours ago he would have thought this encounter would be impossible but now, at last, he was standing in front of him.

Juan-Luis Delgado.

'José,' Delgado said, stepping forward and taking the outstretched hand, covering it with his other hand. 'It has been too long. I don't think I have seen you since Antonio Martinez died.'

'I am glad to see you well, Juan-Luis. This is Colonel Jim Slater of the US Special Forces.'

Delgado pursed his lips, raised his eyebrows, inclined his head, and with elaborate courtesy shook Jim's hand. 'And what is your business here...Colonel?'

Jim could see the doubt in Delgado's behaviour, the way he said 'Colonel' as if he was picking the word up with tongs. He replied, 'On this occasion it is diplomatic.'

'Your Spanish is good, Colonel, but if you have a diplomatic mission perhaps you would be more comfortable speaking in English.'

'If that is acceptable to you...' Jim said, in English.

Delgado switched languages with no apparent effort. 'Evidently you do not know, or perhaps have forgotten, that I studied in England at the University of Oxford.'

'Ah.'

Why the hell didn't Wendell think to mention that? Perhaps he wasn't briefed properly himself.

José murmured something quietly which Jim didn't catch but Delgado did. His eyes switched rapidly from José to Jim.

'Colonel,' he said. 'I would like to speak to José in private for a moment. Would you be so good as to wait outside? He spoke to the two sentries in Spanish, and Jim heard the phrase *'por favor escolte'*. Escort. The meaning was clear enough. The sentries each held an arm and conducted him from the room.

He stood in the corridor with a sentry on either side of him, each still grasping his upper arm. He hadn't heard what José had said, but it had clearly rung warning bells with Delgado. Just at the point that he'd found Delgado it looked like the opportunity was being snatched away from him. Of one thing he was more sure than ever: José simply couldn't be trusted, however much he swore on the life of his mother and all the rest of it. No doubt his hatred and suspicion of Jim had been further fuelled by his undignified defeat and capitulation earlier in the day. Right now José could be settling the scores, telling Delgado that the Colonel was a fake and an imposter, and that he, José, had been forced to bring him here. Jim would be killed, and it would be José who gave Delgado the news about the US invasion and the need to come out of hiding and begin his campaign. In José's own mind he would be the hero and get his revenge on Jim in one move. He could even push Rosa aside and get control of the Guárico cartel. And Jim had helped the man eliminate his one serious adversary: Óscar! None of this must be allowed to happen.

Right now standing here with an armed guard on either side of him was far from ideal. There was, however, something in his favour. They were too close to him and, as they were holding his arms, the rifles were nowhere near ready for use. In fact the Kalashnikovs were entirely the wrong weapon for this situation. If they'd been Federal Agents they'd be standing off, pointing pistols.

He choreographed the moves in his mind and then went into action with lightning speed. He stamped hard on the instep of the sentry to the right and with his weight still on that side delivered a heel strike to the pressure point at the side of the other guard's knee. They both yelled in pain, and the leg of the one on the left gave way under him. With their grip loosened he tore his arms forward and on the back stroke struck the sentry on the right with his elbow. It hit him full in the nose and the man shouted in pain and turned away, a hand to his face. Jim snatched his rifle and swung it by the barrel into the head of the other guard, who was struggling to get up. He collapsed like a rag doll.

Jim turned to the door. There'd been enough noise to warn José and Delgado inside the room. José had been unarmed but Delgado could well have a pistol in that desk. He shouldered the Kalashnikov, flung the door open, and threw himself forward onto the floor, the rifle aimed at Delgado.

The sound was very loud in that small space. A shot had been fired all right, but not by Delgado.

36

Jim switched targets and fired almost before the smoke had left the barrel of José's pistol. José was thrown back against a bookshelf. He sank to his knees, then fell flat on his face. Jim glanced at the rifle. It was set for bursts and there'd been no time to change it. José had taken four rounds in the middle of the chest. One would have been enough.

Jim got to his feet and ran his fingers over the bullet embedded in the wall at the side of the door. A light rain of plaster powdered the dark floorboards. The bullet had been aimed for a target at normal height. If he'd walked into the room instead of diving in he would be the one lying on the floor now instead of José.

'How did he get that pistol?' he snapped, using English.

'It's mine, I threw it to him,' Delgado said calmly. 'I'm not much good with firearms. Well, since you're one of Aguilar's hit men and you've been sent to kill me, you'd better get it over with.'

'Don't be bloody silly,' Jim snarled, still breathing heavily. 'I haven't gone to all this trouble to kill you. I'm here to help you.'

Delgado's brow creased in a puzzled frown.

Jim crossed the room and looked down at José. A glance at the blood seeping into the carpet and spreading through the shirt from the ragged exit wounds in the man's back only confirmed what he already knew. 'You stupid, treacherous, vindictive son-of-a-bitch,' he muttered. 'Do you think I wanted to kill you?' He looked up at Delgado. 'Sorry about this mess. We need to talk. Is there somewhere else we can go?'

Delgado grimaced, but got up and led the way. In the corridor outside he paused to glance at the two sentries, one still cradling his streaming nose, the other unconscious. He raised an eyebrow at Jim, then wordlessly continued further along the corridor. Jim bent over the unconscious sentry and pulled the rifle out from under him before following Delgado. They entered a comfortable sitting-room. Delgado pointed to an armchair, then closed the door and took another armchair himself. Between the two there was a low table with a telephone handset on it. Jim put the two rifles on the floor within easy reach.

Delgado said, 'It is a shame that you killed José. Antonio Martinez relied on his support a great deal.'

'It shouldn't have happened, *señor*. It *needn't* have happened. Antonio Martinez left the organization in the hands of his daughter Rosa. José was loyal to her father, and she believed that he would also be loyal to her. But I am more than ever convinced that she was wrong to trust him. I think he really wanted to take her place and he saw me as one more obstacle in his way. In the end he was not much better than Óscar.'

'Yes, I met Óscar, too. What happened to him?'

'He set up a rival cartel, armed them, and attacked the Guárico headquarters. They were defeated and Óscar was killed.'

'You seem to have learned a great deal about that organization.'

'I suppose I have. Including the fact that they strongly support you and would like to see you take your rightful place as President of this country.'

'Is that what you came here to tell me?'

'I came here to deliver a message direct from the Pentagon, on behalf of the President of the United States.'

'Really?' Delgado inclined his head. 'And the message?'

'I'm to tell you that American troops have taken control of Caracas. President Aguilar has been forced to call a fresh election. We want you to come out of hiding and start campaigning.'

Delgado took a deep breath. 'Colonel, the only reason I am still alive, despite the no doubt strenuous efforts of Aguilar's agents, is that I have made no public appearances and I have kept this location strictly secret. Somehow you persuaded José to lead you here. He is now dead and two of my security staff have been disabled. Why should I believe you?'

Jim said, 'Sir, please ignore whatever lies José handed you. I am Colonel Jim Slater, Commanding Officer of the United States Special Assignment Force. I've been working under cover in your country, so I'm not in uniform and I'm carrying a false I.D. I think it would be best if you had an independent check of my identity and the message I've given you.' He gestured at the handset. 'May I suggest that you phone the Pentagon? Ask to speak to the Secretary of State for Defense, Bob Cressington. If he is not available you can speak to General Wendell Harken.'

Delgado met his eyes for a moment. His lips twitched but he nodded and pressed a combination on the handset. A conversation in rapid Spanish took place, presumably with his PA. It seemed longer than just an instruction to phone the Pentagon. Jim picked up the words *'nuestro invitado'* (our guest) and *'salón'* (lounge) and wondered what that was about. The rifles were close enough to touch with his fingertips. He manoeuvred one so that he could pick it up easily. Having got this far he had no intention of being caught by surprise.

For a while they waited in silence. Jim knew it wouldn't be easy for Delgado's PA to make the phone connection, but both Bob and Wendell were hoping to get this call and it would be put through – unless some asshole of a functionary blocked it. If that happened he had no other way of confirming his identity. What could he do then—?

Delgado straightened up in his chair. Someone was on the line. He said, 'Good morning, General.'

Great, he's through to Wendell.

'I am Juan-Luis Delgado. A man who calls himself Colonel Jim Slater is here. He asks you to confirm his identity for me.'

He handed the phone to Jim. 'He wants to speak to you.'

Jim said, 'Jim Slater here.'

'What's the code name?'

'Hallowe'en. With an apostrophe.'

'Excellent. Have you really found him?'

'Yes, I have. But I need you to confirm my identity.'

'Okay, Jim. You can give the phone back to him. Oh – and well done.'

Jim handed the phone to Delgado. A long conversation followed, mainly from the other end, punctuated by Delgado with an occasional 'Yes' or 'I understand' and frequent glances at Jim. Finally he said, 'Thank you, General, that's what I wanted to know.' He returned the receiver to the handset and looked up. His manner had changed; he was altogether less reserved.

'General Harken confirms you are who you say you are, Colonel. Which makes me wonder why José told me you were an agent of Aguilar. And why did he want to kill you?'

'He said I'd got too close to their organization and too close to Rosa.'

'He said that? When?'

'When he tried to kill me on the way here.'

Delgado's eyebrows went up and his mouth opened. 'He had tried to kill you once before this?'

'Yes. Only I was expecting something of the sort so I unloaded his revolver. The rounds were still in my pocket when one of your sentries checked me outside. They're probably in his pocket right now.'

'I don't understand. What did he have to gain from this?'

Jim shrugged. 'Perhaps he had ideas about bringing you out of hiding himself and using the cartel's people to provide you with protection.'

'I would never have agreed to that! I would have no confidence in such people and it would have placed me in the cartel's debt. Not the best recommendation for someone bidding for the Presidency and promising to clean up government!'

'I knew that, but it seems that José didn't,' Jim said. 'Some people are violent and some are stupid. He was both, unfortunately, and it got him killed.'

'We will deal with that matter later.' Delgado took a deep breath, then went on, 'General Harken informed me about the situation in Caracas. He says that the platoon you requested is standing by and he will ask them to depart immediately. Can you tell me what you have in mind?'

'Our people in Caracas are making arrangements for a free election, and expert inspectors will make sure that this time there is no interference with the votes, the counting, and the recording and reporting of results. If you come out and campaign we are expecting you to achieve a landslide victory. But we know what Aguilar is like and keeping you safe is our top priority. The platoon General Harken mentioned will be flying to Maicao the day after tomorrow. To avoid awkward questions they'll be identified as Drug Enforcement personnel.'

'How will we know when they have landed?'

'When they arrive – which should be the day after tomorrow – they'll use the number of a US cyber group operating in Maracaibo. That group will connect them to me on an encrypted line.' He dipped into his pocket and held up his communicator.

'Do they know where to find us?'

'No, and I don't want a whole convoy turning up here,' Jim said. 'Aguilar's people may have drones in the air looking out for you. I could meet them some distance from here. Where would you suggest?'

'Well,' Delgado said, 'I think it would be best if you crossed the border into Colombia and met them at the airport. I should come with you. I can negotiate the passage through customs into Colombia and back into Venezuela. Then we can pick up your platoon and go straight to Maracaibo.'

'That makes sense. Are there members of your household who could ride with us when we go through the border?'

'Yes, we can travel with two of my security people. They will be armed, of course, because there are bandits along the border.'

'I can get my rifle from the car, too. I don't think your bandits will mess with us – unless they are as stupid as José.'

'So,' Delgado said. 'I will tell the staff and we will prepare for the journey. But there is one thing more, which I would like you to explain, Colonel.'

Jim gestured with a palm. 'Certainly, if I can.'

'I understand from General Harken that an envoy was sent to negotiate with Aguilar's people. What happened to him?'

'They had no intention of negotiating. They were taking him to Buena Vista prison. We reported that to Washington. It was an act that defied every norm of international diplomacy. That's why the US invaded.'

'Yes, but what happened to the envoy?'

Jim paused, then said, 'I'm not at liberty to answer that.'

Delgado threw his head back and laughed. 'That's good, that's very good! You know, Colonel, you sound more English than American. Earlier, for example, you told me not to be bloody silly.'

Jim winced. 'Sorry about that. I'd come close to being shot, so I wasn't in the mood to be polite at the time.'

'Oh, I do understand. But you are English, are you not?'

'Yes, but I've lived in the States for thirteen years now.'

'This envoy. What was his name?'

'It was Dexter Maynard.'

'Dexter Maynard,' he repeated the name in what seemed like an unnecessarily loud voice.

The door opened and a man walked in.

Delgado said, 'This Dexter Maynard?'

'Hallo, Jim,' Dexter said.

37

President Nagel and the White House Chief of Staff, Carol Anders, entered the Situation Room. The President looked round the table, nodded to Admiral Mike Randall, Joe Templeton, Bob Cressington, and General George Wagner.

'Where's General Harken?' she asked.

'Wendell's not here yet, ma'am,' General Wagner answered.

'Very well, we'll start without him. I expect you've heard that the Russian Union tabled a resolution at the UN Security Council condemning our invasion of Venezuela. The Vice-President flew to New York City for the meeting. In the prior consultations he made it clear that we'd be opposing the resolution. The Russians, however, still wanted to bask in the glare of the media, so it went into full session. As expected, Vasily Karagonov, the Russian representative, fulminated for some time about US aggression, disrespect of international borders, flagrant disregard of a country's sovereignty, et cetera, et cetera, and called for an immediate withdrawal.'

There were a few murmurs around the table and George Wagner huffed a short, derisive laugh.

The President went on, 'I imagine you've been too busy to spend time watching the televised proceedings of the Security Council but I thought you might like to see how the VP replied. Carol?'

Carol Anders slipped a memory tile into a reader at the end of the table and the wall screen sprang into life. The picture showed the Security Council Chamber. South Africa had the Presidency this month and Will Engberts invited the United States to respond. The Vice-President got to his feet.

'May I say, Mr President, how much the United States has enjoyed the rich irony of the Russian ambassador's presentation. We are, of course, obliged to listen carefully to what he says, because in the last few years his country has amassed considerable experience of armed incursions into sovereign states. Unlike the Russian Union, however, the United States has no intention of occupying Venezuela permanently. We are in Venezuela because an envoy who was there to negotiate was taken instead to a prison, in naked violation of international conventions of diplomacy. Unfortunately this is typical of the practice of the current administration, which has, we believe, stayed in office only as a result of a falsified election. We intend to stay there only as long as it is necessary to ensure the conduct and reporting of a proper, free and fair election. This election will be overseen by an international team of observers, not just from the United States, but from the United Kingdom, France, and Germany. And we invite the Council to note that we in the United States have been committed to free and fair elections since the founding of our nation. Indeed our experience in these matters is considerably greater even than the experience of armed invasions of their neighbours by our

Russian colleagues. I will be voting against this resolution and I urge all nations who would wish to see a free and fair election in Venezuela to join me.'

The British ambassador raised a hand and was recognized. 'Mr President,' he said. 'In view of the statement by the United States I wonder whether it would be appropriate to defer consideration of this resolution until elections have been held in Venezuela. If, as stated, the United States then withdraws its forces there would be no need to revisit the issue.'

President Nagel signalled to Carol Anders to stop the projection.

'Engberts thought it was a good idea,' she said, 'but the Russians insisted on immediate withdrawal. So it went to a vote and it was soundly defeated. We didn't even have to use the veto.'

Those around the table nodded and smiled.

'As you heard the Vice-President say, the United Kingdom, France, and Germany have all agreed to send inspectors to help oversee the election. That's important, because it makes the scrutiny truly international and the entire election process will be seen to be legitimate.'

Bob Cressington said 'Excellent' and the others murmured agreement.

'What it does say to us, though,' she continued, 'is that it's imperative that we get this election under way. It isn't good for our international standing to be seen to be interfering in the internal affairs of another country and I want to bring the whole episode to a close as quickly as possible. Is there any news of Delgado?'

They shook their heads.

'Very well. Let me know if—'

Wendell Harken entered the room breathing hard. 'Please excuse my late arrival, Madam President,' he said. 'I received a phone call that I couldn't ignore. It was from Juan-Luis Delgado.'

They all straightened up.

President Nagel smiled. 'And...?'

'He wanted me to confirm the identity of the gentleman who'd just arrived. It was Colonel Slater.'

'Outstanding!' General Wagner said.

The President pointed to a chair and Wendell sat down. She said, 'Did you explain the situation?'

'Yes, ma'am,' Wendell said. 'And he's ready to plan his campaign, given our assurances of adequate protection. I told him there was a platoon of crack Special Forces on the way. SAF, of course.'

'Of course,' the President observed dryly. 'Well, that's very reassuring. Juan-Luis Delgado was always a good orator. If he hasn't lost his touch he should secure a majority, and of course that's the outcome we, and just about every other country, is looking for.'

'Everyone except the Russians,' the CSA commented.

The President smiled. 'Yes, George, everyone but the Russians.'

38

Jim leapt to his feet. 'Dexter, what the hell are you doing here?'

Dexter strolled over. He seemed like a totally different man to the exhausted, damp, and dishevelled individual Jim had last seen bidding farewell to Rosa. He was clean-shaven and wore a spotless short-sleeved shirt and lightweight trousers. He stood behind Delgado's armchair and placed a hand on the man's shoulder. 'We're good friends, have been for years. Met when I was an attaché at the US Embassy and we hit it off. I bought this house quite a while before that, when I was conducting business here and in Colombia.'

'What? This house belongs to you?'

'Yes, I bought it from a Colombian drug lord. He'd built it – illicitly of course – in case he needed a bolthole across the border. I expressed interest, he decided he no longer needed it, so it became mine. Then Aguilar became President. He was virulently anti-American from the get-go, closed the US Embassy and chucked the staff out of Venezuela, me included. I had to return to the States but I kept the house on. When Aguilar was re-elected –

fraudulently, this time – I let Juan-Luis move in. I thought he'd be safe here because officially the house doesn't exist.'

'You bugger, you could have vouched for me just now.'

'No I couldn't,' Dexter said. 'I'm supposed to be in Buena Vista prison, remember?'

Jim turned to Delgado. 'You must have known who I was all the time.'

'I could not be sure. And José told me you were a hitman for Aguilar, so I had to confirm your identity. I did it through official channels, because if I'd asked Dexter to do it there would have been some very awkward questions to answer later on. In any case,' he added with a mischievous grin, 'it would have spoilt the fun. I hope you don't mind.'

Jim uttered an uneasy laugh. 'Okay, okay. So what are you going to do now, Dexter? You can't help in the campaign—'

'No, no, if they find out I'm still at large it won't be good for anyone. I'll stay here. It was safe for Juan-Luis, so it should be safe enough for me. And when he's installed in the Palace he won't be needing this place any more.'

Delgado placed his hand over Dexter's, which was still resting on his shoulder. He said, 'Dexter has been more than a friend to me, he has been like a brother. As he says, I have lived in his house safely ever since Aguilar stole the election. He knows that if he ever needs my support or protection he will have it, no questions asked.'

Dexter looked across at Jim. 'I couldn't hear much of your conversation from outside. How will you protect Juan-Luis when he's on the campaign trail?'

'A platoon of my own men will fly in the day after tomorrow. They'll land at Macaio, and we'll meet them there.'

Dexter nodded. 'Riohacha airport. And I expect you'll be accompanying them throughout.'

'I wasn't planning to.'

A short silence hung in the air. Delgado looked at him. 'You weren't?'

'Well, no. The platoon will come in on a military transport, and I can go back to the States on the same plane.'

Delgado said slowly, 'I don't think you should do that.'

'What? Why not?'

'Colonel, the United States has gone to enormous trouble and great expense to secure a new election here. It would be disappointing – would it not? – if, after all that, Aguilar was returned to power.'

'Absolutely.'

'And that's why I think you should remain here. You need to see the whole process through, including the safe conduct of my campaign.'

Jim took a breath. 'I arranged for you to get a platoon of my own men under the command of a lieutenant-colonel. They're perfectly suited for missions of this type. Why do you need me as well?'

Delgado smiled patiently. 'As an American you took a risk coming to Venezuela in the first place. You took an even greater risk when you rescued Dexter from his army escort.'

Jim's eyebrows shot up and he glanced at Dexter.

'Yes,' Delgado said. 'Dexter told me all about it. And it's clear to me now that you took yet another risk when you agreed to let José guide you here.'

242

'So…'

'So you are a man who can survive under dangerous conditions. You think ahead strategically. Just the sort of person I need for my protection. That's why I think you should stay.'

'All right, I'll think about it.'

'Good. Dexter, would you be kind enough to ask the staff to arrange for the Colonel's accommodation tonight and tomorrow night?'

'Certainly.'

'Thank you. Now, we must not forget that a man is lying dead in my study. I will arrange for his burial. It will not be a religious ceremony but it will be respectful.'

Jim nodded.

Perhaps I should be feeling a shred of regret about that but I don't feel anything of the sort. What was it he said? 'May God strike me dead if I harm you.' Well it wasn't God who struck you dead, José, it was me, you lying bastard, and for all sorts of reasons it's a lot better this way.

There was no more discussion that day. Jim noticed a lot of activity about the house as preparations were made for imminent departure. He had a pleasant meal with the others in the evening and a member of staff showed him to the room they'd provided for his stay. It was basic: a bed, a side-table with a reading light, a chair, and a wardrobe. It was already dark outside, but his mental map told him it was at the back of the house. He locked the door, just in case those sentries had recovered enough to think about getting even. He'd hit them pretty hard and he felt some sympathy but that didn't mean he was going to put himself at risk for the third time in one day.

He lay awake for a while, staring at the ceiling and thinking about his options. He'd be going back to the States, no doubt about that; the question was not whether but when? He could return to Fort Piper and resume command there the day after tomorrow. Like he'd said, all he had to do was go back on the military transport that brought Tommy Geiger and the platoon out.

He brushed his hand over the cold, unoccupied half of the double bed. He knew why he was debating this: it was the appeal of returning instead to the cartel's HQ. It would be easy enough. He could drive the vehicle José had used. He'd memorized the route and in any case he had the coordinates on his watch, so he'd have no trouble finding it. Once there he could live under Rosa's sensual spell for a while, and do it without José's malevolent cloud hanging over them. He could make sure she was safe, perhaps help her in her management of the Guárico cartel. He'd take a trip or two to the major cities where Delgado would be holding open-air rallies, as a way of legitimizing his continued presence in the country. He could even smooth the path for Rosa by reintroducing her to Delgado there.

He smiled and shook his head. It was an inviting prospect, but it simply wouldn't be fair to Rosa. They both knew their relationship was over when they parted company. Reviving it for a while would only create more heartache when it had to end again.

So he'd go back on that military transport. Delgado's security would be assured but it would be Tommy, not him, in charge of it.

Even as he made the resolution an image of Rosa came into his mind. He half-closed his eyes, wondering whether he could stick to it.

39

He breakfasted with Delgado and Dexter. Delgado was polite enough to wait until they'd finished eating before asking Jim what he'd decided to do.

'I won't be accompanying you, sir. My men are highly trained and very experienced. Every one of them has been exposed to danger many times and they can anticipate problems and take appropriate action. I'll be leaving you in good hands.'

Delgado shrugged. 'Well, of course I cannot keep you here. But we have a day before your platoon arrives. Perhaps you could give us the benefit of your opinion as we begin to plan the conduct of the campaign.'

'I'd be glad to, if you think that would be helpful.'

'Excellent. I'll introduce you to my campaign manager, Alvaro Gomes.'

'He's here?'

Delgado smiled. 'Yes. You know, the previous campaign was highly successful and would have ended in the Palacio de Miraflores if it hadn't been for the way Aguilar's people manipulated the results. Because of that Alvaro felt that he was a potential target for Aguilar's assassins. He knew they would torture him to ascertain my whereabouts before they killed him. So I offered to accommodate him in this house, and he wisely accepted.'

They went straight to the sitting room they'd used on the previous day. Dexter and Alvaro joined them there.

Delgado began by saying, 'Alvaro is happy if we conduct our discussion in English.'

They nodded.

'I have explained the situation to him. We will meet the platoon at Maicao tomorrow and proceed with them to Maracaibo, where we will start the campaign.'

'Yes,' Alvaro said. 'My main concern is security. Colonel, this platoon that is arriving. How many people is that?'

'In this case it's eighteen.'

'And is that enough?'

'Oh yes. Those men are from my unit, the Special Assignment Force. They'll be Spanish-speaking and they're ideal for a protection detail like this. They'll be well equipped: they'll carry weapons, of course – conventional and crowd control, but they'll also have surveillance and attack drones, and surface-to-air missiles in case of an attack from the air, all standard on such an operation. They won't be working alone, either. A group in Maracaibo will be listening for radio activity from Aguilar's people and the Venezuelan army; they'll keep us informed if they're up to any dirty tricks. And when you are in the coastal area you'll have the support of the US Army force down there as well.'

'Thank you, that is reassuring,' Alvaro said. 'What about the Guárico cartel? I'm sure they would be willing to help with security.'

Delgado shook his head. 'No, Alvaro. People have had enough of cartels in the service of the President. I want to distance myself from that sort of thing.'

'I understand. So, we start in Maracaibo. That will be a good base for us, won't it, Juan-Luis?'

'Yes,' Delgado said. 'We could use the hotel we had before. You should book the whole of the top floor. Then we can accommodate the soldiers and our staff as well.'

'What about security there?' Alvaro asked.

Jim said, 'Our people will certainly be mounting guards on the elevators and fire stairs. And maybe someone to watch the entrance.'

Alvaro nodded. 'Good. Well, we should start with a television campaign. There is a well-equipped television studio in the city, so we can transmit from there. You can make speeches, Juan-Luis, and hold interviews with journalists.'

Jim said, 'The US Army has control of the national television stations so they can make sure you get good coverage. And of course my platoon will provide protection, wherever you go.'

'May I?' Dexter asked.

'Certainly,' Delgado replied, opening a hand.

'I think we shouldn't underestimate the difficulties, Juan-Luis. This won't be like the last time. It's several years since that last election and you haven't been in the public eye for the whole of that time. Some people may not remember you or what you stood for. Others will remember you, but they'll think you're totally out of touch. You'll need to show them that you know what the problems are for the country, the effect it's having on the citizens – and how you can change it all. You have to be recognizable as a person and as a credible opponent of Aguilar and you have to do it all over again. In marketing terms you have to re-establish your brand.'

He translated this quickly into Spanish for Alvaro, to make sure he understood. Jim noticed how effortlessly Dexter spoke the language.

Alvaro nodded vigorously. 'You are right, Dexter. I can help with that. I have good contacts in Maracaibo and Caracas and I will put together a team who will go out and talk to local people: fishermen, farmers, housewives, leaders of industry. We will find out, Juan-Luis, what their problems are so that you can show that you care and understand and will look after them.'

Delgado said, 'Thank you, that is very important. I have tried to keep in touch with developments here and abroad, of course, but the local newspapers are controlled by the administration. In better times I used to take the *Washington Post*. There was often a useful column in there commenting on Venezuela and Colombia.'

Jim smothered a smile, recognizing the reference to Aidan Somersby's reports.

'Of course there will be posters everywhere,' Alvaro said, 'a good picture of you, Juan-Luis, and something like "Vote for a better Venezuela, vote Delgado". When we have generated a little excitement we will arrange for you to address an open-air meeting.'

Jim said, 'I assume your staff can erect a podium with a bullet-proof glass screen?'

'Yes, all that is normal,' Alvaro said. 'We will need good security, of course. It's best to use the stadium, then we can control the entrances and make sure the scanners are working. After Maracaibo, we will do something similar in Barquisimeto and we can end up at Caracas. My staff may suggest other venues along the way. They will make all the arrangements.'

'What about a debate with Aguilar?' Dexter asked.

There was a short silence. Then Alvaro raised his eyebrows and tilted his head. 'I think that would be a good idea. What do you say, Juan-Luis? The debate went well for you when we did it last time.'

'Certainly. It's the only chance the people get to compare the candidates side by side. So if he challenges us to have one, we will accept. If he does not, we will challenge him.'

'Don't do it in person,' Jim said. 'He will simply interrupt and shout you down. I suggest you do it virtually. You make the rules: each of you is allowed a maximum of two minutes to speak. If that is exceeded your microphone will be muted, and the other speaker will have his turn.'

Delgado laughed. 'That will infuriate Aguilar.'

'Yes, and it will also unsettle him, which is good. Even so, a man like that won't leave the debate, he would lose too much face.'

'Have you got that, Alvaro?' Delgado asked.

Alvaro grinned. 'I have.'

'Is there anything else?'

Jim thought for a moment. 'I suggest you take your house staff with you on the campaign. Even in the hotels I advise you to accept only food and drink they have purchased themselves and prepared.'

Delgado gave him a rueful smile. 'Yes, I can see the sense in that. But you know, all my staff have been very loyal over these years and if I am elected I will transfer them to the Palace to serve me there, too.'

'That's generous of you, sir.'

'Oh, it's no great sacrifice. I have a very fine cook and she knows exactly what I like.'

He rose to his feet and they all followed suit.

'Well,' Alvaro said, 'I must arrange for our stay in Maracaibo. When we have settled in we can make more detailed plans.'

Dexter said, 'I'll be off for a while, visiting some friends around here. I guess you'll be back in the States by the time I return, Jim, so I'll say goodbye now.'

They shook hands and Dexter met Jim's eyes and held his hand a little longer. 'Thank you for giving me my life back, Jim,' he said softly, his voice close to breaking. 'It was just about the finest thing anyone could do.'

Jim smiled. 'Good luck, Dexter.'

40

At three o'clock the next afternoon Jim's communicator buzzed. He switched it on.

'Jim Slater.'

'Colonel, it's Harry.'

'Go ahead, Harry.'

'Your platoon's landed at Maicao, Riohacha airport. Shall I put you through?'

'Yes, thanks.'

There was a pause, then a familiar voice came on the line. 'Jim?'

'Hi, Tommy.'

Jim pictured him at the other end of the line: Lieutenant-Colonel Tommy Geiger, with his compact build and earnest expression that easily broke into a smile. No doubt he'd be smiling right now. He did a fine job as second-in-command back at Fort Piper but he'd be delighted to have this mission for a change.

'Hi, Jim. Got a bunch of good guys here. Where do you want to meet up?'

'Stay where you are, Tommy. We'll come and meet you at the airport. I'll have Delgado with me and a couple of his security guards. They'll conduct you through the border and down to Maracaibo. That'll be your base to start with.'

'Great.'

'Who did you leave in charge at Fort Piper?'

'Well I left Bagley to stall any routine enquiries. General Harken knows the situation so he won't be putting any more missions our way at the moment. There's an outside chance we might get something from the CIA. If we do, I told Bagley to direct it to Major Veratti.'

'That's fine. Is the transport that brought you still there?'

'Yeah, I told them to stay put until I contacted them again. I thought you might need a ride.'

'That was good thinking. I'll fly back with him.'

'Sure you don't want to come with us? It'd be good to have you on board.'

'Thanks, but I think I've done enough here. I'll leave you to handle it Ask the pilot of that transport plane to wait for us.'

'Will do. See you later.'

*

Either there were no bandits at the border or they were deterred by the rifles extending from their vehicle's windows and stayed well hidden. Delgado conducted his small party smoothly through the border control into Colombia and they drove to the airport. Tommy was waiting for them and Jim brought him over.

'Tommy, this is Juan-Luis Delgado. Señor, I'd like you to meet Lieutenant-Colonel Tommy Geiger.'

Delgado extended a hand. 'I am pleased to meet you, Colonel.'

'You can call me Tommy, sir. Don't worry, we're going to take very good care of you.'

'Tommy,' Jim said. 'I don't want to keep that aircraft waiting any longer. Would you join your guys for a moment while I take my leave here?'

'Sure thing.'

As Tommy was walking over to his platoon Jim shook hands with Delgado. 'I hope all goes well, sir,' he said. 'If we should meet again I expect to be speaking to the President of Venezuela.'

Delgado smiled. 'We have some way to go, Colonel, but if that happens you will be always be a most welcome guest.'

'Thank you.' He took a breath. 'There's just one more thing. We spoke earlier about the Guárico cartel, and I do understand your reservations – that outfit has the usual history of unpleasant activities. But Rosa's a smart businesswoman and she's taking steps to move her people away from those areas into legitimate enterprises. She's totally committed to seeing you in the Miraflores Palace – in fact it was Rosa who told José to bring me to you. What I'm saying is, when you become President the time may come when her support wouldn't be a political embarrassment.'

Delgado nodded. 'Thank you. I will remember that.'

Jim hesitated for a moment. Then he said, 'I expect you'll meet Rosa in due course. I hope you can tell her about José, and how he got himself killed. And, well, I'd like you to explain that I had to return to the United States, and… and I…' He looked down, then took a breath. 'I guess that's it.'

Delgado smiled. He'd got the message.

Jim went over to Tommy. 'Okay, I'll go now. You know the score: protection at all times, especially in any public places.' He paused. 'The main threat will come from...'

He looked up at Tommy, staring so intensely that his colleague's head jerked back. 'I've changed my mind. Tell the pilot he can leave. The job's not finished.'

41

The convoy rolled on to Maracaibo. Alvaro led the way in the four-wheel drive that José had driven to Delgado's house. Behind him were four armoured vehicles and an armoured truck for the heavier equipment, all bearing the insignia of the Drug Enforcement Agency. Delgado was in one of the armoured vehicles.

Jim, who was in the passenger seat next to Alvaro, said little. He was angry with himself. He'd found Delgado, seen to it that the campaign had started, and arranged for close protection. Yet all this time he'd been neglecting the bigger picture. He closed his eyes and shook his head. Up to that moment at the airport he'd been so preoccupied with whether or not to see Rosa again that he'd completely lost sight of the chief danger. Well now he was going to put that right.

On arrival in Maracaibo they promptly occupied a sizeable chunk of the hotel's car park. As soon as they'd checked in Alvaro went back to work on the organization of the rally and the television broadcasts. Jim gave his uniform – damp, creased, and muddy – to hotel staff to be cleaned and pressed. Then he took one of the rooms and remained there to make phone calls and notes, leaving Tommy to supervise the installation of Delgado and his staff, and the SAF platoon. They met up later for a meal, most of which the kitchen staff had brought with them.

'How are you getting on, Alvaro?' Jim asked over coffee.

'All is in progress now. I made a lot of preparations before we left.'

'And the rally?'

'That has been the biggest problem. Did it really have to be the day after tomorrow, Jim? It would have been much easier if we had more time.'

'Sorry, yes. I'll explain why later.'

'Well,' Alvaro said with a shrug, 'the company I use is doing their best to print the posters quickly but they may not be ready in time. I have arranged for announcements to be made on television and by loudspeaker vans touring the streets.'

'Excellent idea. Now would it be possible to leave your assistants to handle things tomorrow?'

Alvaro raised his eyebrows. 'Why, what is tomorrow?'

'I'd like you and Tommy to come with me to Caracas. I've set up a meeting with Colonel Philip Weaver. He's in overall command of the American forces here.'

*

Although Jim hadn't been to Caracas before he could bet things never looked like they did today. In the city centre there were military vehicles buzzing around and US soldiers in evidence on the streets. Security was, as expected, particularly tight at the Miraflores Palace, but Jim had anticipated that by making prior arrangements. The sentries did no more than check I.D.s before raising the barrier and waving them in. They parked the car and walked across an open area now occupied by tanks and khaki vehicles with the big white star on the door. American flags fluttered in a feeble breeze. As they approached the building Jim noted the bullet marks on the façade and on the massive doors. A corporal stepped forward and saluted.

'Colonel Slater, here to see Colonel Weaver. These are my associates.'

'Yes, sir, we were told to expect you. I'll take you there.' He shouted to a private. 'Sean, take over the door, will you?'

As they followed the corporal, Alvaro looked about him wide-eyed. The interior of the building still breathed opulence – thickly carpeted corridors, decorated ceilings, statues in niches, paintings and costly fabrics – although it was badly scarred in places by the recent conflict. They stopped outside an office door on which an improvised notice had been pinned.

COLONEL P.G. WEAVER

The corporal knocked, opened the door, and announced, 'Colonel Slater for you, sir.' Then he nodded to the visitors and left.

Weaver came out from behind a desk to shake hands. He was stocky, somewhat ruddy in appearance. His moustache was greying but his hair, though thin, was still dark. His shirtsleeves were neatly rolled back above the elbows. Jim saw the tunic hanging on the back of his chair. He shook hands vigorously with Jim, and with Tommy and Alvaro as they were introduced. Then he indicated chairs in front of his desk and returned to his own.

'General Harken told me to expect you,' Weaver said. 'It's my understanding this has to do with a candidate in the coming election who the US administration wants to protect. The General's orders were very clear: give you any assistance you request.' He leaned forward, placing thick forearms on the table, and his voice became strident, as if addressing a company rather than three people sitting on the other side of his desk. 'Colonel,' he said. 'I have just conducted an invasion of this goddamned country, directing and coordinating a force that comprises US Navy, Marines, infantry and paratroops of the US Army. We have taken over the airports, the television stations and the seat of government, including this here Palace, with, I might add, minimal casualties—'

'Three dead, eight wounded,' Jim put in quickly.

Weaver raised his eyebrows, evidently registering that Jim had access to the highest security levels, which was exactly what Jim had intended.

'Well, yes,' Weaver said gruffly. 'Light casualties for such a comprehensive operation.' His voice rose again. 'So let me level with you. Bearing all this in mind, I do not believe it's actually beyond my abilities to mount a straightforward protection detail. Which leaves me wondering why I need the help of goddamned special forces down here.' He sat back in a single, emphatic movement.

Jim smiled. 'Colonel, I congratulate you on conducting a first-class – one might say text-book – operation. I can assure you that no one doubts your abilities to mount a straightforward protection detail, least of all me. The question is: is it really straightforward?'

Weaver frowned. 'You saying it's not?'

'Yes, I am. You probably know what's been going on in this country over recent years. President Aguilar doesn't tolerate opposition; he's had any serious political contenders jailed and tortured to death. The one exception is Jean-Luis Delgado, who would be President now if Aguilar hadn't rigged the election results. The US and about fifty other countries want Delgado instated, and the election process is now in train, thanks to your ultimatum to President Aguilar.' Again Jim saw that this high-level intelligence was not lost on the Colonel. 'Delgado has come out of hiding to campaign in the election, at considerable personal risk. It's up to us to make sure he stays safe. If we don't, Aguilar will be returned and this superb operation of yours will be for nothing.'

'Shit, Colonel,' Weaver said impatiently. 'I know all that.'

'Of course you do. You also know that Aguilar's tactics are crude: arrest by soldiers or armed police, or assassination – a sniper at a rally, or a pistol or knife at close quarters if a suitable fanatic can be found to do it. He could blame any of it on a drug cartel. That's the kind of thing you're familiar with, and I'm sure you can handle it.'

'Damn right I can.'

'The real problem is the Russians.'

Weaver's face went blank for a moment. 'Russians?'

'Yes. Russia wants a foothold in South America and for some time that foothold's been Venezuela. Right now, for reasons which may emerge sooner or later, they have an even stronger stake in the country than ever before. They're not going to give it up easily. If Delgado comes to power they'll be forced to, no question about it. That would represent a major setback for them. The easiest solution would be to assassinate Delgado before it can happen.' Jim leaned forward. 'The Russians are a very different proposition to Aguilar's thugs. Their methods are subtle and they've perfected them over many years. That's what we could be up against and that, Colonel, is what you may not be ready for.'

Weaver chewed his lip thoughtfully. Then he said, 'All right, what do you propose?'

'They normally use a couple of agents,' Jim said. 'First question is: how are they going to get here? They're not going to land at the airports, because you have total control of the traffic.'

'They'll fly as passengers into a neighbouring country like Brazil or Colombia, rent a car, and drive in.'

Jim was gratified to see that Weaver was engaged now, entering into the thought process.

'Okay, so we can't stop them coming in. What we have to do is make it harder for them to predict where Delgado will be next.'

Weaver nodded.

Jim turned to Alvaro. 'You see why the rally in Macaibo has to take place as soon as possible? It'll take at least a couple of days to get a couple of assassins into the country, so we've got a breathing space, but only a short one. After that you'll have to abandon the hotel in Maracaibo. Don't cancel the booking, though. If someone checks they'll think he's still there. That gives us a little more time.'

Alvaro said, 'I see.' He was taking notes.

'After the rally we need to move on. Wherever we go, we travel in a convoy and put Delgado in different vehicles each time.'

'Give him a helmet to wear?' Weaver suggested.

'Excellent idea. If anyone's waiting with an RPG they won't know what to aim at. It won't even be clear whether he's on the move or not.'

Weaver gave a wry smile.

'Hotels,' Jim said. 'Alvaro, make reservations at the last minute. There shouldn't be a problem about it; there'll be plenty of vacancies at the moment. Always do the booking in person. No conversations on open lines. We'll make it hard for anyone to know where Delgado is and where he'll be next.'

'Okay,' Jim went on. 'Next, television. We don't want to book studios everywhere you stop – gives the assassins too many opportunities. Alvaro, see if Juan-Luis will make a whole batch of videos while you're in Maracaibo. They can be shown one at a time throughout the campaign.'

'Okay,' Alvaro said. 'I'm sure he will agree to do that. What about the debate?'

Jim turned to Weaver. 'There's going to be a television debate between Delgado and Aguilar,' he said. 'But it'll be done virtually, not face-to-face. Alvaro, it would probably be best not to film Juan-Luis in a studio. You have a good camera team. They can do it in his hotel suite. We'll have to set up network connections there.'

Alvaro nodded.

'You can't keep Delgado's location secret all the time,' Weaver said. 'I guess he'll be addressing meetings and rallies. You have to let the public know, and you're telling the agents at the same time.'

'That's right, Colonel,' Jim said. 'The main danger is a contact poison. Can you lay your hands on some surgical gloves?'

'Sure, the medics will have plenty.'

'Okay. We'll get Delgado to wear them wherever he goes. He can take them off before he appears in front of cameras or when he's in his own quarters.' Jim turned to Alvaro again. 'Obviously there must be no mingling with crowds or shaking hands.'

'He likes to do that, so I'll tell him,' Alvaro said, and scribbled some more.

Jim returned to Weaver. 'Lieutenant-Colonel Geiger here is in charge of the SAF contingent, but he only has eighteen men. We really need a much bigger presence, to police the rallies, escort the convoy, and provide security at the hotels. That's where I'd really appreciate your input.'

'No problem about that, you have it. I'll assign a company to this and get the captain to liaise with you.'

'Excellent. Well, I think that's all, Colonel. I'm very grateful for your help.'

They all stood, and Weaver shook hands with them across the desk. 'Colonel Slater, Colonel Geiger, Mr Gomez, thanks for coming. I'm glad to know what we could be up against.'

When they were outside Tommy Geiger blew out a breath. 'My God, Jim, I'm glad you were here to talk to that guy. I couldn't have managed it the way you did. And all that stuff about the Russians – I didn't know any of that.'

Jim smiled. 'I suddenly realized it wouldn't be fair on you. I have access to information which you don't, and anyway Weaver was more likely to listen to someone of his own rank.'

'So, we going back to Maracaibo?'

'Yes. We'll update Jean-Luis later today.'

*

An hour after they'd left the Miraflores Palace, Vicente Torres, President Aguilar's campaign manager, arrived at the entrance. He found his way blocked by the usual pole barrier, but it was manned this time by a US sentry. The sentry stepped forward.

'I.D.'

Torres placed his card in the waiting hand and watched the soldier check it. 'I have an appointment with President Aguilar,' he said.

'Moment.'

The sentry turned away and took a cell from his pocket. He spoke for a while, then came back. 'Okay,' he said, returning the I.D. 'One of the soldiers at the door will take you up.'

'Thank you.'

His eyes widened as he emerged into the familiar apron, now occupied by tanks and other American vehicles. At the entrance he was challenged again, patted down, then conducted to Aguilar's office.

'Vicente!' Aguilar said expansively. 'Come in, take a seat. You know Javier.'

Torres nodded to Javier Arellano, head of the Los Feroces cartel. Arellano was wearing jeans and a high-necked black sweater, and he was sitting in front of the massive desk with his legs stretched out in front of him. He acknowledged the new arrival with a slow closing and opening of his eyes.

To Torres nothing in here seemed to have changed. The office was the same as before, and Aguilar seemed unperturbed by what had been happening outside. His straight hair, a dull black from constant dying, was combed back; his moustache, also dyed, was carefully trimmed; his deeply-tanned skin was shiny and tight, thanks to his plastic surgeons. He wore a creaseless dark grey suit with the jacket unbuttoned. Torres sat down awkwardly in the empty chair next to Arellano.

'So, Vicente, you knew I would be calling upon you.'

'Yes, Señor. I saw your announcement of the election.'

Aguilar made a throwaway gesture with one hand. 'I did it to satisfy these American fools and get them out of our country. We will run the election like we did last time. Javier will handle my security – I can't trust the Army, they're too incompetent even to take a couple of prisoners to jail. There will be observers this time, but so what? Apart from me there are no realistic candidates.'

Torres moistened his lips. 'Sir, there's Delgado. He's out, and he's campaigning.'

Aguilar's bonhomie vanished. His face set and his eyes bored into Torres. He placed both hands flat on the desk and spoke slowly. 'When did this happen?'

To Torres' relief Arellano answered. 'They moved into a hotel in Maracaibo yesterday.'

'How come you know this and my secret police do not?'

Arellano smiled. 'I thought the election announcement would bring him out. I had some observers in Maracaibo – that's where he based himself last time.'

'So kill him. Or take some police and arrest him, then kill him.'

265

'Not so easy,' Arellano said. 'He has an escort of American Special Forces and it looks like they're well equipped. I expect they'll be reinforced by some of the troops they landed last week.'

'He'll hold rallies.'

'They'll hold them in stadia and turn away anyone who triggers the metal detectors.'

'A drone strike?'

'A protection detail like that will have missiles.'

'Put a bomb in his car? Or put a grenade under it when he's on the move?'

'It's a bit obvious, don't you think? In any case the Americans will be looking out for tactics like that.'

Torres noticed how relaxed Arellano seemed to be. He only wished he felt the same way.

'Señor,' Torres said, 'you have a good following, and Delgado hasn't been seen for some time. Most people have forgotten him. It will surely satisfy the Americans if you fight the campaign and beat him.' Seeing Aguilar's features darken he added quickly, 'As you will.'

There was a short silence, during which he again faced that penetrating stare.

'All right, Vicente. We will run a strong campaign…'

Torres saw what was coming and quickly took out his notebook and pen.

'You will have access to an unlimited budget,' Aguilar said. 'We will have big rallies, fifty thousand or more – Javier, your people will protect me. Aircraft will trail banners across the sky. Parades in the streets, at least ten thousand people, the army marching with them, carrying flags. Have them in every major city, everyone chanting

"Americans, Out, Out, Out, Aguilar, In, In, In" '. He paused and nodded. 'That's good. Have you made a note of all this, Vicente?'

Torres was writing as fast as he could, despite gripping the pen so hard that his knuckles had whitened.

'The Americans have taken over the television stations,' Aguilar continued, 'but we will tell them it's only fair that I have equal time.' His mouth twisted. 'That is a great weakness of the Americans: they worship fairness. Vicente, I'm depending on you to organize all of this.'

Torres felt a churning in his stomach. Nasty things happened to people who Aguilar decided he could no longer depend upon.

Aguilar sat back. 'Delgado will have nothing like our resources. His campaign will look feeble by comparison. We will wipe the floor with him.'

*

After dinner Jim sat down with Alvaro and Tommy to update Delgado on their conversation with Colonel Weaver. Delgado looked very grave and took all the points on board. The first of the television speeches would be broadcast the following day, and he went off to make a list of the topics he'd cover when he recorded the series of videos. They would be transmitted at intervals as the campaign progressed.

That evening a Captain Nowicki phoned Jim and told him he'd been put in charge of the infantry company assigned by Colonel Weaver to the protection operation. They arranged to meet up at the stadium early next morning. Things were beginning to fall into place.

42

They were ten days into the campaign.

The first television broadcasts had gone out, and everywhere they went there were posters up, loudspeaker vans in the streets, and leaflets being distributed. As anticipated, Aguilar challenged Delgado to a debate, and Delgado accepted the challenge but set the rules. It would be held virtually.

Jim had no doubt that the Russian assassins were already in the country, probably plugged into Aguilar's surveillance systems or possibly their own, waiting for their opportunity. But thanks to Jim and Alvaro's careful organization, Tommy's SAF squad, and Captain Nowicki's infantry company, they'd been given no such opportunity and the campaign was now well under way.

Today they were in Barquisimeto, a key city for them. The rally here seemed to have gone well although, as in Maracaibo, turnout hadn't been as large as they'd hoped.

After dinner Jim went to the sitting-room with Delgado and Alvaro to discuss progress.

'What do the polls look like, Alvaro?' Delgado asked as they sat down.

Alvaro sighed. 'I'm afraid it's still in the balance, Juan-Luis.'

Delgado frowned.

'I thought it was going pretty well,' Jim said. 'What's the problem?'

'We have support,' Alvaro said. 'Our problem is getting them to turn out. After the previous election some people think voting is a waste of time because Aguilar will rig the result anyway. Others have been swept along by the anti-American sentiment Aguilar has stirred up. They are quite prepared to believe that the US is entirely responsible for the state of their economy and they resent the invasion of their country. Then you have Aguilar's power base: the army, the better-off – most of them in Caracas, the people who have been awarded contracts and given bribes by his government and the cartel that supports him—'

'Los Feroces,' Jim said.

'Yes, Los Feroces,' Alvaro said. 'They will all cast their votes for Aguilar.' He shrugged. 'That's how things stand.'

'You must not worry, Alvaro,' Delgado said. 'Tomorrow we will be in Caracas, and the next day we will have the debate. After that, things are going to change. You'll see.'

*

'What are the polls looking like today, Vicente?'

Aguilar was holding his daily meeting with Vicente Torres and Javier Arellano.

'You have a clear lead, Señor,' Torres said. 'Everything is going well.'

'And in two days' time we will have our debate and that will be the end of Delgado.'

There was a short silence.

Arellano said casually, 'I wouldn't underestimate Delgado. In the last election he came out of the debate pretty well.'

Torres swallowed. It took someone in Arellano's position to even suggest such a thing to Aguilar. Curiously, though, Aguilar didn't erupt in his usual way. He gave them a one-sided smile, but his eyes were dead.

'Don't worry,' he said. 'I have friends, some very good friends. They are going to make sure that things go well in the debate.' He shrugged and the smile spread further. 'If there is a debate.'

43

Delgado's campaign was progressing as planned but the polls continued to be deeply disappointing. He received each set of figures with a calm confidence that seemed to Jim misplaced, and at times infuriating. On current ratings Aguilar would be the clear winner with all that meant for this country, for the reputation of the US, and the families of the US soldiers killed or injured in the invasion.

Had the CIA miscalculated? It certainly wouldn't be the first time. The huge rallies and marches orchestrated by the incumbent President's campaign managers were only part of it; Aguilar was riding a wave of anti-American sentiment. The people didn't want him, but they wanted the Americans in their country even less. He'd projected himself as the candidate who would get them out, and that was the message he was driving home in his television speeches and his long addresses to the rallies.

Delgado's rallies were on a smaller scale, his television appearances lower-key. Jim couldn't see them changing anything. Their one slender hope rested on the forthcoming debate. The ground rules for the debate would help Delgado. He was a skilled and articulate speaker, nimble on his feet, and he'd have no problem making telling points within his two minutes. Aguilar on the other hand, relied on bluster. If he behaved in his usual domineering manner he'd run out of time. And while his opponent was speaking his own mic would be muted, so there was no way he could shout him down. Delgado should emerge well – *if it was a level playing-field*. That was the part that worried Jim. So it was time to take the initiative.

He used the computer in his room to assemble a list of the larger hotels, then drove to Caracas armed with the list and a map of Caracas.

He started with a hotel not far from the Miraflores Palace. As he got out of the car he was met by the usual wall of hot, humid air. It was a relief to step inside the air-conditioned interior of the hotel. At the reception desk he explained that he had to make a reservation for a large party and he wanted to inspect their best accommodation. The receptionist summoned one of the managers.

'Please come with me, sir,' he said, leading Jim to the elevator.' He pressed the button for the top floor and they emerged into a carpeted corridor.

'On this floor most of the rooms are suites, sir,' he explained. 'Would you like to see inside one?'

'No, that won't be necessary.' He pointed to an elevator with a smaller door. 'Is that a service lift?'

'Yes, sir.'

'What's it used for?'

'Cleaners, room service, and the man who deals with the minibar.'

Jim looked up and down the corridor. He said, 'Okay, I've seen enough.'

'Would you like to make your reservation now?'

'Are you heavily booked?'

The manager smiled. 'In the current circumstances, no.'

'Then I'll just take details and make any reservation by telephone. Thank you for your trouble.'

'No trouble at all, sir. We look forward to seeing you.'

In fact what he'd seen didn't suit Jim's purposes at all, and he walked to the next one on the list.

The next five he visited were also hotels of recent vintage, and none were suitable. The seventh, called 'The Excelsior', looked more promising. It was clearly a much older building, perhaps a government building or embassy in its day that had been converted to a hotel.

When the manager arrived at reception he glanced at the uniform and said 'May I help you?' in good English.

Jim replied in English. 'I'm here on behalf of some senior people. I'm looking for suitable accommodation. We would need an entire floor. Possibly more than one.'

The manager kept a commendably neutral countenance. 'That would not be a problem at the moment, sir. These are not normal times and we have a lot of vacancies. Please come with me.'

They began the tour. Jim didn't want to use the elevator, so they ascended a curved staircase that featured an ornate wrought-iron balustrade.

There were five floors, and on each floor the rooms were accessed via a gallery. They paused on one gallery so that the manager could show Jim a typical room. While the manager was opening the door behind him Jim leaned on the wrought-iron balustrade and looked down on the stairwell and the floors below. He turned to see the man waiting at the open door, so he went in and inspected the room, which was high-ceilinged and well appointed.

'Where are the suites?'

'There is one on each of the top two floors.'

'Excellent. We would take both floors.'

'Very good, sir.'

He pointed to the service elevator. 'Where does this go?'

'To the kitchen and service area.'

'The people I represent are high-ranking – you understand? – very high-ranking. They are fussy about cleanliness. Can we go down to those areas?'

The manager raised his eyebrows, then shrugged. 'Certainly, if you wish.' He summoned the elevator.

The lift made slow, slightly lumpy, progress. Then it stopped and the doors opened into a large room. The long walls were occupied by shelves and large refrigerators. On the shelves Jim saw bath towels, hand towels, face flannels, bottles of liquid soap, boxes of tissues, cleaning materials, complimentary toiletries, and more. The manager opened the door of a refrigerator; it contained bottles of white wine and miniatures of the kind used to fill minibars. He closed the door. Between the facing walls was an arch, through which Jim glimpsed a good deal of stainless steel and deduced that it was the kitchen. In the opposite direction he noted what looked like a door to the outside. He pointed.

'Where does that go?'

'To the car park, sir. It's the staff entrance.'

Jim nodded his approval and continued to look around. There were trolleys standing around, presumably for room service and to top up the minibars. Everything looked clean. He indicated an array of small steel doors fitted with locks.

'What are those?'

'Those are the lockers for the staff.'

'Just in case we need early room service, what time do they get here?'

'Six o'clock every morning, sir. But it is best to order the night before.'

'The reason I'm asking is, on the first day we may be arriving very early, very early indeed. Will we be able to enter the building and the rooms?'

'There are no night staff. But when you have made your reservation it will be possible to collect the proximity keys for the entrance and the rooms beforehand. They are, of course, only valid for the days of your reservation.'

'That's excellent. Well thank you. All this is very satisfactory. We'll be in touch with you very shortly.'

The manager bowed, then conducted him to the foyer, where he gave him a brochure and wished him a nice day. Before he left Jim had a look at the car park, a large open area at the back, and checked the access from the road. He also saw the entrance to the kitchen and service areas, which carried a notice 'STAFF ONLY'.

He had found what he was looking for.

*

Back in Barquisimeto Jim knocked on the door of Alvaro's hotel room and went in.

Alvaro, who'd been sitting at a desk littered with papers, stood to greet him.

'Was it a useful trip to Caracas, Jim?' he asked.

'Yes, very useful.' He handed Alvaro the brochure from The Excelsior, the last hotel he'd inspected.

'Book this one, Alvaro. Take the whole of the fourth and fifth floors.'

'Do we need both floors?' Alvaro asked.

'No, we'll only occupy the fourth floor. But book both, and make the reservation now.'

Alvaro's eyes widened. 'Now?'

'Yes, now. Use your cell.'

'But it is an open line! You said we should always—'

'I know, I know. I have something different in mind this time. There's a suite on that floor. Make it very clear to the booking clerk that we must have that suite. Okay?'

'That is for Juan-Luis?'

'Not yet,' Jim said. 'Put Juan-Luis, Colonel Geiger, and six of our SAF men in a different hotel until I give the word. Book that one quietly, in person, in the usual way. Nothing fancy, you understand? Somewhere modest.' He crossed to the door.

Alvaro shook his head. 'I don't know what you are doing...'

Jim paused at the door and looked round with the hint of a smile. 'Don't worry about it, Alvaro. I'm playing a little game. You could call it Russian Roulette.'

44

It was four am, and still dark, when two people carriers pulled up outside The Excelsior hotel. Jim and twelve armed SAF soldiers got out and moved quickly and quietly to the entrance. The two vehicles drove away. Jim used the proximity key he'd been given when he'd called the previous day and they went inside. The hotel was silent; if any of the rooms were occupied the guests were doubtless asleep. They mounted the stairs to the fourth floor, their soft boots making no sound, and assembled in the middle of the gallery.

'Okay, listen up,' Jim said into his helmet mic, keeping his voice low. 'Matt and Ashley, upstairs to the fifth floor balcony. Sight your rifles where we are at the moment. Marco, you go with them. You've set the video to record time and date?'

'You betcha.'

'Good, check in with us every ten minutes – and immediately if you see something. I've got the proximity keys for the nine rooms on this floor. Jay, go to the room at that end and try them out. When you find the one that works for you give the bunch to the next guy and tell him to do the same. Continue until we've got all nine rooms occupied.' As they were starting to move off, he said, 'Look, guys, before you take up your positions. There are no guarantees. This operation may come up totally blank. You can set a trap but you never know if it's going to catch something. I just have a hunch, and my hunches have been known to pay off. Okay, deploy now.'

They dispersed up and down the corridor. All along the floor, doors were quietly opened and closed. One of his soldiers handed him a proximity key. 'These'll be the ones for your room and the suite, Jim.'

'Thanks, Maria.'

Jim glanced up at the fifth floor and saw Matt and Ashley settling into prone firing positions, the long barrels of their sniper rifles extending by about a foot beyond the balustrade. Between the two, Marco, also lying prone, was focusing his camera.

He waited for Maria to go to her room, confirmed that the corridor was now empty and everyone was in place, then walked to the far end. The first of the two keys produced a click, and a green light signalled that the door had opened. This was the suite that Delgado would be using. He had a quick look round. He was standing in a thickly carpeted sitting-room with several comfortable armchairs, a desk and chairs, dressing table, and a coffee table that incorporated a console for the wall screen. Heavy curtains hung on either side of the windows. On an adjacent wall there was a large electronic picture of a landscape: the type that changes slowly between daytime and night-time. The sitting-room opened into a double bedroom with a large, canopied bed and fitted furniture. The en-suite bathroom had two sinks, a copious supply of toiletries and towels, two bathrobes, and two pairs of slippers. He lifted one of the bathrobes off its hook and put it on over his uniform, fastening it tightly with the belt. Then he dragged an armchair nearer the door to the corridor.

Marco's voice came over the headset. 'Comms check.'

'Jim?'

Jim spoke into the helmet mic. 'I copy.'

'Maria?'

'I copy.'

'Jay?'

'I copy…'

One by one they all checked in.

'All good,' Marco said.

Jim settled down to wait.

Ten minutes later, Marco's voice again. 'Nothing so far.'

Jim sank further into the armchair. It was very quiet. From time to time a car or motorcycle passed on a neighbouring road, the sound rising then falling. Once there was the heavier rumble of a truck or a military vehicle.

Ten minutes passed and Marco repeated the message. And ten minutes after that. And four more times.

Jim drummed his fingers lightly on the armrest. Was the trap going to spring or not? He'd dangled a juicy bait, and it would surely have been picked up by Aguilar's surveillance systems, if not by the Russians. He could do no more.

He looked at his watch. Five o'clock. In one hour the hotel's staff would arrive. He decided to pull everyone out in fifty minutes' time. By then he'd know that nothing was going to happen.

At five minutes past five the message changed.

'Service lift doors just opened. Two people. Look like staff. Both wheeling trolleys.'

Jim got to his feet.

'Coming along the corridor now. Nearly halfway.'

Jim put his helmet on the chair and stepped out into the corridor.

The two stopped dead. He walked up to them and spoke in Spanish. 'Good morning.'

The man answered, 'You asked for room service, *señor*?'

'Ah, room service,' Jim said. He looked at the trolleys. The woman's was loaded with a variety of drinks and some miniatures. The man's had an insulated jug, presumably for coffee, cups and saucers, and a metal dome, which Jim lifted, revealing some sandwiches. These guys were well prepared.

'You want we go to the room?' the woman asked.

They spoke the language with heavy accents. Jim smiled and wagged a finger between them. 'You are not from here. Where are you from?'

'Poland,' the man said.

'Both of you?'

'Yes.'

He smiled. 'Guests have to be so careful these days. Can I see your I.D.s?'

The I.D. cards were hanging from blue lanyards. The man waved his briefly, but Jim stopped it with his fingers.

'Not a very good likeness,' he said. 'And "Ortiz" is a Spanish name, isn't it?' His voice hardened. 'You should have stolen a better one from the lockers downstairs. Something that sounded Polish.' He looked up at them. 'Or Russian.'

The woman's hand darted to a pocket in the front of her apron.

'Hold it right there!'

Their heads jerked towards the shout and their faces went slack as they registered the two rifle muzzles pointing at them.

'They are very good shots,' Jim said quietly. 'Do as they say or they will blow your heads off.'

Their heads jerked round as eight doors opened all along the fourth floor, and eight helmeted soldiers fanned out with automatic rifles trained. By the time the two had turned back Jim had discarded the bathrobe and stood in front of them in his SAF uniform. Marco came down the stairs still filming.

Jim said to the woman, 'Now let go of whatever is in that apron and take your hand out slowly.'

She glared at him and her hand emerged.

'Put your hands behind your backs, both of you. Do it now!'

They did as they were told.

'Maria, clip their wrists.'

Maria busied herself and Jim saw the two wince as the cable ties were zipped tight.

'Now,' Jim said, turning to the trolleys. 'Let's see what we have here. Oh, how convenient!' He pointed to a box of disposable gloves on the drinks trolley, took a pair out and put them on.

'Marco, are you filming this?'

'I sure am.'

Jim dipped into the woman's apron pocket and came out with a snub-nosed automatic. Handling it by the grips, which

281

were of no value for fingerprinting, he put it on the trolley. It wasn't unexpected but it wasn't what he was looking for.

He turned to the other trolley and lifted the sandwiches, which they'd probably bought the previous day. Nothing there. He lifted the coffee jug, keeping the two Russians in his peripheral vision but there was no reaction. He poured some coffee into a cup then set the jug down.

He turned to the woman's trolley with the drinks and began to push around the miniatures with one finger. In the centre was a slightly taller bottle.

He held it up by the cap, then showed it to the camera. 'The label says "Glen Mohr, Single Malt Scotch Whiskey."' He looked at the two. 'It looks nice. Would you like to join me in a drink?'

The woman passed her tongue over her lips.

'No?' Jim said. He paused, turning the bottle around in his hand. 'Probably wise. You know, your people at the GRU ought to know that in Scotland "whisky" is spelt without the "e".' He shook his head. 'You bastards, there's enough contact poison in this bottle to wipe out the entire staff of this hotel, not just the guest you were targeting. Maria, call in the vehicles. We're taking these two to campaign headquarters. Colonel Weaver can decide what to do with them.'

*

In the circumstances Colonel Weaver didn't mind being raised from bed a little earlier than usual.

'Caught in the act, eh?' he said when they met up. He was grinning from ear to ear. 'There'll be some folks in Washington rubbing their hands with glee over this. I'd say

282

that you just made your Señor Delgado's life a whole lot safer, Colonel.'

'I hope so. Assassins like these usually work in pairs. I shouldn't think they sent any more than those two and it's too late now to ship out any others. I think the whole idea was that Delgado would miss the debate because he'd be dead or dying or he'd turn up so ill he couldn't perform at his best. Aguilar's going to be really disappointed when he sees him there looking fit and well. Where are the man and woman now?'

'In a basement room under armed guard.'

'What are you going to do with them?' Jim asked.

'I guess that's for someone else to decide. There's no actual government in Venezuela at the moment, and no functioning judicial system – if there ever was. We could keep them here until there's a new government but if Aguilar does get re-elected he'll release them right away. I wouldn't want that to happen.'

'Me neither. You'll probably be asked to ship them to the States to stand trial for attempted murder.'

Weaver nodded. 'Seems likely. I'll contact the USACID. If the folks there can't make a decision they may take it to the Attorney General. Of course,' he added, 'the Russians will say it's all fake news.'

Jim smiled. 'They'll have a job to make that stick. Even if they say the footage was staged or the date and time stamps were added afterwards, those two were in possession of a handgun and a quantity of contact poison, probably both with their fingerprints on them. The hotel manager will no doubt confirm that they broke into lockers in the staff area before the actual hotel staff arrived and stole those uniforms and I.D. cards. A court of law in the States wouldn't have a problem convicting on that evidence.'

'You and I know that, but this may end up in the political arena, not the courts.' He stood up and they shook hands. 'Well, thank you, Colonel Slater. It's been a pleasure. I thought I'd headed up a pretty good operation, but you just put the cherry on the cake.'

45

It was the day of the debate. Delgado and his entourage had been transferred to The Excelsior, and Alvaro was with him in his suite as the technicians set up cameras and lights and trailed cables out of the windows to an outside broadcast vehicle in preparation for the afternoon. They would start transmitting live at two o'clock and the programme would be recorded and repeated in the evening.

The hotel manager had agreed to the security cordon Jim wanted around the hotel. He wasn't hard to persuade: there weren't many guests apart from the Delgado party and Jim had offered a quid pro quo – Delgado would mention at some stage that he was speaking from the Excelsior Hotel.

Jim stayed around Delgado's suite until close to two o'clock and then went downstairs to inspect the cordon. Captain Nowicki came over to speak to him.

'No problems so far, Colonel, and if there are any I reckon we can handle them.'

Jim smiled. Even at a glance there had to be at least fifty soldiers as well as a good deal of weaponry. 'It certainly looks like it. Well, we appreciate your help, Captain. I know it seems like pretty dull stuff as assignments go but you're already doing a great job just by being here. Shall we talk to some of your guys?'

Jim walked round with the Captain, speaking to some of the soldiers and making sure they knew what they were looking out for. He hoped this would help to boost morale and vigilance. Finally he felt there was nothing more he could do, so he joined Tommy Geiger in his hotel room to watch what was left of the debate. Most of their party would be watching it in the other rooms.

'How's it going, Tommy?'

'Okay, I guess. They've talked about the economy, shortages of goods, inflation, stuff like that. Delgado's on good form, scoring points hand over fist. Aguilar looks unsettled to me. He keeps going off on one of his rants and gets muted every time.'

Jim took a chair and sat down to watch the programme with him. The television crew had arranged for the candidates to appear side by side on a split screen. This switched from time to time to the moderator, who was posing questions sent in by the public. Delgado looked very relaxed in an open-necked short-sleeved shirt. He spoke to the camera as if he were having a conversation with the person who'd raised the question. Aguilar was wearing an immaculate suit, shirt and tie, but he looked ill at ease; his face was flushed and his eyes darted about. Any time he tried to shout Delgado down he was muted, and after a while he grimaced and stopped trying. When he was given his opportunity to speak he rambled and constantly over-ran his allotted time.

Tommy got up and went to the minibar. 'Beer, Jim?'

'Sure.'

He took out a couple of bottles, and picked up an opener for the crown caps. 'To be honest,' he said, 'I find this political banter pretty boring.'

'I know, but it's necessary. It's bringing out what a mess Aguilar's making of the country. And—'

He paused. Delgado wasn't speaking to the public now, he had turned his head as if he was speaking direct to Aguilar.

'So, that being the case, President Aguilar, may I ask why you made an agreement with the Russians that allows them to build missile sites on our coast?'

Tommy froze, the bottle in one hand and the opener in the other. 'Holy shit!' he gasped. He looked at the television.

Aguilar's jaw had dropped. He stuttered, 'How…?' then seemed to pull himself together. He waved a hand dismissively. 'Lies, all lies. You're losing this election, Delgado, so now you're concocting fake news. It's all lies.'

'Is it? I don't think you'll convince the people who've noticed that the coastal road in that entire area is closed. Or the ones who've seen a lot of Russians in Maracaibo. They're wondering what they're doing there.'

'The Russians are our allies. They're advising on trade, investing in our economy—'

'And is that why the Americans sent an invasion force?'

Aguilar passed his tongue over his lips. 'Typical American aggression. A violation of Venezuelan sovereignty. And my priority is to get them out of our country, which I can't do while I'm bandying words with you.'

'But is it any wonder they're here? Wouldn't you feel the same way if someone was erecting missile emplacements on our doorstep?'

'That's not why they're here—'

'So you admit missiles are being installed here?'

'No, I—'

Tommy looked at Jim, eyebrows raised. 'Oh dear. Delgado's got him wriggling on a hook and he's reeling him in.'

Jim grinned. 'I think this campaign could be turning a corner.'

Tommy uncapped the two bottles and handed one to Jim. 'Let's drink to that!'

When the debate was over two election addresses appeared on television. Aguilar's was substantially the formula he'd used before, banging the drum for Venezuela to be freed from the American invaders. But Delgado's was one of those recorded in a studio at Maracaibo. He'd clearly been thinking well ahead.

He soon worked around to his main message.

'Yes, my fellow countrymen, missiles on our coast, pointing at the United States of America. You don't believe me? Have you been in Maracaibo lately? Have you noticed an unusual number of Russian visitors there? Have you tried to drive along the coast road? Try it. You can't. You'll be diverted because the Russians don't want you to see the missile silos they are constructing.'

And now he pointed a finger at the viewers, stabbing it repeatedly at them.

'How do you feel about that, my friends? How do you feel about being the number one target in a nuclear war? Is there any benefit to this country? Will there be any benefit to you, the people? Will there be any benefit to you, the companies trying to import goods and spare parts with bolivares that are worthless on the world stage? No. Will there be any benefit to you, the farmers, the shopkeepers trying to sell goods to people who can no longer afford them? No. Will there be any benefit to you, the fishermen, trying to secure a live catch in a lake that is poisoned with oil? No. Will there be any benefit to you, the people who have no clean water to drink because the rivers are polluted by gold-mining? No.'

He opened his hand. 'So who will benefit? Who? You know who will benefit. It will be President Aguilar and his hangers-on, who can fill their pockets with Russian bribes.'

He pointed at the viewers again. 'I promise you this. Elect me, not for my sake but for your sake and the sake of this country. Elect me to put an end to missiles, so that the Americans can go home. Elect me to put an end to corruption, an end to economic sanctions, and an end to the neglect that has left so many people without even the basic necessities of life. This could be the most important vote of your life. Vote for a new Venezuela. Vote for me.'

*

That evening Jim, Tommy, and Alvaro sat down with Juan-Luis in his suite. They were full of the success of the debate and the powerful speech he'd followed it up with.

Tommy said, 'I didn't know there were missiles going up here. Did you, Jim?'

'A lot of people didn't know,' Jim replied.

Tommy frowned. 'You dodged the question.'

'That's right, I did.'

Delgado chuckled.

'It was a shock for me,' Alvaro said, 'so it will be a shock for everyone. This could make all the difference.'

'But will it be enough?' Jim said.

'Perhaps,' Delgado said. 'Perhaps not. Aguilar will still have strong support from the army, Los Feroces, the businessmen who are favoured with his contracts and kickbacks. This news will make no difference to them. It is the ordinary people who count now. Unfortunately they may not be taking any interest in the campaign. I will be repeating that message again many times before we go to the polls, but if those people don't turn out to vote…'

'We will do our best to get them out,' Alvaro said. 'I have people going from door to door, and on the day we will have loudspeaker vans in every major centre of population. But you know, Juan-Luis, even if they have not been watching your videos up to now I think the word will soon get around.'

Delgado shrugged. 'Let us hope so.'

After a while Jim said, 'I didn't want to say anything before the debate, but I think it's time I told you what happened at The Excelsior yesterday morning.'

They turned to him and he gave them an account of the successful arrest of the two Russian assassins.

'And that's about it,' he said finally. 'Colonel Weaver now has two unhappy Russians on his hands. They'll probably be shipped to the States.'

'That was my main worry,' Tommy said quietly, 'and you put it to bed.'

Delgado looked pale. 'I have much to thank you for, Jim. And not just for my life: many innocent people could have been poisoned.'

'Now I see why you wanted me to book that hotel on an open line,' Alvaro said, 'and they fell for it! The Russians can't influence the election now, it's too late.'

'That's right.' Jim took a deep breath. 'You know, from now on it's a routine protection detail. There's not much more I can do here.'

'You going back to Fort Piper then, Jim?' Tommy said.

'Yes. There are military transports coming and going all the time at Caracas airport. There's one going to Andrews, and they're prepared to drop me off at Raleigh-Durham. I'll arrange to be picked up from there.' He looked at Delgado. 'You do understand, don't you, sir?'

Delgado smiled. 'Of course. Thank you for everything you've done. I hope we will meet again.'

They stood and shook hands. Then Jim shook hands with Tommy and Alvaro and left the room.

46

'You been following the news, Jim?' Wendell asked, looking across his desk. They were in his office at the Pentagon for Jim's final debriefing.

'Yes, I have. Decisive victory for Delgado.'

'And the international inspectors have told the world that the election was fair and free, which clinched it. That's the end of Aguilar and his administration.'

'They got off too lightly,' Jim said. 'They should have been put on trial at the Hague for crimes against humanity.'

Wendell nodded. 'We'd have loved to do that, Jim, but politics is the art of compromise.'

'Will they compromise with the Russians on those two assassins I brought in as well?'

'Who knows? It's a massive international embarrassment for the Russians, but they'll live it down. Still, if those two or their bosses want to do a deal you can bet we'll extract something worthwhile in return.'

Jim grimaced.

'Take heart, Jim. By trapping them you secured the safety of Delgado. That was a good outcome. Anyway, right now there are a lot of smiling faces in the White House Situation

Room – which makes a pleasant change. For a while back there the atmosphere was pretty strained.'

'You mean when Delgado didn't show?'

'Yes. The one credible opposition candidate wasn't making an appearance. It started to look like we'd gone through this whole costly caper only to preside over a re election of Aguilar. You solved that problem for us. How did you find him?'

The question was expected and Jim had improvised an answer of sorts, based on the kind of approach he'd have used if Rosa hadn't been there to help out. 'I assumed he must have a household to support as well as himself, and that meant he was probably being supplied by local farmers. There weren't too many in that area, so I made some enquiries. Eventually it led to him. He was well guarded, though, so I had to be careful.'

'Well, great job,' Wendell said. 'Everyone round the table wanted me to pass on congratulations, especially President Nagel and the Chief of Staff. Still, that wasn't the end of our problems. We thought he'd walk the election but we were looking at the polls and the outcome wasn't anywhere near certain. That all changed with the debate.'

'Yes. it was a key moment.'

Wendell sat back, tapping his fingertips together. 'I have to say this missile business was news to me, but it makes sense, doesn't it? All the same, there's something curious about it. We presented them with a deal, which presumably offered them trade agreements and inward investment if they'd dismantle the sites. They didn't accept it, so an invasion couldn't be avoided. But the whole plan was absolutely top secret. Only a few people were in on the whole thing – just a few at the very top – and they're keen to know how Delgado found out.' He raised his eyebrows. 'Any ideas, Jim?'

Jim smiled. 'Delgado had been in hiding, but I imagine he still had his sources.'

Sources like Maynard Dexter, who those 'people at the very top' think is either dead or rotting in a Venezuelan prison. It's okay, Dexter. Your secret is safe with me.

'Mmm. Well I can see now why it was so important to have you and the other three on the ground out there. The envoy's imprisonment was the justification for the entire operation. Does that surprise you?'

'Not really. Previous experience tells me not to be surprised by anything the CIA cooks up. And as you say, once the deal was turned down we had no choice; we had to force regime change there.'

Wendell seemed to be deep in thought. Finally he said, 'Well, that's it. Delgado's in the Miraflores Palace. Our troops are pulling out – President Nagel's pleased about that; she never wanted us to be there at all. And I doubt that even Russia will have the brass neck to bring their complaint back to the Security Council. They'll be keeping their heads down now, especially after you caught those two assassins red-handed. What did you think of Delgado, by the way?'

'He's charismatic and he has good intentions. But the economy is the key. Unless he can bring that under control there's a limit to what he can achieve.'

'We'll step in, of course, drop sanctions, renew trade links, make loans. A lot of other countries will do the same now there's been a fair election. We might even buy some of their oil, although God knows we don't need the stuff. It'll take time, of course.'

He gripped the edge of his desk and Jim, who was familiar with Wendell's preparations to rise, got to his feet. Wendell saw him to the door.

'Well, Jim,' he said. 'Good mission in very difficult circumstances. I expect you're glad to be back?'

'Yes, there's not much out there I'll miss.'

Not much, he mused, as he descended the stairs to the Pentagon's concourse. *Just one thing. A hell of a remarkable young woman.*

*

At Washington Dulles Jim boarded his plane and settled in for the flight back to Raleigh-Durham and his return to Fort Piper.

His mind was still dwelling on Rosa. At least he felt comfortable in the knowledge that her position would be secure now that Óscar and José were both out of the picture. A fair election had given Delgado the Presidency, and there was a good chance he'd revive the fortunes of their country and restore it to the community of nations. Rosa would rebuild the Guárico cartel as a business organization and they would be in a good position to help one another. It would take time, as Wendell had said, but the future looked promising.

His thoughts turned to Dexter. In many ways it had been a dark episode. The man had acted in a moment of extreme provocation. He'd killed someone, someone who had betrayed him, embezzled their company's funds, stolen his wife, and then mocked his gullibility. But Dexter had paid a heavy price: two years in prison under sentence of death.

The CIA, on the other hand, had cold-bloodedly used him as a human sacrifice. Their plan had succeeded in its object of overturning Aguilar's regime, and they were now basking in its success. If – as Jim fully expected – Delgado opened the gates of Buena Vista and the detainees came pouring out into the waiting arms of their families, Dexter Maynard would not be among them. Nobody would be surprised: he was just one of the many *desaparecidos* whose bodies would never be found. It was part of the CIA's trade-off: Dexter would be tortured to death while ex-President Aguilar, a man responsible for many hundreds of grisly murders, would walk free.

The engine note rose for take-off and the aircraft roared down the runway, rose into the sky, and gained altitude. Jim watched the landscape fall away below them with a mixture of feelings. There'd been little moral high ground in any of this, but what there was he felt he'd taken. Dexter would be safe now, living quietly in his house near the Colombian border, and Jim was glad.

It was very unusual, perhaps unique, for someone to escape to freedom from Death Row. Perhaps Dexter had set some sort of record.

If so no one would ever know.

Printed in Great Britain
by Amazon